The
SAFE
HOUSE

Also by Kiki Swinson

The Playing Dirty Series: *Playing Dirty* and *Notorious*
The Candy Shop
A Sticky Situation
The Wifey Series: *Wifey, I'm Still Wifey, Life After Wifey,*
Still Wifey Material
Wife Extraordinaire Series: *Wife Extraordinaire* and
Wife Extraordinaire Returns
Cheaper to Keep Her Series: Books 1-5
The Score Series: *The Score* and *The Mark*
Dead on Arrival
The Black Market Series: *The Black Market,*
The Safe House, Property of the State
The Deadline
Public Enemy #1
Playing with Fire

ANTHOLOGIES
Sleeping with the Enemy (with Wahida Clark)
Heist and *Heist 2* (with De'nesha Diamond)
Lifestyles of the Rich and Shameless (with Noire)
A Gangster and a Gentleman (with De'nesha Diamond)
Most Wanted (with Nikki Turner)
Still Candy Shopping (with Amaleka McCall)
Fistful of Benjamins (with De'nesha Diamond)
Schemes and *Dirty Tricks* (with Saundra)
Bad Behavior (with Noire)

Published by Kensington Publishing Corp.

The SAFE HOUSE

Kiki Swinson

DAFINA

www.kensingtonbooks.com

DAFINA BOOKS are published by

Kensington Publishing Corp.
119 West 40th Street
New York, NY 10018

Copyright © 2019 by Kiki Swinson

All Kensington Titles, Imprints, and Distributed Lines are available at special quantity discounts for bulk purchases for sales promotions, premiums, fund-raising, and educational or institutional use. Special book excerpts or customized printings can also be created to fit specific needs. For details, write or phone the office of the Kensington special sales manager: Kensington Publishing Corp119 West 40th Street, New York, NY 10018, attn: Special Sales Department, Phone: 1-800-221-2647.

The DAFINA logo is a trademark of Kensington Publishing Corp.

ISBN: 978-1-4967-2004-7
First Kensington Hardcover Edition: July 2019
First Kensington Trade Edition: January 2020
First Kensington Mass Market: December 2021

ISBN: 978-1-4967-2005-4 (ebook)

10 9 8 7 6 5 4 3 2 1

Printed in the United States of America

1

MY AFTERLIFE

I felt my consciousness slipping into a quiet place. It almost seemed weird because there was no noise around me. It felt soothing to finally be in a peaceful place. There was no one in this dark place but me. Why hadn't I done this before? Why was I afraid to leave that other world? Here I have no worries and I'm pain free. I was told all my life that it was wrong to do what I did. They said that you'd be condemned. But then I realized, it was my way out. In fact, it was a win-win for me. I would get the chance to see my grandmother and my cousin again and they were all that mattered to me, since my life had gone to complete hell. Who would've thought that I would screw my life up? I went from being a college graduate in the field of pharmaceutical science, and working as a pharmaceutical tech, to being a fucking murderer and informant.

I'd been wanting to work in the medical field for as long as I could remember, but I ruined my life by stealing prescription drugs for my drug addict–ass cousin, which led to a robbery gone bad. Not only that, I fucked around and murdered my ex-boyfriend—but in self-defense. But who's gonna believe that? Especially since I paid some-one to discard his body. What has happened to me? Why have I allowed these things to corrupt my life? I was doing good for myself. But look at me now. I'm a fucking idiot with a target on my back. What are the odds of me getting out of this? Slim . . .

"Got an A-24! In the bedroom. Need some help!" I heard faintly, and then everything went silent.

Wow! This place is nice. Everything is so white and clean. It kind of has the feel of a hospital, but with no one around.

"Hello," I said, but no one answered. I traveled down what seemed like a hallway, but there was no floor. It felt like I was floating around on thin air. Now, how was this possible? I didn't have superpowers. Nor was I immortal. So, what was going on?

"I can tell you what's going on," said a voice behind me.

I turned around and, to my surprise, my grandmother was standing behind me. Oh my God! Seeing her standing there before me dressed in all white took my breath away. "Grandma, is that you?"

She smiled. "Yes, it is, sweetheart!"

When she confirmed to me that it was, in fact, her, I leaned in and embraced her. "I thought I lost you," I told her while I held on to her as tight as I could.

"No, baby, you will never lose me," she assured me.

"But I thought you were dead? The agent said that you and Jillian were both murdered."

"Yes, that's true—" she started, but I cut her off.

"What do you mean 'that's true'? And where is Jillian?" I wanted to know. Things she was saying were not adding up.

"I have passed on, darling. And as far as Jillian is concerned, I don't know where she is. But I'm sure she's around here somewhere."

"So I'm dead too?"

"Not quite. You're in a realm that is called the After Life."

"I don't understand."

"Listen, baby, I'm just a messenger that was sent to tell you that your work on earth is not yet done," my grandmother told me, and then she smiled.

"What do you mean that my 'work on earth' isn't done? What am I supposed to do?"

"Misty, God has a calling on your life, so He will not allow you to die. You can't get into heaven by committing suicide. He said that He's going to give you another chance to do it right."

"Do what right, Grandma? You're scaring me."

"There's no need to be scared, darling. You're gonna be okay."

"What am I supposed to do?"

"You're gonna have to help those agents bring those mafia guys to justice. Those guys have killed over a dozen people. They're into human trafficking amongst some other things. They are some very dangerous people. And then you're gonna have to make it right with Terrell's family. You're gonna have to tell his mother that you killed him and show them where his body is."

"I can't do that. I would go to prison for life if they found out what I did."

"I'm sorry, Misty, but you're gonna have to make it right. You won't be able to see me again if you don't."

I covered my ears with both hands and tried to block out every word she uttered. I mean, what kind of demands were these? I couldn't go back, testify against those guys, and then turn my own self in. Who would do that? I refused to snitch on myself. The end result of that would mean that my life would be over.

"Misty, I know that you don't wanna hear what I am saying, but there's no other way around it."

"Please let me stay here with you." I began to sob. Tears started running down my face uncontrollably. I leaned into my grandmother again and embraced her. But this time, I held on to her tighter. In my mind, I wasn't going to let her go.

Somehow she managed to push me away from her. "I'm sorry, baby, it's out of my hands. I can't help you right now. You gotta do the right thing," she said, and then she started stepping backward.

"Grandmom, where are you going? I'm not done talking to you."

"I have to leave now, darling. Do as I instructed you, and you will be fine. Also tell your mother that despite how she felt, I always loved her," she told me, and before I could utter another word, she disappeared into thin air.

I stood there with a troubled mind and broken heart. Here I was standing in the After Life with my grandmother, hoping to join her, but was told that now wasn't my time. And then to be told that I had to help the agents take down Ahmad and his family, and reveal to the cops that I murdered Terrell. I'd really be committing suicide then. The whole thing was unfathomable.

While I tried to piece together my next course of action, I started hearing voices around me. I heard a woman say: "We just updated her vitals. She's stable and breathing on her own now."

"So, when will I be able to talk to her?" I heard a male's voice ask.

"It's all just a waiting game now," the woman continued.

"Will she remember what happened?"

"Yes, she will."

"Okay. Great. Thank you for your time."

"You're welcome, sir," the woman replied, and then I heard two sets of footsteps. It lasted for a few moments and then I didn't hear it anymore, so I opened my eyes slowly to prevent any light from blinding me. Halfway into full focus, it became apparent that I was in a room, but it wasn't the same room I talked to my grandmother in. This room was different. This room looked like a hospital room. In fact, it was a hospital room and I was hooked to every machine placed around my bed. "Oh no, I'm here. Back here alive," I whispered after I opened my eyes completely. Instantly anxiety consumed my entire body. I didn't want to be here. I wanted to be where my grandmother was. This godforsaken place was nothing short of hell. Bad people lived here and they made sure everyone knew exactly who they were.

"What am I gonna do? I can't be here," I continued to whisper. My heart became very heavy.

"Who are you talking to?" a female's voice asked me.

I looked in the direction in which the voice came from and realized that a nurse had walked into my hospital room. The woman smiled as she walked toward me dressed in her scrubs.

"I was talking to myself," I told her, feeling very saddened that I was lying in my bed alive.

"How are you feeling?" she asked me while she stood alongside my bed. She checked my IV to make sure that it was intact.

"I don't wanna be here," I got up the nerve to say.

"You mean here in the hospital?" she questioned me again. I figured this was a test question, a suicidal test question.

"No, I mean *here*. On this freaking earth," I boldly replied.

"Why don't you wanna be here?" Her questions kept coming.

"Because there's nothing left on this earth that I want to live for. My grandmother is gone and so is my cousin. I wanna be in heaven with them."

"So you are aware that you tried to commit suicide?"

"I wasn't trying to commit suicide. I was only trying to exchange my life with my mother's."

"Well, I'm sorry to hear that."

"Don't feel sorry for me. Just disconnect me from all of these freaking needles and tubes so I can get out of here," I said quietly, but in an aggressive manner.

"I'm sorry, but I can't do that. You're gonna have to speak with your doctor. He's the one that would be authorized to discharge you."

"Tell him I need to speak to him right now."

"I'm afraid he's in surgery right now, but I will let him know when he's done."

"Yeah, whatever," I said, and turned my focus to the window in my room.

"Is there anything else I can help you with?"

"No, you can't. Just leave me alone."

"There are a couple of federal agents outside the door, and one of them instructed me to let him know when you wake up. So I'm going to go outside and let them know."

"No, don't tell them anything. I just want to be left alone. Tell him I'm still asleep."

The nurse took a deep breath and then she exhaled. "As you wish," she said, and then she opened the door to my room. While she tried to leave, Agent Sims met her at the door because he was trying to come in the room himself. "Excuse me," he said to the nurse.

"No 'excuse me,'" she replied while she scooted by him.

Agent Sims smiled as he approached me. "I'm glad to see you up and alert," he commented.

"I'm not."

"Come on, Misty, it cannot be that bad," Agent Sims responded.

"You wouldn't have the slightest clue," I replied sarcastically, because he didn't. I had a bunch of mess going on in my life. Shit, that would make me look like a heartless bitch. But more important, I would have been in jail for the rest of my life.

"Want to talk about it?"

"No, I don't. But I do want to get out of here."

"I'm sorry, but it's not going to be that simple."

"Explain that to me."

"Do you realize that you tried to commit suicide? If I hadn't come in that bedroom, when I did, you'd be dead right now."

"What'cha want me to say, thank you for saving my life?"

"We can start from there."

"News flash, I wanted to die. And I'm glad I did it too, because I saw my grandmother and we had a nice time talking. She held me in her arms and told me how much she loved me."

"So you're telling me that you went to heaven and came back?"

"Why are you smiling? You think I'm a freaking joke?"

"No, I don't think you're a joke. I just never talked to someone that went to heaven and came back. You know, I see people on TV claiming that they've done it."

"Well, I have, and I'm going back."

"If you went there, and you liked it so much, then why did you come back?"

"Because my grandma said that my work here on the earth wasn't complete."

"She's talking about this case, huh?"

"Oh, shut up! And get out of my face."

"Is your life that screwed up, that you want to die?"

"Give me another chance and I will prove it to you."

"Your doctor has you under suicide watch so you won't try that stunt again."

"Are you done? Because let's keep it real, you only want me to be alive so I can help you put those guys away in prison."

"You're a very smart girl."

"So this is funny to you? You're holding me hostage so I can testify against Ahmad and the rest of his family?"

"This isn't just about putting Ahmad and his family

behind bars. Remember, you're getting a get-out-of-jail-free card."

"Are you kidding me right now? You think you're doing me a favor by testifying against those people? Do you know that I lost my grandmother and cousin behind this bullshit?" I spat, the volume of my voice got louder.

"If you would've kept your hands clean and never taken any prescription drugs from the pharmacy, then we wouldn't be having this conversation."

"You know what, fuck you! Fuck you and the boat you got off of."

Agent Sims chuckled. "Don't get upset. It's not healthy. And besides, I don't want to be the reason that you try to commit suicide again. I wouldn't be able to look at myself in the mirror anymore."

"You're so fucking phony."

"What gave you that idea?"

"Will I be free to go on with my life after this case is over?"

"That depends on if you go into witness protection."

"Well, let me be the first to tell you that I won't need you guys' protection. I'm gonna move so far away it would take one of those drones in space to find me."

"Are you sure you wanna do that? Those guys have ties to contract killers all over the world," Agent Sims warned me.

"I'm gonna be fine. Thank you," I assured him. "Has the doctor said when I would be released?" I changed the subject.

"No, he hasn't. I believe he wants you to speak with a psychiatrist before he can make a medical prognosis."

"Fuck a prognosis! I'm fine and I'm ready to get out of here."

"I'm sure you are, Misty. But we have protocol here."

"So you say," I commented, and then I turned my focus back toward the window in my room. Looking outside at all the birds flying back and forth was more entertaining than Agent Sims. All he wanted to do was talk about my testimony for his case. He couldn't care less about anything. But whether he knew it or not, I had a trick up my sleeve, and he and no one else was going to hinder me from doing it.

"Listen, I'm gonna let you get some rest. There are two agents outside of your door, so if you need anything, you let them know."

"Yeah, right," I said nonchalantly as I continued to look in the opposite direction.

2

NEWS FLASH

I lay in my hospital bed and tried to come up with a plan on how I was going to get out of here without the agents knowing. Let's not forget the hospital staff too, especially since they're the ones that had me on suicide watch. *Ugh! I hate when I can't do what I want to do.*

A couple hours passed and I was still trying to mull over ways that I could make a successful escape. But that all went down the drain when I got a knock on the door. "Coming in," I heard a woman's voice say. I immediately turned my attention toward the door and in came my mother. She rushed over to my bedside and gave me a big hug and a kiss on my forehead.

"Ah, baby, look at you. Are you all right?" she asked as she looked at me while combing my hair with her hand.

"Mom, I am so glad to see you," I told her.

"I'm glad to see you too, baby girl. How are these people treating you in here?"

"All right, I guess. I like that pink fingernail polish on your nails."

"Thank you," she replied, and then she switched the subject. "So, what is going on with you that would make you attempt to commit suicide?"

"I just got a lot on my plate, Mom, and I was tired of dealing with it."

"You know I was hurt when I got a call from that agent telling me what you tried to do."

"I know you were. And I'm sorry, Mama, but I'm tired. I just want to live in peace. Look at what happened to Jillian and Grandma. They didn't have to get killed like that."

"You're right. But there's other ways to work through obstacles that come into our lives."

"So, what'cha want me to drink my problems away like you do?" I replied sarcastically, because who is she to try and give me advice? Her life was more fucked up than mine. She can keep her advice to herself.

"Really, Misty, did you have to go there?!" my mom said. I could hear the hurt in her voice.

"Ma, I'm sorry for saying that."

"It's okay, darling. I know you didn't mean it," she said, trying to cut through the tension I had just created. "Carl says hello and that he hopes you get well soon."

"Where is he?"

"He's downstairs in the waiting room on the first floor. Seeing all the cops standing outside your door made him feel uneasy."

"You are staying with his family, right?"

"We haven't officially moved in with them yet. But don't worry, most of our things are in his car, so as soon as we leave here, that's where we're heading."

"Mom, please do. If I lose another person I am going to lose my mind."

"Don't worry about me. Carl and I can take care of ourselves. You're the one that needs to be looked after."

"Have you thought about who's going to help bury Grandma and Jillian?" I asked her, forcing her to talk about my grandmother, since she hadn't mentioned her from the time she walked into my room up until this very moment.

"Misty, I can't deal with that right now. You're asking too much of me. I've already agreed to leave my house because of something you did. And now you want me to take on the task of handling my mother's burial arrangements. Now, how selfish is that?"

"Mom, do you hear yourself?"

"You damn right, I hear myself. I will not take on that responsibility. That woman didn't love me. She only loved my brother and his damn daughter."

"Mom, will you please give it up? It's not about you anymore. Your mother was killed by the people that are looking for me, so have some freaking compassion."

"Didn't you just say that she was killed by people that were looking for you?"

"Yeah," I said, trying to hold back my tears.

"Then you take care of their funeral arrangements because I'm out of here," she replied, and then she kissed me on my forehead and exited the room.

After the door closed, I couldn't hold back my tears any longer. The hurtful words she uttered from her mouth stabbed me like a dagger in my heart. I mean, how heartless could she have been? She acted as if my grandmother hadn't given birth to her. Despite what my mother had said all her life, my grandmother was a good woman. And she was selfless. So to see my mother carry on like she just did sent me into a deeper depression than I was already in.

"Are you okay?" a black guy asked me. I suspect that he was one of the agents Agent Sims had sitting in on my watch. He was dressed in casual clothing from head to toe and was a clean-cut–looking guy.

"Who are you?" I asked him while I wiped the tears away from my eyes.

"I'm Agent Taylor. I'm assigned to protect you during your stay here at the hospital."

"Where is Agent Montclair?" I wanted to know, trying to figure out how many agents were standing outside my room.

"Agent Montclair is downstairs in the cafeteria getting us something to eat."

"How long are y'all supposed to watch me?"

"I'm not sure. Our details change every minute, it seems like," he said.

But I didn't believe him. He was full of shit. I knew he knew what his schedule was for my detail. He just didn't want to tell me, for fear that I'd try to hang myself again. "Did you hear my mother get upset before she left?"

"Yes, I did. But that's family business. That's where I draw the line."

"Do you know when I am getting out of here?" I asked him, testing whether or not he was going to spill the beans.

Once again, he kept tight-lipped. "No, I'm afraid not."

"What the hell do you know?" I snapped, because I knew he was lying to me.

"All I know is that I was told to keep an eye on you, that's it," he replied.

"Yeah, right. You're a bullshitter, just like Agent Sims."

Agent Taylor smiled. "I'm sorry that you feel like that, ma'am."

"Please, you could care less," I told him. "I'm done talking. You can leave now." I continued while I grabbed for the TV remote to change the channel.

Thankfully, he listened to my instructions and exited my room. If he would've given me a hard time, then I would've done something extreme, like yelling out to hospital staff, accusing him of screaming at me and causing me mental anguish. Believe me, it would've been classic, to say the least.

Immediately after he left my room, I stopped sifting through the television channels after seeing a very familiar face plastered around the TV screen. I turned up the volume to listen: "My son Terrell would not get up and leave town without telling me or his family. We all have a good relationship. People tell me all the time that he was a mama's boy, so if he hadn't said anything to anyone else, he would've at least called and told me. But I do have a strong suspicion that his ex-girlfriend named Misty Heiress had something to do with his disappearance. The police tracked his phone and the last pinging alert was a cell phone tower only a mile from her apartment. Now I've talked to her a few times and she's done nothing but lie. So I'm standing here and pleading to anyone that knows his whereabouts, please call the police. You don't have to leave your name. Just call us if you heard or seen anything," she said as the tears from her eyes flooded the cheeks of her face.

I instantly saw the pain in Mrs. Mason's eyes. She was doing everything in her power to find her son, and if that included throwing me under the bus, then so be it, I'm sure she thought. After the news break ended, I got sick to my stomach. All I could think about was what were the chances of them getting a search warrant to search my apartment? And what if they gained access to my apartment and found traces of blood on the living-room floor or my bathroom left by Terrell's body? The thought of that happening consumed me. Fear stricken, I closed my eyes and started praying silently. At this point, that was all I could do. No one could save me now but God. He was the only one.

Of course, God knew that I had killed Terrell, but He also knew that He had forgiven me for the act. But getting arrested for it right now isn't in the plan. My grandmother told me that I had several jobs to do and confessing the murder wasn't the first thing on my list. What I needed to do now was concentrate on helping these loser-ass agents so they can convict Ahmad and his family. After I'm done with that, then I'll wait on God to tell me what I needed to do next. But in that order.

3

ON PINS & NEEDLES

I swear shit can't get no worse than it already has. I hate not being in control. This mess is running me crazy. Why can't I just snap my finger and disappear from this place? I would go off to a far land, where no one would be able to find me. Ever!

A few hours had gone by and I had a total of six visits inside my room, all of them where hospital staff checked my vitals and monitored my blood pressure. I even got a visit from the resident psychiatrist. She introduced herself as Dr. Mary Gleason. She was an older white woman that looked to be in her late fifties. She had a small frame, but she looked like she had a lot of fire in her. She came in my room, asked me a few questions, like "Have you ever tried to commit suicide before this last time?" Then she asked, "Do you have plans to do it again?" I told her no. I was done with it. She also asked me if I had a family that would come here and talk to her. I told her no. And she asked me why. So I told her that I had just lost my grandmother and my favorite cousin, and the only person left in my family was my mother and we weren't on good terms as of this moment. "Is there something you want to talk about?" she asked me.

"No, not really," I told her after she sat down in a chair near my bed.

"Well, can we talk about the incident that happened last night?"

"What? About me hanging myself?"

"Yes."

"There's nothing to really talk about. I did it and now I'm here because of it."

"Are you having thoughts of doing it again?" she asked, pressing me.

"No, I'm not."

"Would you tell me how you felt when you regained consciousness?"

"I didn't feel anything," I lied. I was not trying to open up a can of worms so she could dig around in it. I really wanted her to get lost because she was wasting my time.

"Well, I was told by Agent Sims that when you were away from us for those two to three minutes, that you saw and spoke with your grandmother. Was that true?" She kept on, pressing me.

"Yes, I told him that."

"Was it true?"

"Yes, I saw my grandmother, and I spoke with her too."

"Do you mind telling me what you two talked about?"

"She told me she loved me, and that it wasn't my time to come where she was, and that I had to come back."

"Were you disappointed?"

"Of course, I was. I didn't want to come back to this godforsaken place."

"Did she tell you why it wasn't your time to stay where she was? And I'm presuming she was talking about heaven."

"No, she really didn't." I lied to her once more. I wasn't going to divulge my conversation between my grandmother and me. Was she insane or what?

"Did you talk about anything other than you not being able to stay with her in heaven?"

"If you want to know if she and I sat down, had a cup of hot tea, and talked about how great the weather was, then that's what it was. I mean, come on, I wasn't with her that long."

"I'm sorry if I'm upsetting you, but I have to ask you these questions so I can get a sense of where your state of mind is," she tried to explain.

"But I didn't ask you to do that. I told you that I was fine."

Dr. Gleason paused for a moment and then she said, "Will you please help me so that I can help you?"

"What part of 'I don't need your help,' don't you understand? I am fine!" She was wrecking my nerves. I swear, I wanted to wrap my hands around her neck and choke the shit out of her.

"Listen, Misty, all I'm here to do is help you overcome any issues that you may have. I want to see you well or at least heading in that direction." Dr. Gleason wouldn't let up.

"Will someone come in here and get this fucking lady out of my face! She's getting on my nerves!" I yelled at the top of my voice.

She immediately stood up. "Misty, there's no need for that. I'll leave, but if you change your mind and want to talk, then have the nurse page me," she said as she was walking toward the door.

When she opened the door, Agent Taylor bumped into her. "Is everything all right in here?" he asked, looking at me and then at Dr. Gleason.

"She was harassing me, so I told her to get out, but she wouldn't listen. So that's why I yelled for help."

"Don't worry. I'm leaving," she told Agent Taylor as she stepped by him.

"She's leaving, okay," Agent Taylor said as if he was trying to defuse the situation. But he didn't do anything but tell me what I had already witnessed.

"Will you close my door?" I instructed him, and then I turned my attention back toward the television.

Approximately thirty minutes after the psychiatrist left, Agent Sims came storming through the door, looking like he was mad at the world. "Have you seen the news?" He didn't hesitate to ask me.

"Yes, I did. Why?" I asked him. But I knew where he was going with this.

"What's this I hear about your ex-boyfriend being missing?" he continued after he stood next to my bed.

"What about it?" I replied nonchalantly. I knew I had to control my actions around him. Didn't want to let on that I had something to do with Terrell being missing.

"Misty, don't play games with me. Your ex-boyfriend's mother was just on TV asking if anyone knows anything about her missing son. So, if you know something, I suggest you tell me right now."

"I don't know anything," I told him, trying to hold on to the same facial expression.

"You better not be bullshitting me! Because if I find out otherwise, I'm going to personally give local authorities permission to bury your ass in a maximum-security prison for the rest of your life!" he roared, looking like he was about to lose his mind.

"I told you I don't know anything, so leave me alone about it."

"When was the last time you saw him? Because if my memory serves me, he was visiting you when Agent Montclair and I stopped by there."

"That day you stopped by was the last time I saw him," I lied. "And when he stopped by that day, he came without an invite," I continued, talking with the utmost sincerity.

"Well, tell me why I found footage of Terrell from the cameras inside the pharmacy?"

"Once again, he came by uninvited. And if you saw the whole thing, you'd see that he and Ahmad were having words with one another. Terrell was being really disrespectful to Ahmad, so Ahmad told him to leave."

"Is that during the time Ahmad grabbed for his handgun?"

"You saw that on camera?"

"We kind of knew what it was, when Ahmad took a step toward Terrell."

Hearing Agent Sims say that he saw Ahmad reach for his gun, while confronting Terrell, gave me an idea. "Think he may have had something to do with Terrell's disappearance? I mean, Terrell did say a lot of slick shit out of his mouth toward Ahmad." I threw that out there, hoping Agent Sims would take the bait.

He stood there a moment and then he said, "That's a good possibility."

"Do you remember the last thing Ahmad said to Terrell?"

"I remember Ahmad telling him to leave the pharmacy."

"And what did Terrell say to him?"

"Terrell tried to act tough, but after he saw that Ahmad was packing a gun, he told Ahmad that he wasn't trying to make any trouble and left."

"Was that all the dialogue they had? Because they were talking for at least two minutes, so I believe that you're not telling me everything. You're leaving something out, so I want you to think long and hard—and not to leave anything out this time."

"What do you mean? That was everything."

"Tell me what Terrell said to Ahmad, after Ahmad walked into the pharmacy?" Agent Sims asked me. He gave me this stern look. Somewhere inside his mind told him that I could be bullshitting him. "Think long and hard."

"But I told you everything." I tried to reason with him, but he wasn't falling for the whole banana in the tailpipe.

"Misty, think long and hard." He wouldn't let up.

It felt like I was carrying a lot of weight on my shoulders and I wanted it off. And the only way I'd be able to do it was to tell Agent Sims everything. I took a long sigh and then I said, "When Ahmad walked in the pharmacy and noticed how Terrell was harassing me, he asked him to leave, but Terrell told him in so many words to mind his business because I was his girlfriend. So I interjected and told Ahmad that I wasn't Terrell's girlfriend and that I wanted him to leave. Ahmad turned toward Terrell and told him to leave, and Terrell asked him, 'Who are you?'

Ahmad told him that he was the owner of the pharmacy. Immediately after Ahmad said that he was the owner, Terrell said, 'Oh, so you're the one selling prescription drugs out of here?'"

"What did Ahmad say?"

"I'm not sure Ahmad understood what Terrell said, because he asked Terrell to repeat himself. But I prevented Terrell from saying anything else by grabbing him and escorted him to the front door of the pharmacy."

"Do you really believe that Ahmad didn't hear or understand what Terrell said?"

"There's a possibility that he could have."

"Why had you not told me this before?"

"Because I didn't think it was important."

"Every word of dialogue is important when it's coming out of the mouths of those mafia guys."

"Well, you should've mentioned it."

"Misty, we've been telling you this from day one."

"Yes, you have, but you didn't spell it out to me this way."

Agent Sims turned his attention to the birds flying outside of the window. After they disappeared around the building, he turned his attention back toward me. "Are you prepared to tell the detectives the same thing you just told me?"

"No, I won't. They'll try to trick me into saying something they want me to say and I can't let that happen. And especially without a lawyer present."

"I will be there with you, if they decide that they want to talk to you," he assured me. But I wasn't giving in to that lame-ass alternative. What did he think—I was stupid or born yesterday? It may not look like I have a bit of sense, but trust me, I do.

"No, if I don't have a lawyer, then there's nothing else to talk about," I said, making it plain and clear.

"As you wish," he replied, and changed the subject. "How was your visit with your mother? The agent outside your room told me that she visited you."

"What do you want me to say? She came in, she said hello, and then she asked me, how was I doing?"

"What did you tell her?"

"There wasn't much for me to say. Seeing me lying in this bed speaks for itself."

"Were you able to talk her into going into witness protection?"

"We didn't talk about it. She was more concerned about why I tried to kill myself than anything else."

"Is she still planning to go to her boyfriend's family's house?"

"Yes, she assured me that she would."

"I hope she does. If she doesn't, then she could be signing her own death certificate."

"Is that all you can think about? I'm so sick of hearing about people dying," I stressed to him.

"I'm sorry, but that's the world we live in."

"Look, can we talk about something else, please?"

"Well, what do you want to talk about?"

"Anything but that."

"Okay, well, let me be the one to tell you that immediately after you arrived here at the hospital, we had the doctor discharge him so we could transfer him to the federal holding facility."

"Is that supposed to make me feel good? Or am I supposed to say thank you?" I replied sarcastically.

"Listen, I'm only trying to keep you informed as we proceed with this investigation."

"Why don't you do me a favor and bring my grand-mother back!? Bring my cousin Jillian back too, while you're at it."

"Oh, don't try to put that blood on my hands. You're responsible for the death of your cousin. Remember, she and two other guys came to your place of employment to rob it. Now she'd still be alive if things hadn't gone down the way it did."

"I told you I had nothing to do with it!" I roared. The fact that he was trying to get me to confess that I had something to do with the botched robbery made my blood boil. I'm sure he knew I had something to do with the robbery. Any blind man could see it. But as long as I could hold on to my freedom, the more time I'd have to take care of what I needed to take care of.

4
PLEAD THE FIFTH

Agent Sims could not have left any sooner than he had. The sight of him was making me become nauseated. While I lay in the bed, I tried to watch TV, but I couldn't focus. Instead, I continued to sift through all the channels. I finally settled on watching a TV movie about a woman recently diagnosed with HIV and hospitalized while she was pregnant and in her last trimester. The night-shift nurse and the woman became very close. Knowing that the nurse couldn't have babies, the woman started the adoption process so she could gift her baby to the nurse. The movie was great and it invoked a lot of feeling inside of me. I cried at the end after the woman with HIV died. The nurse was brokenhearted when the woman died, but she was totally grateful that the woman had gifted her that beautiful little girl.

All and all, the movie was great. It was also an eye opener for me: the fact that that woman died, but still had love and compassion in her heart. People like her come a dime a dozen. My takeaway from that movie was not to take things for granted.

After the movie had gone off, I found myself a little restless, so I turned the volume of the television down a little and closed my eyes. While I was lying there with my eyes closed, I heard two voices outside of my room door. One of those voices I knew belonged to Agent Taylor. The other voice came from a woman. Before I could decipher what they were saying, the door to my room opened and in came two plainclothes detectives wearing their badges strapped to their belts. I was not happy to see them. "I already told Agent Sims that I didn't want to talk to y'all. So please tell me why you are here?" I asked sarcastically.

"Ms. Heiress, my name is Detective Belle, and this is my partner, Detective Caesar," she said, extending her hand as she approached my bed, while her male partner smiled.

"I don't shake hands," I told her while I gritted my teeth at her and him.

They were both cops that looked like they weren't a day over thirty years old. "Will you give us just a couple of minutes to ask you a few questions?" he spoke up, pleading.

"I don't have anything to say," I replied.

"Can we at least tell you why we're here?" Detective Belle pressed the issue.

"Look, I saw you on the news standing next to Mrs. Mason."

"Yes, we were there. And that's why we're here. Hoping you could shed some light on where Mr. Mason could be," the female detective said.

"I told Agent Sims that I haven't seen Terrell since the other day."

"And what day would that have been?"

"Ask Agent Sims."

"Where is this Agent Sims?"

"Ask the agent sitting outside my room, he'll tell you."

"Could you think of anywhere Mr. Mason could be? His family would greatly appreciate it if you could help us find him."

"That's bullshit and you know it. His mother was talking shit about me on live TV. She basically said that I knew where he was, because the last time she spoke to him, he said that he was on his way to my house."

"So you didn't see him the night that he disappeared?" she asked me.

"I don't know what night that was."

"We're guessing it was the night of the last time his cell phone pinged at the cell phone tower near your apartment building," she explained.

"Once again, I don't know what night that was. I told Agent Sims the thing I'm telling you now. The last time I saw him was the day the agents came by my apartment to talk to me. Now, I don't know exactly what day that was, but that was the last day I saw him," I lied. As much as I tried to prevent myself from giving these detectives any information about the last time I saw Terrell, they managed to get it out of me anyway.

"Does he have any enemies?" the female cop asked me.

"Who doesn't have enemies?" I said nonchalantly.

"I don't have any," she said.

"Neither do I," Detective Caesar interjected.

"Oh yes, you do, you just don't know it." I made them painfully aware of that.

"Has Terrell ever been abusive to you?" Detective Belle asked.

"What do you mean, when you say 'abusive'?" I wondered out loud.

"Has he ever beaten or attacked you?" she clarified.

"No, he never put his hands on me," I told her. I saw where she was going with this question. If I told her that Terrell and I had fought before, then she would suspect that if something happened to him, I could be behind it.

"That's not what his mother said," Detective Caesar said.

"Look, I don't care what Mrs. Mason said. He and I have argued over a dozen times, but we never had a physical fight!" I roared, because by this time, they had pushed me to the limit.

"Misty, I'm sorry. Detective Caesar and I didn't come all the way here to upset you. We came here today so you could clear up some things for us. That's it. So, if there's anything else you could think of, we'd really appreciate it," she said, changing her tone to a meek and calm woman. She knew that she had to change the tone of her voice so that she could continue to get me to answer her questions. She had no idea that I saw right through her bullshit-ass antics.

"I told you all I can tell you," I told them. I figured if I kept talking to them, they'd get more information out of me that I didn't want them to have. And who knows? I could possibly put my foot in my mouth and incriminate myself. They'd put handcuffs on me faster than I could blink my eyes.

"Can you tell us why you and Terrell broke up?"

"It was because he couldn't keep his dick in his pants."

"How many times had he cheated on you?"

"Let's just say that it was a lot."

"Do you know any of the girls that he cheated on you with?" Detective Caesar wanted to know.

"What do you think, I walked around with a pen and clipboard?"

"Most women I know would know these things," Detective Belle said.

"I stopped counting after he cheated on me for a third time, causing me to have a miscarriage."

"I'm sorry to hear that."

"Don't feel sorry for me. Not having a baby with him was the best thing that could've happened to me," I told them. Finally acknowledging verbally that I had a major loss sank deep into the pit of my stomach. No one knew this but Jillian and me. Terrell hadn't even known this. If he had, I knew he'd have tried to kill me sooner than he tried the night I took his life.

"How did he take it when he found out that you had a miscarriage?"

Becoming frustrated, I said, "Look, I've answered enough of your questions. I'm done. So, will you please leave?"

"Sure, we can do that. But would you take a polygraph test for us?" Detective Caesar asked me.

"Hell nah, I'm not taking a polygraph test. Are you motherfuckers crazy?" I roared. Now they had really crossed the line. "Agent Taylor, would you please remove these cops from my room?!" I yelled loud as I could.

"Well, tell us what you're involved in that would have

US Marshals babysitting you?" Detective Caesar asked. He was acting really petty.

"What I'm doing for them doesn't have shit to do wit you," I spat.

"It would give us an idea of what kind of person we're dealing with," Detective Belle chimed in. By this time, Agent Taylor had opened the door to my room. "What's going on?" he asked as he stood in the entryway of the door.

"Get these rookie-ass cops out of my room. We've talked enough."

"Don't mind us, Agent Taylor, my partner and I are leaving now," Detective Belle said as they both began to walk toward the door of my room.

"You should've left when I told you the first time!" I yelled.

Before Detective Belle walked completely out of the room, she looked at Agent Taylor and handed him her card. "If she decides that she wants to talk to us further, please call me."

"Agent Taylor, you might as well throw that card away, because I don't have anything else to say to them. I don't know where Terrell is, so leave me alone."

Agent Taylor took the card and shoved it down into his pocket.

After both detectives left my room, Agent Taylor stood at the doorway and said, "What happened?"

"If you were in here, then you'd know," I replied sarcastically, and then I turned my attention right back toward the television. Instead of commenting, Agent Taylor closed the door.

5

AN UNEXPECTED GIFT

After those detectives left my room, everything from there calmed down, just like I wanted it. I was surprised that Agent Sims hadn't come back to the hospital to check on me. But what he did do was swap Agent Taylor out for another agent. He walked into my room and introduced himself as Agent Fuller. He was an older black agent, and in my eyes, he was an Uncle Tom. A kiss-ass, if you will. Immediately after he made the introduction, he asked me if I needed something and I told him no, and that's when he exited my room.

The following morning I woke up very early. It was six o'clock, to be exact, and I felt rejuvenated from the day before. The nurse that was assigned to me, along with the medical tech, came and went at least five times. Thank God for His angels, because He sent one in here with my breakfast in tow. When it's time to eat my food, the ladies always gave me my space.

I powered on the television while I ate my food. First I watched *The Price is Right* and then I tuned into the reality show *Shahs of Sunset*. I swear that is one of my favorite reality shows on Bravo. As soon as that show ended, I flipped the channel again to watch *The Wendy Williams Show.* That show is another one of my favorite reality shows. While I was caught up in the drama that those women also found themselves in, the local news station interrupted the show for an emergency broadcast.

"Just over an hour ago, the remains of a decapitated male were found inside of a heavy-duty satchel in the crematory area of Webbers' Funeral Home during a routine inspection by the Virginia Beach Fire Marshal Department. From what the marshal told us, the remains were badly decomposed, which means that the body had to have been there for more than a few days. When we spoke to the owner of this family-owned business, he said that he'd been out of town for a week on business and that he left a trusted staff member to run things while he was away. He also expressed that nothing like this has ever happened before and that he would cooperate fully to help Virginia Beach Police solve this gruesome mystery. No one knows the identity of the male, but Virginia Beach Police said that they will work tirelessly to find out. My name is Tonya Spaulden and you're watching *Ten on Your Side.*"

Anxiety paralyzed me instantly. It felt like I couldn't breathe and that all the walls around me were collapsing. "Oh my God! That's where Tedo and that girl took Terrell's body to." I whispered so that only I could hear me speak. Lying in the bed made me feel helpless. If only they would've done what they were supposed to do. *Now I'm fucked!*

"Come on, Misty, you got to think of a master plan and pray that that body doesn't belong to Terrell," I spoke in a whisper-like manner.

After mulling over every word that the news reporter had uttered, I completely lost my appetite. I mean, who would want to eat after seeing their life flash right in front of them? There was no way in the world that I was going to get out of this situation. With Tedo dead, all I had to worry about was homegirl April. Because if the cops found out that she had something to do with Terrell's body being there, then I knew that she was going to throw my ass underneath the bus.

The lady that had brought my breakfast came back to pick up the tray. "You hardly touched your food," she commented.

"I know. I just lost my appetite."

"Would you like for me to get you a cup of ice?"

"No, I'm good. Thanks," I told her, and then I watched her as she walked out of my room. "Misty, what the hell are you going to do?" I started whispering to myself again while I searched my mind for a flawless plan so I wouldn't get sucked into that murder case. I just hoped that even if April got caught, she wouldn't remember who I was and would take the fall herself. I knew that was wishful thinking, but anything other than getting charged with murder sounded good to me.

I finally got my anxiety under control and was ready to think clearly, until Agent Sims showed his face. As soon as he knocked on the door and I gave him the green light to open the door to walk in, I zoomed in on his facial expression and body language and immediately knew why he was here.

"Are you coming in here to tell me that I'm leaving this place?" I asked him, knowing that wasn't what he had come here for.

"Did you see the news?" He got straight to the point.

"No, I haven't. What has happened now?" I replied, disinterested.

"Local authorities found a decapitated male body inside of a funeral home."

"Where are you going with this?" I asked him, trying to play it cool. Didn't want to come across as afraid or nervous. Sims was a great judge of character, so if I showed him anything other than me being unfazed by what he had to say to me, he'd know on the spot that I had something to hide from him.

"I just want to know how you'd feel if that body is, in fact, Mr. Mason."

"I really wouldn't have any feelings about it either way you put it."

"So you wouldn't be upset about it?"

"Of course, I'll be hurt by it, but with everything I've got going on, I can't think about him. And speaking of which, why did you allow those Virginia Beach detectives to come here to talk to me, after I told you that I didn't want to talk to them?"

"Sorry about that. I never got a chance to inform the agent on duty yesterday that that interview shouldn't have happened."

"Yeah, tell me anything," I commented.

"So, how did it go?" he questioned me.

"Well, it was two detectives. One of 'em was a lady, and the other one was a man. The woman did the most talking."

"So, what did she say?"

"She basically wanted to know when was the last time I saw or spoke to Terrell. So I told her the last time I saw him was when you and Montclair stopped by my house."

"But that's not accurate. Remember, we've got footage of him stopping by the pharmacy right after we saw him at your apartment," he corrected me.

"Okay, well, my bad. I forgot."

"Well, you know that I'm gonna have to give them the correct information, huh?"

I became frustrated. "But what difference does it make? I was only a day off."

"I understand that, but I'm an officer of the courts, so I can't withhold that information from them, especially since there's an open investigation going on."

"See, I knew I shouldn't have talked to them. You were supposed to keep them from confronting me. I'm in your care. Not the other way around!" I snapped. I was pissed off.

"Let's not get emotional."

"There's no other way to be but to get emotional. You left me amongst a pack of wolves."

"Look, did they put you in handcuffs and read you your rights?"

"No."

"Well, lighten up. It's not the end of the world."

"You're such an asshole!"

He smiled at me. "You know what? I've heard that twice today already."

"Then it should mean something."

"Not really," he replied nonchalantly.

"When am I getting out of here?" I changed the subject. "I'm so tired of being confined inside this room. I wanna go outside and get some fresh air."

"I'm getting ready to speak with the doctor on duty in a few minutes. I'm sure he's going to release you today, because you've been here for two days, and by law a suicidal patient has to be in the hospital and under watch for forty-eight hours."

"I've told everybody that has come in here that I won't ever try to commit suicide again."

"I'm sure you won't. But a lot of people say the same thing you're saying right now, which is why medical professionals are placed in situations like yours, just in case circumstances change."

"Look, do what you have to do so I can get out of here."

"Will do," he said, and then he exited the room.

While Agent Sims went to go and talk to the doctor on call, I sat there with all kinds of emotions ricocheting inside of me. One minute it felt like I was having an anxiety attack, then feeling optimistic. But then my feelings changed again. I knew it would be hard, but I wanted to be at peace. Be at peace with everything going on around me, regardless of my outcome. I guess in time, I might get just that.

It didn't take Sims long to come back to my room. "Got some good news," he said, giving me the phoniest smile he could muster up.

"So I'm being released today?"

"Yes, you are. The doctor said that he'll fill out the discharge papers by lunch and then you can leave." I looked at the clock and it read: 9:50. That meant that I was going to be in this hellhole for another two hours. "I've gotta be here for two more hours?" I complained.

"He gave a window of two hours, just to be on the safe side. I'm sure he's gonna let you out of here within an hour. So let me run back to the office and get a few things so we can take you to a safe house."

"Please don't take long, because I am ready to get out of here."

"I will be right back. But if you need anything, Agent Montclair is standing right outside your door," he assured me, and then he left.

Once again, I found myself sitting alone, trying to figure out my next step, especially since there's only an amount of time before the cops reveal that they have Terrell's remains. And when this happened, there'd be a strong possibility that they're gonna want to come back and talk to me. Now I can't allow those rookies to play me like they did the first time. I'm gonna have to be on my A game. At this point, I can't afford to take any losses.

I started preparing myself mentally, since I was leaving this godforsaken place. It didn't feel like I was in a freaking institution versus a hospital. I figured it probably felt that way because I couldn't leave and go as I pleased. In addition, the fact that I was monitored closely swayed me to feel that way too.

It had been almost an hour since Agent Sims left my room. He said he had to run to his office to get some paperwork and then he was going to head back my way, so I watched the clock on the wall like the staff was watching me. While doing this, I decided to get dressed. I grabbed my purse too. I wanted to be ready when I was officially escorted out of this place.

Moments passed and I heard someone standing outside my door talking. A couple of seconds later, the door to my room opened, and in came the nurse that took care of me. She was smiling from ear to ear, carrying a beautifully wrapped gift box. "Got some chocolate-covered sweets for you," she announced as she walked toward me.

I smiled and zoomed in on the box and noticed that it was from a locally owned gourmet chocolate shop. They were known for their chocolate-covered strawberries, bananas, and pineapples. "Where did it come from?" I asked as she placed the gift box on the wheel table in front of me.

"A young lady dropped it off to the nurses' station and asked me if I could bring this gift to you."

"Really?!" I said, wondering who could've bought me this edible arrangement. Curious as to what chocolate-covered fruits were inside, I pulled the box closer to me so I could open it.

"Enjoy!" the nurse said as she exited my room.

With anticipation, I took the bow off the box and lifted the top up slowly. Instantly I screamed. *"Ahhhhhhhhhh!"* I pushed the box onto the floor.

Alarmed by my yell for help, Agent Montclair burst into my room with his gun drawn. "My mama's hand is in that box. Oh my God! They got my mama." I began to sob hysterically. I jumped up from the bed and rushed toward the door. By this time, the nurse had turned around and come back to my room. "What's going on?" she asked.

Meanwhile, Agent Montclair was picking up the box

and my mother's hand with a surgical glove he got from the box near my bed. "My mama's hand was in there. They got my mama! We gotta help her before they kill her!" I started crying uncontrollably as I pointed toward the floor.

"Did you say your mother's hand?" the nurse asked me while she stood in the entryway of the door.

"Agent Sims, you need to get back here ASAP." I watched Agent Montclair speak through his cell phone. "Grab her things and get her out of here!" Agent Montclair instructed the nurse.

"Where do you want me to take her?" the nurse wanted to know.

"Put her in another room!" he yelled at her.

"Wait! Who's gonna get my mama back? They gon' kill her if we don't hurry up and get her back!" I yelled. I wanted everyone in the freaking hospital to hear me.

"Come on, let's go," the nurse said after she grabbed my purse from the chair near the bed. "I'm gonna put her in the medical suite," she informed Agent Montclair, and then she grabbed my hand and pulled me into the hallway.

Scared and panic stricken, I followed the nurse down the hallway. "What's going on, Pamela?" another nurse asked.

"Get on the radio and call security," the nurse with me said.

"What should I tell them?" the other nurse asked.

"Tell them we have a Code 33. And tell security to locate a young, small-framed white female wearing a blue T-shirt and white jeans. Don't let her leave the hospital."

"Okay, I'm on it," the other nurse said as she raced in

the opposite direction. It was apparent that she was on her way toward the nurses' station.

Meanwhile, the nurse with me continued on our walk toward the other end of the hallway. The moment after we arrived at the room I was supposed to stay in, the nurse unlocked it and pushed the door open. "This is where you'll stay until we are told otherwise."

"Okay," I said, still sobbing from the images I had in my head about my mother's hand. I took a couple of steps toward the bed in the middle of the room and then I took a seat on the edge of it. I watched the nurse close the door and lock it while I scooted around, trying to find a soft spot on the bed.

As I sat there, all I could do was cry and wondered why my mother's hand was chopped off and sent to me in a fucking chocolate box. It wasn't a secret about who did it. The answer I needed was why? Why cut off my mother's hand and send it to me? I also wondered what kind of message they were sending. And what state was my mother in? Was she dead? Or was she alive? I needed these questions answered? And I needed them now.

Trying to juggle every thought in my mind, I wondered how those motherfuckers found her. And if they also had her boyfriend, Carl, too? If they did, why take him? He had absolutely nothing to do with what I had going on. Nor had my mom. Now I've got to figure some things out.

I continued to cry my eyes out when I heard the lock on the door click and then it opened. When I looked up, Agent Sims walked in. I sat there and bawled my eyes out.

"How are you feeling right now?"

"I just opened a box and found my mother's hand inside of it, and you want to know how I'm feeling? What kind of question is that?" By this time, my tears had saturated my face. Moments later, I got up from the bed and started pacing the floor in that room.

"How do you know it's your mother's hand?"

"Because when she came to see me yesterday, I complimented her on the color of her fingernail polish." I cried even harder.

"We took the hand down to our office so we can get a forensic professional to examine it."

"What is there to examine? I told you, that's my mother's hand. So what you need to be doing now is getting a team together and going to look for my mother," I snapped. Agent Sims was surely testing my patience.

"Listen, Misty, I know you're upset, but I'm gonna need you to calm down so I can get your full cooperation," he said.

"Is it about my mother? Because I don't want to hear anything unless we're talking about how we're gonna get my mother back. Getting her back is all I care about."

"Don't worry about your mother right now. I've got another team of agents searching for her at this very moment."

"Do they know where to go? Or where she is?"

"We got some very good leads, so let us handle it. Right now, we need to concentrate on getting you out of the hospital and into a safe house, at least until all of this is done and over with."

"Are we leaving now?"

"Yes, we are. So let's go."

6

MOVE INTO ACTION

Still sobbing my eyes out, I stood up and proceeded to the door. Sims snatched a couple of tissue papers from a napkin box near the door. After he handed them to me, I wiped my eyes and my cheeks. By the time Agent Sims and I walked into the hallway, two other agents were waiting for us there. The only one I recognized was Agent Taylor. The other one I hadn't seen before. "We're gonna take her down to the basement and exit the left wing of the hospital adjacent to the coroner's office," Sims said.

"Let's move it," Sims continued, and then he led the way to the stairwell. It was me with a total of three agents escorting me down to the basement. I had a mixture of emotions while the agents and I raced toward the nearest exit. My tears wouldn't stop. They started coming with every step I took. And all I could think about was where my mom was and if she was still alive.

We finally made it to the basement garage of the hospital and Sims started giving the other two agents instructions. "Taylor, you stay here with me while Kennedy goes and gets the car," he said.

"I'm on it," the very tall, medium-build Caucasian man said, and then he walked off.

While Agent Kennedy went to fetch the car, Agent Sims and Agent Taylor started a dialogue. I stood there and wallowed in my own state of emotions and misery.

"Do you have a location yet?" Agent Taylor asked Sims.

"Yes, it was just confirmed about five minutes ago," Sims told him.

"When we find my mama, will she be able to come where we're going?" I threw out there. I wanted to know if they were hatching out a plan for her.

"Misty, I can't confirm that right now. Let's focus on getting you safely out of here and then discuss getting your mother next," Sims said.

"That's not good enough. You guys pulled me into some bullshit-ass drug investigation, when I wanted no part of it. And when I was forced to be your eyes and ears, I realized that I didn't have a choice. On top of that, I lost my grandmother, my cousin, and only God knows that I could have lost my mother too. But do y'all care?"

"Yes, we do."

"That's bullshit! All you care about is arresting those drug dealing–ass killers and putting them in prison. Outside of that, it doesn't mean shit to you!" I shouted while I sobbed even more.

"Will you shut the fuck up with all that crying! You've been running your mouth since I met you. And it's getting old!" Agent Taylor shouted, and then he pulled his government-issued handgun. Shocked by his sudden outburst, Agent Sims and I looked at him like he had just lost his damn mind. We both looked at Agent Taylor's gun and then we looked him in the face.

"What are you doing?" Agent Sims asked him.

"Yeah, why the fuck you got a gun pointed at us?" I asked, trying to see through my glassy eyes.

"Didn't I tell you to shut up?!" Taylor roared. I could see the veins protruding through his forehead.

"Taylor, what's going on?" Agent Sims wanted to know. Sims even took a couple of steps toward him with his hands half up, like he was trying to play it easy and not cause any trouble.

"Stop right there. Don't move another fucking inch or I'm gonna have to take you out," Taylor warned Sims.

"I knew there was a reason why I didn't like you. You're a fucking traitor!" I spat as I gritted my teeth.

"Call me what you want, you fucking informant. I'm gonna get one million dollars to deliver you to the Malek family. And do you know what I am going to do with that money? I'm gonna get on a one-way flight out of here and never look back," Taylor explained.

"What about your wife and kids?" Sims asked him.

"What about her? She a low-down, dirty bitch!"

"Come on, Taylor, don't say that."

"Don't tell me what to say. Do you know that those two kids aren't really mine? Now, could you imagine how I felt when I found that out?"

"No, buddy, I can't. But I promise you, if you put your gun away, I will make sure that you get the best therapist so they could help you cope with what's going on at home." Sims was trying to reason with him.

"I don't need you to help with shit. Just take your gun from your waist, put it on the ground, and slide it over to me," Taylor told him.

"Please, Taylor, don't do this," Sims said carefully, still trying to play it easy.

"Look, I'm gonna only say this one more time. Take your gun from your waist and slide it on the ground toward me." Taylor was repeating himself, and I could tell that he was getting agitated by Agent Sims.

"All right, all right," Sims said, and slowly removed his pistol from the waist area of his pants. I watched him as he kneeled down to place his gun on the ground, and immediately after he slid the gun across the concrete floor, we heard the car that Agent Kennedy was driving. It was coming in our direction. Agent Sims and Agent Taylor and I looked back at the car to see how far it was from us. This took the focus off Agent Sims's gun, so when they realized how close Agent Kennedy was, they turned back around simultaneously. Agent Sims rushed toward Agent Taylor and they started wrestling each other for the gun Taylor had in his hands. Seeing this gave me my way out. Before Agent Kennedy got any closer, I took off running back toward the door that led to the stairwell. As the door closed behind, I heard two gunshots. *Pop! Pop!* Alarmed by the sounds, I raced back up the stairs and only traveled up one flight of steps. Panting and breathing erratically, I knew that I had to calm down and act normal when I opened the door to the first floor and walked through the lobby. So that's what I did.

I wiped my eyes as the door closed behind me. I was fortunate that only four people were sitting around near the front entrance of the hospital. I could tell that the three people sitting down near the help desk were family.

The older woman had to be the grandmother, the second person was the mother, and the last person was the daughter. Three generations of love. I would do anything to have that right now. The other person was an old black man that looked like he was waiting for his wife to come back from the bathroom or something. He was reading a newspaper and was the least interested in what was going on around him.

I continued toward the front door, and luckily by the time I had walked to the curb, I saw a taxicab dropping two people off. I took a couple of steps and leaned into the passenger-side window. "Could you please give me a ride?" I asked him, hoping he'd say yes, considering he could've taken another call before he dropped these two people off now.

"Where are you heading?" the white man asked me.

"Anywhere but here," I told him without giving it much thought. My only mission was to leave this place before the agents came looking for me. Knowing that Agent Taylor had agreed to bring me to the Malek family for $1,000,000 was horrifying to think about. I mean, who could I trust now? If the Maleks managed to get Agent Taylor to work for them, then who else had they put on the payroll? *Damn! My life is worth that kind of money?*

I jumped in the taxi and instructed the cabdriver to head toward I-64. "Copy that," he said.

I sat in the back seat and found myself looking out the back window at least over a dozen times. The cabdriver noticed and asked me if everything was all right. I let out a long sigh. "Yes, it is. I'm just making sure that my boyfriend wasn't following us," I managed to say. That answer was the only thing I could come up with.

"Listen, lady, I don't want any problems. Men can be really crazy and dangerous. I see it all the time when guys beat up on their wives and girlfriends."

"Sir, I promise you don't have to worry about that."

"That's what they all say."

"I'll tell you what, after you get on the highway, take me straight to the IHOP restaurant on Military Highway."

"Okay, we're on our way," he said, and then he pressed down on the accelerator a little harder. While en route to IHOP, I couldn't help but tear up again. I was an emotional wreck right now. My mind was going in circles and my anxiety level shot through the roof. How could a young woman like me manage all this stuff that I was going through? Coping with the murders, now I sat in this back seat and wondered if Agent Sims had been shot. I do know for sure that someone had to have taken that bullet. I'd find out later who it was, I guess.

The cabdriver finally dropped me off at the IHOP, and before he pulled away, I paid him and included a tip. He was pleased and told me to take care of myself. I told him I would, and then I headed into the restaurant. I waited inside the IHOP in the sitting area and watched the cabdriver as he drove out of the parking area. As soon as he was completely out of sight, I headed back outside and flagged another taxi driving by. When he saw me waving, he slowed and came to a complete stop alongside Military Highway and Raby Road.

"Where to?" the cabby asked.

"Take me downtown," I said.

"Where exactly?"

"Down on Cleveland Street."

"North or south?"

"South," I told him, and then we were off.

I sat there with my head resting against the headrest of the back seat. I racked my brain trying to piece all my thoughts together, but I couldn't. *Here I am sitting in the back seat of the taxi, trying to figure out where to go or where to hide, because there is a gang of mercenaries and dirty cops looking for me. How has my life come to this?*

I knew I'd done some bad things in my life, but I'd never done anything that would warrant me to be in this situation. My heart ached because I didn't know what kind of state my mother was in. For all I knew, she could be dead, just like my grandmother and my cousin. Not only that, but I had blood on my own hands. So when the authorities figured out that they had Terrell's body, I was going to have to figure out how I was going to deal with that.

My whole life was screwed up because I stole a couple of muscle relaxers, which I gave to my cousin. How stupid could I have been? My only hope right now was to find a way to get through all of this bullshit before the cops found out that I had killed Terrell.

"We're here, ladybug," the cabdriver announced.

I lifted my head and noticed that we were in the downtown area, traveling down Cleveland Street. I looked around at the different people walking around on this busy street. Cleveland Street had a multitude of restaurants, retail shops, and grocery stores. ALDI was a grocery store located two miles from my apartment. I frequented this place when I wanted fresh seafood. My purpose for driving by was to check out the scenario before I had the cabdriver circle around the outskirts, near my place. I would not have asked the cabdriver to drive down my street, no way. That would've been a dummy move! But I did have him cruise the area so I could see what was going on. I figured that there could be a possibility that the DEA could have a couple of agents posted up around here, waiting to see if I pop up out of nowhere—or so they thought.

"Will you slow down?" I asked the cabdriver after he zoomed up on an older lady walking out of the grocery store. I looked at her twice and realized that I was looking at my neighbor Mrs. Mabel. My heart stopped. I wasn't sure if I wanted the driver to stop and let me out or have him continue driving. After I thought about it, my gut told me to get out of the car. "You can let me out here," I instructed him.

When I stopped the cab, I paid him and then I exited the car. I walked with my head down as I pursued her. I had no idea what I was going to say to her, which was scary because what if she screamed for help and grabbed the attention of the people in the immediate area. "Misty, just remain calm. She's not going to give you any problems," I whispered quietly to myself.

By now, I was within a few yards of her, and she was stuffing grocery bags into the trunk of her car, so I began to rehearse what I was going to say to her. Everything in my head said that if I stay calm, then she'll cooperate with me. But it seemed like the closer I came to her, all that confidence went out of the window.

Within a matter of minutes, she had put her grocery bags into her car and had made her way into the driver's seat. I had no other option but to call her name. "Mrs. Mabel," I said, loud enough for only her to hear me.

And even though she heard her name being called, she had no idea where it came from.

She turned around and looked to the right side of her

car and then she looked behind herself, failing to look to the left. "Mrs. Mabel, I'm right here!" This time she heard me and sat there like she was paralyzed. Thankfully, she didn't drive off. "What are you doing around here? Do you know that police detectives have been all around the apartment complex? They've been asking all the neighbors questions about you," she told me as I stood before her.

"Mrs. Mabel, whatever the cops are saying about me is a lie. They're trying to make me look like a bad person, but I'm not," I began to explain to her.

"Why don't you get in my car before someone recognizes you," she insisted as she removed her purse from the passenger-side seat. After I climbed into the seat, I leaned the seat back a little, just in case I had to duck down.

"Mrs. Mabel, you have no idea what I have been through these last few days, so I really appreciate you talking and letting me into your car."

"It's okay. I know you do," she said to me, and then she drove out of the grocery store parking lot. "So tell me what's going on, because cops have been on high alert these last couple of days."

I knew I had to choose my words carefully before I uttered anything. Mrs. Mabel was an elderly woman, and she had to be at least sixty-five years old. If I told her that I was involved in a drug heist gone bad, and I'd also managed to kill my ex-boyfriend on top of that, this lady would probably call the cops on me in a heartbeat. And looking at it from her perspective, I wouldn't blame her. After thinking about what would be more appropriate to say, I told her that the cops were looking for me because they thought I had something to do with my ex-boyfriend going missing.

"You know what? That's exactly what the police said when they came by my place," she acknowledged.

See, I knew it. I knew that if I had said anything about the DEA drug bust, how my grandmother and my cousin were murdered as a result of it, this lady wouldn't have let me into her space. In her mind, the cops can't convince her that I had something to do with Terrell's disappearance because that's not the person she sees me as. She sees me as this very polite young lady that lives alone and aspires to be a pharmacist. That's it.

"When did they come and speak with you?" I asked her.

"They stopped by yesterday. It was very early in the morning. It was about eight. I had just prayed and read my Bible. It was a white woman and man. They were both nice. I asked him if they wanted to come in, so I let them in. The woman did the most talking."

"What did she say?"

"She wanted to know how long you been living in the building. Then she showed me a picture of your male friend and asked me when was the last time I saw him with you—"

"And what did you say?" I cut her off.

"I told them that I didn't remember. But I did tell them how disrespectful he was toward you. I even told them how I've seen him push you around outside your car a few months ago."

"You saw that?" I asked her.

"Yes, I saw it. I've seen and heard some other things too, but I knew what to say and what I shouldn't. See, I was a victim of abuse at the hands of my first husband forty years ago. One day I woke up and said that I wasn't going to let him put his hands on me anymore. And he didn't."

"What did you do?" I wanted to know.

"I tried to take his head off his shoulders with our son's baseball bat. After he fell down on the floor, I called the cops and told them what I did and where he was."

"What happened when the police got there?"

"They didn't do anything to me because a week earlier I filed a restraining order, so by him coming into our house, he violated the order, so I had just cause to defend myself."

"Where is he now?"

"He died a few years ago due to colon cancer."

"Oh, I'm sorry to hear that."

"Don't feel sorry for me. I'm living my best years right now."

"So where is your son?"

"He lives in California with his wife and kids. And they are doing wonderful."

"You mentioned that that guy was your first husband. Where's your second husband?"

"He died in a car accident ten years ago."

"Wow! You've been through a lot," I commented. I mean, she'd been through more drama than I had. She was definitely a strong woman. While she gave me some backstory on her life, I realized that we were driving around in a circle, and I pointed that out. "Are you sure that we should be doing this?"

"What's wrong with me doing this?"

"I don't wanna bring any attention to your car, just in case the cops are hanging out around here."

"Would you feel better if I pull over?"

"Yes, please," I replied.

"Will it be all right if I park in the shopping center across the street?"

"Yes, Mrs. Mabel, that would be great," I told her.

Having her take instructions from me, I felt even more comfortable being in her presence.

Right after she found a parking spot in front of Carlo's Bakery, she powered off her car. "So, what are you going to do? Go back to your apartment?" she questioned me.

I thought for a second, and it was only because I needed to come up with a plausible answer. After hearing stories from her past, I now knew that she was a very smart lady, and she wouldn't take shit from anyone. So, after mulling things over, I said, "I figured that if I go home, the cops are only going to harass me, and I can't have that kind of drama in my life. I just want to be left alone."

"I can understand that," she agreed. "Why don't you go to your grandmother's place?"

"She's in the hospital. I literally just came from seeing her," I lied, trying to sound as sincere as possible.

"What is going on with her? Will she be all right?"

"Yes, she's going to be fine." I lied once more. What I really wanted to do was get off this subject concerning my grandmother. I was really hurting inside just thinking about the fact that she was dead.

"So, what about your mother? Why don't you stay over there for a while?" Mrs. Mabel suggested.

"My mother is out of town and she left her boyfriend at the house, and see, he and I don't get along, so I'd rather just stay away from over there. At least while she's gone." My lies continued. I swear, I had no idea how I was so able to come up with these stories so quickly. My only hope was that I would remember these same lies if I was confronted with them later.

"I'll tell you what, why don't you stay at my place for a while. At least until your mother comes back," she offered. I couldn't believe that she uttered those words from her mouth. As much as I wanted to take her up on her offer, how was I going to sneak into her house without anyone seeing me?

After thinking about it for several minutes, I said, "Okay, I will stay with you, but I cannot let anyone see me."

"So, how are we going to do that?"

"Okay, I'll tell you what, since we don't have parking garages and only carports, I want you to drive back home and act normal, just in case the cops are watching our building. Park in your designated spot, get your things from the trunk, and go into your house like everything is cool. And while you're doing that, I'm gonna stay inside your car and wait until nightfall before I get out. After I get out, I'm gonna duckwalk the entire time, until I get to your front door. So make sure you keep watching out for me. As a matter of fact, when you see me coming toward your apartment, shut off the light so no one will see you opening your front door," I instructed her.

"All right, I can do that."

"Well, then, that's our plan," I said.

"But wait, do you really think you can stay in my car all those hours. It's just after two o'clock now."

"Don't worry about me. It gets dark around five thirty or six, so I will be fine," I assured her.

Mrs. Mabel let out a long sigh. "Okay, I guess you know what you're doing," she commented, and then we put our plan in motion.

7

SCARED SHITLESS

Ms. Mabel and I did a little small talk until we got in front of our apartment building. We stopped talking immediately after she put her gearshift in Park. "Well, we're here," she said without a lot of movement from her mouth. A lot of people can read lips, so this was why she used that tactic to communicate with me. And before she got out of the car, she told me to be careful not to let anyone see me. I promised her that I would do just that. I also thanked her for helping me out. After she told me "you're welcome," she closed the driver's-side door and walked away from the car. From there, the time started ticking.

I knew I had at least four hours to hide out in this car before I would be able to exit. I thanked God for the cool weather outside, because if it had been a typical summer day, I'd be in a world of trouble.

While I hung out in Mrs. Mabel's car, I heard several

comments from one of my neighbors as she walked by Mrs. Mabel's car and stood thirty feet from it. The voice sounded familiar, and as I continued to hear it, I realized that it was my neighbor Candace. Candace lived in the building next to Mrs. Mabel and me. She was a small-framed black woman. She and I never talked really, but we did do the introduction thing, which was why I knew her name. I also found out that she was married with three kids, and that she was middle-aged, with a bum for a husband. All of her children were in middle school, so I knew that they were young. Unlike her, her husband was very social. I saw him canvassing the neighborhood many times to see who he could flirt with while Candace was at work. He never tried to flirt with me, because if he had, I would've hurt his feelings.

Candace was talking on her cell phone. I couldn't hear the other person, but Candace sure made up for it with the juicy details of a fight she had with her husband. Judging from her conversation, I figured the fight with her husband started because he called her a ho! "I told him that he better not ever call me a ho again. Or I was going to put him out of the house for good," I heard her say.

She fell silent for about eight seconds and then she said, "The only reason why I am still with him is because of the kids. If we didn't have the kids, I would've divorced him long ago." Once again, she fell silent. But after a few more seconds, she said, "I told him he needed to go and live with his mother because I am so tired of coming home every day and seeing him sit on the sofa playing video games. This is not the life I signed up for after I married him," she continued. The rest of her conversation started fading away because she had started walking toward her apartment building.

After sitting on the passenger-side floor for some time, my back started hurting, so I climbed into the back seat of Mrs. Mabel's car. This freed my legs up, so I was able to stretch them out.

An hour and a half later I heard voices again. This time it was two guys walking by. Thankfully, they didn't walk directly by Mrs. Mabel's car, because if they had, I wasn't sure if they'd see me or not. I was able to eavesdrop on their conversation. Well, at least seven seconds of it. "Yo, dude, what was the last time you seen that chick that lives in that apartment building?" one guy asked.

"I don't know. Maybe a few days," the other guy answered.

"Did you hear that she probably had something to do with her boyfriend going missing?" the first guy said, but I still wasn't able to recognize either one of their voices. I peeped between the two front seats and was able to get a look at them both. To my surprise, they were my neighbors Sid and Lloyd. They were roommates and college students at one of our local universities. Both of them tried to flirt with me, on more than one occasion, but after I assured them that I would never date either one of them, they stepped back and gave me some space. But according to another neighbor, those two said that I tried to flirt with them and they told me that I wasn't their type. Fortunately for them, I decided not to confront them. Because if I had, I would hurt their poor little feelings.

"I can't picture her doing that. But you never know," Lloyd said as they walked on toward the apartment building.

After I analyzed the conversation between the two, the one thing I could take away from it was that when people heard that I might have had something to do with Terrell going missing, they didn't believe it. That, of course, was a good thing in my eyes. I just hoped the detectives saw it that way too.

No one else walked into the area of Mrs. Mabel's car, so I was forced to lie back on the floor and reflect on my life. I remembered growing up with both my mother and my father in the same home. A lot of my friends didn't have that, so I was fortunate from that aspect. The unfortunate thing about it was that I found my mother and me fighting for my father's attention. My mother has always thanked my dad for coming into her life when he did. She would tell him all the bad things my grandmother did to her as a child after my grandfather had passed away. My grandfather was a savior in my mother's eyes. So she felt like she had to fight my grandmother for my grandfather's attention. And because of it, that behavior trickled down to my mother. She found herself fighting me for my dad's attention. It was one bad cycle. I just wished that my mother would've had a healthy relationship with my grandmother. If she had, my relationship with her wouldn't be strained. And to know that she could be somewhere dead, that caused me so much pain that I couldn't live with right now. "God, please help me," I said aloud. "God, if You help me to get out of this situation and find my mother, I will be in total debt to You." I started praying aloud. "And, Lord God, I know it seems like I only come to You in prayer when I need something. But I really don't feel that way. I just know that You can handle my situation better than I can. So I beg You right now, to help my mother and Carl. Because they shouldn't be punished for something I did wrong. They don't deserve it. They need You, Lord God. In Jesus' name, I pray. Amen."

After my prayer to God, I closed my eyes and thought

about how I cannot be spotted getting out of Mrs. Mabel's car. I was gonna have to stay as long as I could on the ground while traveling up to her front door. But what was most important was not allowing my neighbors to see me too. Not all of them like me, or know me, for that matter. So, if they saw me and watched me go into Mrs. Mabel's apartment, they could report me to the cops. And the last thing I wanted to do was get picked up by the cops. After seeing Agent Taylor turn on Agent Sims for a million-dollar payoff, I cannot trust anyone with a uniform or badge. For all I know, all the cops and agents are crooked. So falling into their hands would end dangerously. And I couldn't have that. Not today or tomorrow.

I looked up at the sky and saw how the sun was beginning to set. And, boy, was I happy, because I had to pee like a little kid that had just consumed a gallon of Kool-Aid. It was that bad.

Fortunately for me, though, Mrs. Mabel decided to walk back out to her car. She got in the driver's seat, placed her purse on the passenger-side seat, and then started up the ignition. "I want you to keep still and stay where you are," she instructed me.

"What's wrong? Is everything all right?" I questioned her from the back seat.

"Those same detectives are camped out on the other side of the street so they can see if anybody comes close to your apartment."

"You're kidding, right?" I asked her, even though I believed her already. I just needed her to confirm what I had just heard.

"No, I am not kidding. I have to drive by them, so stay calm."

"Will they be able to see me in the back seat?"

"No, but we can't take any chances."

"So, where are we going?"

"I'm taking you on a ten-minute ride so we can get you a wig and another set of clothing. That way, when we come back, you won't have to stay in the car. You'll be able to walk in my house with me," she explained.

I was partly relieved that Mrs. Mabel cared for my well-being more than I thought, but the other part of me was scared that her plan for me might not work. What would be the chances if the cops saw me walking into her apartment? Boy, that would be devastating.

"Do you know how long they've been out here?"

"It's been a little over an hour. I saw another car drive by our building too. But they didn't stay. They did stop alongside the other detectives' car for a few minutes and then they sped off."

"Did you see which direction the other cop car went?"

"They headed in the opposite direction of where you and I are going," Mrs. Mabel said, and then she fell silent. I, on the other hand, became a nervous wreck. Every thought in my head began to spin around in circles. I couldn't think straight at all. I almost told Mrs. Mabel to drop me off at the nearest police station. But when I thought about the possibility that my mother could still be alive, I decided against it. I figured I would be of more help if I stayed out on the street, instead of in jail. I was my mother's only savior, so I knew I had to remain strong and figure this thing out.

While I was still lying on the backseat floor, I heard Mrs. Mabel pulling into a shopping center parking lot. She told me that she would be right back. I lay on the floor of her car for about ten minutes, if that. As soon as she got back into the car, I heard her scrambling items around inside of a plastic bag. Couple of seconds later, she handed me a wig and a jacket. "Put both of them on. Now, I know it ain't fashionable like the wigs that you young girls wear, but it'll do what it is supposed to do," she instructed me. A few minutes later, she pulled her car up to the side of the road and told me to get in the front seat. And I did just that. After I closed the passenger-side door, she sped off.

I turned around and faced her. "How does it look?" I wondered aloud.

"It looks perfect," she replied, and then she smiled.

"Now, when we get back to the apartment building, I want you to walk directly beside me and pretend like we're having a conversation. Don't look at anyone but me. Got it?"

"Got it," I assured her.

As planned, Mrs. Mabel drove back to the apartment building. Immediately after she parked the car underneath our carport, she and I got out of the car and headed toward her apartment. Thankfully, we didn't see those detectives sitting in their parked car across from our building. And even though they weren't around when we came back, something in my gut told me that they were somewhere near. "Come on, we only got twenty yards left before we get to my apartment," she coached me.

It seemed like with each step I took, the closer we were out of the woods. I couldn't help but look at my front door as I approached the building. From the outside, everything looked intact. The kind of look like no one lived there. And what's crazy about it is, the apartment belonged to me. I lived there. Everything I owned was inside and I couldn't get to it. Now, how messed up is that?

"Here we are," Mrs. Mabel said as we walked up to

her front door. I stood beside her while she unlocked the door. "Come on in," she continued after she walked through the entryway. I followed her inside. And when I stepped to the side, she closed the door behind me and locked it. I let out a sigh of relief. I couldn't believe that I had made it inside of my neighbor's apartment without being detected. It felt like a whole bunch of weight was lifted from my shoulders.

"Can I use the bathroom?" I asked her immediately after she locked the door.

"Sure, honey, it's right there to your left," she pointed out, and then she walked into another room in her apartment.

It didn't take me long to use the bathroom. After I washed my hands, I headed into the front area of Mrs. Mabel's apartment. She was in the kitchen pouring a cup of hot water. She didn't hesitate to ask me, "Want a cup of hot tea?"

"No, I'm fine. Please let me thank you again, Mrs. Mabel. You are a lifesaver. I really appreciate everything you did for me today. You went over and beyond for me. And I can't thank you enough," I expressed, getting a little teary-eyed.

"Why are you about to cry? Is everything all right?" she asked me while she added a tea bag to her coffee mug.

"I'm not about to cry," I lied while I wiped my glassy eyes with the back of my hand.

"It sure looks like you're about to cry, to me." She handed me a paper napkin from the paper towel holder near the kitchen sink.

"I'm just tired. Tired of everything I've got going on with my family. I wish I could go on a vacation and just forget about all the drama I have in my life," I told her after I took the paper napkin from her.

"Whatever you got going on, baby, you can always count on God to make everything right."

"I talk to God every now and again."

"What you need to do is talk to him every day. Three times a day if you have to."

"I know. I'll get better at it," I assured her.

"Come on into the living room so we can sit down and watch some TV together. What kind of TV shows you like? And don't be talking about the reality shows. I don't watch that mess. Those people be airing all their business on TV. I know their parents are ashamed of them. I know I would be if my child was up there. I will cut their butts off and change my number."

Mrs. Mabel was an old soul—a woman with years of experience and wisdom. So to hear her talk about how the new generation of children is today gave me a warm feeling, because she spoke from the heart. Looking at her made me think about my grandmother. Lord knows what I would do if I could have her with me right now. Life with her would be really good.

"I know this may shock you, but I like this show called *Shark Tank.* A person can learn so much by watching that show," I said.

"I watched it a couple of times. The episodes I saw were good. But I don't know if it's on right now."

"I'll watch anything you wanna watch. Just as long as it is not the news. I've been watching the news channel for two days straight and I am so tired of seeing or hearing one bad thing after the next."

"If you don't watch the news, then how are you going to keep up with what's going on around the world? It's important to stay informed, especially since I live alone," she said.

"That's understandable," I said. But on the flip side, I wasn't interested in watching anything being broadcast from a news station. If Mrs. Mabel saw my face plastered across her television screen, along with the journalists reporting that I escaped federal custody and was a person of interest involved with Terrell's disappearance, I knew she would change her mind about me. And how could I come back from that? And who could blame her? I would probably act the same way. So, to prevent any of this from happening, I just prayed that my name didn't get mentioned while we were watching TV.

She and I agreed to watch the movie *The Green Mile*. When the movie started, she didn't like it at all. But I talked her into giving the movie another ten minutes. She did and eventually began to like it. Unfortunately for her, she fell asleep on the couch before the movie ended. I started to wake her up, but she looked so peaceful that I left her alone.

While she was asleep, I tried watching another movie, but I couldn't give it my full attention. Every time I heard noise, loud or small, I found myself peeping through Mrs. Mabel's window blinds. Nothing significant was going on outside. A few neighbors from the other building walked by to either go to their cars or take their trash to the nearby Dumpster.

During my peep shows, I found myself watching my apartment too. I couldn't see my entire apartment from the window I was looking through, but I was able to see my kitchen and living-room window. All the lights were off, of course, but somehow I was still able to make out a few things I had propped up near my windows.

Sitting here and being able to watch my apartment made me homesick. I was also sick because I wasn't aware of my mother's state. I could only hope that she was still alive, despite my seeing her hand cut off and placed in a fucking treat box. I swear, if I found out who did that to her, I was going to fuck them up. And that's my word.

8

BLINDSIDED

Mrs. Mabel woke me up the next morning with the smell of bacon and eggs. I had fallen asleep on the couch so I could be close to the front door. I figured if I stayed on the sofa, I'd be able to hear all the movement coming from the other side of the front door.

"Hungry?" she asked me after she noticed that my eyes were open.

"Kind of," I told her as I sat up on the couch.

"Well, go on in the bathroom and freshen up. I've got clean wash towels on the vanity next to the bathroom sink. There's a bottle of mouthwash underneath the sink," she replied while she continued shuffling plates and forks around near the stove.

"Okay, thank you," I said, and then I headed in the bathroom. I peed, washed my face, and gargled a mouthful of mouthwash. As soon as I was done, I headed back into the kitchen with Mrs. Mabel. She had two plates of food on the table when I walked into the kitchen. "This food looks so good," I commented as I approached the table.

"Well, come and have a seat. We can't let the food get cold," she instructed me as she was taking a seat at the table herself. I took a seat next to hers. "Come on, bow your head so we can pray."

Upon Mrs. Mabel's request, I bowed my head, closed my eyes, and then I let her take it away. Her prayer consisted of thanking God that she woke up this morning. She even thanked Him for keeping her with a sound mind. I said a quiet prayer. And my prayer was that God would allow me to look for my mother without getting hurt. I even asked God to cover me from the dirty cops, the dirty DEA agents, and the Malek family. Those guys didn't play fair, so I would need to stay on my A game and try to stay alive as long as possible. The slightest slip and fall would definitely cause my demise. And I couldn't have that.

My prayer was simple and quick. Mrs. Mabel's prayer was a few minutes longer than that. She ended it by thanking God for having me as company and she told Him to guide my steps. Her words were touching. I got filled up with emotions. And immediately after she said the word *Amen,* I thanked her.

"Oh, sweetheart, you don't have to thank me. Thank our Lord and Savior. I'm just His vessel," she explained as she picked up her fork.

I picked up my fork too and started eating. After I put the first forkful of eggs in my mouth, it melted on my tongue. "Hmmm, Mrs. Mabel, your eggs are so good."

"Thank you, darling, but you haven't tasted my bacon yet."

"I'm about to do so right now," I assured her while I broke the bacon in half and stuffed the first half of it into my mouth. Just like the eggs, it also melted in my mouth. "I haven't had eggs like this in a long time."

"I'm glad you're enjoying them," she said while she continued to eat. "Did you get a good night's rest?"

"Yes, ma'am, I did."

"I heard you talking in your sleep a few times last night."

"I was told that I do that from time to time."

"You better stop it. Because one day, you might say something and the wrong person could be around to hear it."

"I know," I agreed.

But before she uttered another word, we heard a knock on the door. I went straight into panic mode. My heart fell into the pit of my stomach. I placed my fork down on my plate of food and stopped chewing, thinking that it could be heard from the other side of the front door. "Are you expecting any company?" I whispered.

"No," she whispered back, and then she stood on her feet.

"Please don't let anyone know that I'm here," I begged her, pressing my hands together like I was beginning to pray.

"Don't worry. I won't," she assured me, and walked away from the table.

Instead of staying at the kitchen table, I hid myself in a small room in the kitchen that she used for storing her food. It was just big enough for me to fit in there.

"Who is it?" I heard her yell to the person outside her front door.

"I'm Agent Sims, and I'm with Detective Belle. We

were wondering if we could ask you a few questions," I heard Sims say.

I also heard when Mrs. Mabel opened her front door. That move scared the crap out of me. I felt that in any moment, Agent Sims and that local cop could walk into the house without giving Mrs. Mabel consent and find me hiding in this closet. Boy, would my life be over.

"How you doing, ma'am?" I heard Sims say.

"I'm doing well. Now, what can I help you with?" Mrs. Mabel got straight to the point.

"Detective Belle and I are looking for the young lady that lives in this apartment next door to you. So we were wondering if you've seen her."

"No, I haven't. And what are you guys doing in her apartment?" I heard Mrs. Mabel ask. She seemed alarmed by it.

"Ma'am, it's official police business," Agent Sims said.

"Police business, my foot. You just can't go into her apartment like that," Mrs. Mabel protested. I heard the anger and frustration in her voice and she was upset.

"Listen, ma'am, it's really important that we find her, because she may be in serious danger," I heard Detective Belle say.

"Wait a minute, why are you guys taking fingerprints and stuff? Who's gonna clean up all that black dust on her door and in her apartment?"

"Ma'am, wiping away fingerprint dust is the least of our worries. We need to find Misty before someone else does," Agent Sims chimed in. "Here, take my card, and if you hear anything, please call me," he continued.

"I sure will. And when I talk to her, I will definitely let

her know how you're messing up her apartment," Mrs. Mabel warned them.

"Thank you for your time," Detective Belle said.

"Yes, thank you," Agent Sims spoke up.

After I heard her close her front door, I walked out of the food pantry and took a seat back at the kitchen table. She walked back into the kitchen and placed the business card down on the kitchen table. "Did you hear what they said?" she wondered aloud after she sat back down in her chair.

"Yes, I did."

"They said that your life may be in danger."

"They're lying, Mrs. Mabel. They're just saying that as a tactic to get you, and whoever else, to help them find me. And look at me! I'm here with you. So, how could I be in danger? They are full of lies." I was trying to convince her.

"You know, they're messing up your apartment with all the black fingerprint powder?"

"I heard."

"You know that stuff is really hard getting off."

"I'm sure I'll find a way," I said nonchalantly, even though I was on pins and needles. I began to rack my brain, trying to figure out why they're dusting my apartment for fingerprints. And then it hit me that they can't be looking for anything else but Terrell's fingerprints. This realization shot my blood pressure through the roof of Mrs. Mabel's apartment. The thought of them using forensics gave me a ton of mixed emotions. I knew that before they left my place, they were going to find every piece of DNA they could find. And before I knew it, I was going to be on the FBI's Most Wanted poster. *Fuck! Fuck! Fuck!*

Mrs. Mabel dug back into her food, but to save my life, I couldn't lift the fork from my plate. I had literally lost my appetite. "You're not gonna eat the rest of your food?" she wanted to know.

"Yes, I'm gonna eat it," I told her, but in reality, I wasn't. My mind was too fixated on them motherfuckers that were looking for me. *Why won't everybody just leave me alone?* I'm speaking of Sanjay's family, the homicide detectives, the DEA agents, and the people who have been ordered to kill me. And in the mix of things, I now found myself trying to cope with the death of my grandmother, my cousin, and maybe my mother. *How much longer am I gonna have to go through this?* I was a strong woman, but I still have weaknesses. So, if I'm given enough strength to go forward, then I will do that and see where it takes me.

"Will you excuse me?" I asked her.

"Sure, honey," she replied.

I stood up from my chair. "Is it all right if I look out of your living-room window?" I asked.

"Sure. You go right ahead," she insisted, and then she stood up behind me. "When you look out the window, look through the blinds this way," she instructed me as she pointed at the side she wanted me to touch.

"Mind if I sit on the arm of the sofa?"

"Sure, honey."

Taking directions from Mrs. Mabel, I sat on the arm of her sofa, giving it just a small amount of pressure; then I pulled back the blinds on the right side of the window. Once again, I couldn't see the front door of my apartment, but I got an eyeful of traffic patrolling the sidewalk and grass that led to my apartment. I didn't see Agent Sims or the other detective, but I saw a team of forensic investigators and two uniformed policemen. I saw them looking around their surroundings. I saw one of them look at the window I was looking out of. I pulled the blinds closed a little to prevent either one of them from seeing me. You can never be too careful.

Mrs. Mabel sat on the couch and began watching TV. She asked me a few questions while I peered out of her window. "Have you wondered what they could be looking for? They're over there going all over your personal things. I know if they were going through my stuff, I would go over there and put a stop to it."

"See, that's what they want me to do. But I won't give them the satisfaction," I reasoned. I had no other choice but to come up with that lame-ass rebuttal. I just hoped that Mrs. Mabel bought it.

"The police officer that said her name was Belle was the one that stopped by here before, asking me when was the last time I seen my ex-boyfriend."

"Oh, so that was who you were talking about?"

"Yep, that was her," she confirmed.

Hearing Mrs. Mabel confirm that Detective Belle was one of the cops that talked to her about Terrell put a big perspective on what was going on at my apartment. I now knew the reason why they were in my place. They just found out that they did have the remains of Terrell's body, so now they needed to trace his DNA to something or someone. But guess what? If they did, I could argue the fact that he and I used to date. And even after we broke up, he still came around. The only way they'd be able to link him to me was if Tedo's homegirl April stepped up to the plate. Otherwise, I was good.

I sat at that window for at least two hours and watched the cops and the forensic team sift inside and around my building. I even saw local cops talking to a few of my neighbors. I noticed a couple of them creating dialogues with them, but the rest of my neighbors weren't that interested. That made me feel safe and secure.

After fishing around my apartment for almost three hours, those cops finally left. It was a weight lifted when I saw them leave, but it also gave me a feeling of anxiety. Being in the dark about things concerning you can be torture. The only thing good that came from the knock at Mrs. Mabel's door was that I finally found out that Agent Sims was not shot when we were in the underground garage of the hospital. I was now left to wonder what happened to Agent Taylor. I mean, I was not concerned for that traitor. But I am curious to hear if he was shot or killed. I was sure that information would come in due time.

9

TAKING NO PRISONERS

I sat around on the couch and watched a few TV shows, but I wouldn't be able to tell you anything about them. Mrs. Mabel hopped in the shower and changed clothes. When she reappeared in the living room, she asked me if I wanted to take a shower too. "I need a change of clothes," I told her.

"Well, I'm too big for you to wear my clothes."

"I see that."

"Why don't you go over to your place," she suggested.

"I was just thinking that. But what if one of those detectives is watching my apartment?"

"What's the worst thing that could happen?"

I wanted to tell her that if I was caught, I'd be locked up on sight. I also wanted to tell her the reason why they would lock my ass up was because I'm a person of interest concerning Terrell's murder, and I was a government informant for the DEA. But let's not forget that I'm also supposed to testify against several members of a mafia family. But I knew she would freak out if I had, so I left well enough alone. Instead, I said, "I just don't like them harassing me is all. But what I will do is when it gets dark, I'll sneak over there and get some things then."

"Okay, well, I got a doctor's appointment, so I'm gonna head on out. If you need something, call me."

"You don't mind leaving me here in your place by myself?" I asked her. It was shocking to see how trusting she was of me.

"What are you going to do? Rob me of my millions of dollars?" she joked.

"Oh, stop it, Mrs. Mabel. You're being funny now."

"No, you're being funny!" She smiled. "Remember, if you need anything, give me a call," she continued.

"I will," I assured her.

I watched Mrs. Mabel as she headed out her front door. I even watched her as she headed down the walkway toward her car. After she got into her car, she sped away. Seeing her go made me begin to miss her, even though she had only been gone for a second. It felt good to have her stick by my side. This time yesterday, I left the hospital and had no idea where I was going. Now I'm here in the comfort of my neighbor's house, with access to views of my apartment that I would not have had if she hadn't opened her doors for me.

I sat there at the window and gazed out into the neighborhood and watched everybody come and go as they pleased. It's funny how we take the small things for granted. I would love to leave here and take a stroll down the road and take in some of this fresh air. But since I can't, staring out this window will have to do.

Unexpectedly, an unmarked car pulled up and the driver parked it alongside the street directly across from this apartment complex. My heart began to race uncontrollably. Not knowing who was in the driver's seat concerned me, especially since all the windows were up and tinted. Being that I couldn't get a look into the car, I stepped back a few inches from the window, just in case whoever was in the car had binoculars and was able to see me from that distance. While anxiety filled my entire body, I wondered how long those people in that car planned to be there. *Damn! It sure sucks being a wanted woman.* Just think, a month ago, I was happy to go to work, enjoyed talking to the customers, and relished the fact that one day I was going to be a pharmacist. The head pharmacist, at best.

But no, I ruined those chances by getting caught up in the illegal prescription-drug ring. How stupid was that? Now I sit here taking the repercussions like a boxer would take a jab to the face. Unfortunately for me, I didn't know how to fight back. And that's why I was in this situation.

While I sat there and watched the car, I noticed the similarities of this car and Agent Sims's car, and that's when I realized that this was the same car. Agent Sims had to be somewhere inside of it. Knowing this, I got an eerie feeling in my body. My stomach and my head were so screwed up, I needed some antidepressants to calm me down and put me to sleep. In the back of my head, I could hear Agent Sims saying, "Misty, you gotta be straight up with me. And if I find out that you're doing anything different, I'm gonna lock you up and you will never see daylight again."

He always found a way to threaten me, so I could service him with all his needs, which included being an in-

formant. He didn't care about me. All he cared about was
a victory in court and locking everyone up that I testified
against. That's it. That's all he wanted. Which is why I
believed he was sitting in that car. He was sitting there,
and hoping that I would come back to the area, so he
could take me back into his care. But I couldn't let him do
that. Not today. Not tomorrow. I'm gonna need to be on
my own so I could figure all of this stuff out.

After sitting there for over two hours, the unmarked
car finally drove away. But I knew he was coming back. I
couldn't say when, but I knew for a fact that he was. I was
his meal ticket for a promotion, so he was going to pull
out all the stops, so he could stuff me right back into his
back pocket.

I stood up from the arm of the chair and headed into
Mrs. Mabel's kitchen. I hadn't worked up an appetite
from my surveillance duties, but I was thirsty. I poured
myself a glass of juice and tried to enjoy every ounce of
it. And when I was done, I rinsed the glass out and placed it
in the dish rack. Right when I was leaving the kitchen, it
hit me that right now would be the perfect time to sneak
into my apartment. The agents had left and might not
come back until later on. *Come on, Misty, you can do it.* I
began to give myself a silent pep talk. *If you go there
right now, it will only take you three minutes at the most
to grab a few things to get out of there.* I continued to en-
courage myself.

While I began to mull over whether or not I was going
to go into my apartment, I looked back out the window,
just to make sure the car hadn't circled back around.
When I noticed that it hadn't, I raced over to the sofa,

grabbed my shoes, and placed them on my feet. Then I grabbed my house keys from my purse. Unsure as to whether or not I planned to go into my apartment, I raced back over to the window and gave it another look. Once again, the car hadn't circled back around, so I felt like I was good. *If I'm gonna do it, I need to do it now.*

Come on, Misty, you can do it. Is gonna only take you less than three minutes.

I raced for the front door and snatched it open. To my surprise, someone was already standing at the front door. "Hi, ma'am, would you like to buy a chocolate bar?" a little boy asked me while he held out a box of different kinds of candy bars.

Unsure as to how to answer this cute little boy, I paused and then asked him how much it cost. His answer was one dollar. I hurried over to the couch, where my purse was, grabbed one dollar from my wallet, and then I raced back to the door and handed it to him.

"Which one do you want?" he asked me.

"It doesn't matter. Just give me one," I told him.

After he handed me the candy bar, he thanked me and then walked away. I watched him as he headed to my front door, so I stopped him. "No one is there," I told him.

"How you know that?" he asked me.

"Because I live there."

"If you live there, then what are you doing over here?"

"Because I'm visiting my neighbor."

"What is all that black stuff on the door?"

"Just some black dust. It can be wiped off," I assured him.

"Cool," he said, and then he walked away.

I watched the little guy as he headed to another neighbor's apartment. I smiled at him because he was learning the hustle at a young age. He couldn't be older than eleven years old. Seeing him get his hustle on put a huge smile on my face. Boy, what would I give to be his age right now? He had no worries. No bills. No girlfriend problems. Nothing. And here I was with the world on my shoulders while everyone died around me. How fucked up was that? Hopefully, one day I'd have that same measure of peace that little boy had. *Wishful thinking, huh?*

"Hey, you better watch out where you're going!" I heard someone yell. I couldn't see who said it, but it brought me back to reality.

My main focus was to get into my place, grab a few pieces of clothes, and get the hell out of there. Time was of the essence, and I had to make it count. "Let's get it," I said, and then I rushed over to my front door, grabbed the doorknob with the bottom of my shirt, and then I used my other hand to unlock the door. Within seconds I had opened my door. I pushed it open just a tad bit to scope out my living room. When I felt like the coast was clear, I looked back at the street, to make sure no one was watching. When that checked out, I pushed the front door in, even farther, and scrambled inside.

As I got farther and farther into my apartment, I saw how those fucking cops had ransacked it. *How dare they have all my stuff out of place like this? Are they freaking crazy? Just look at the pillow cushions from the sofa on the floor, black dust all over my doors and doorknobs. Who they think is going to clean this shit up? Ugh!*

As the anger built up inside of me, the more my blood started boiling inside my veins. And as bad as I wanted to clean up the mess they made, I knew that I couldn't. I only came in here to get a couple of outfits, so that's what I was about to do.

I made my way into my bedroom and grabbed one of my overnight bags from my walk-in closet. After I tossed it on my bed, I grabbed one of my perfume bottles from my vanity, my deodorant, a couple pairs of jeans, shirts, panties, bras, and socks. Whatever I could grab, that's what I did. Once my bag was filled to the rim, I picked it up from the bed, turned around, and headed toward my front door. Three steps in, I heard a voice coming from outside my apartment, so I stopped in my tracks. While my heart rate tripled in speed per minute, an overwhelming amount of anxiety consumed me. "Stay calm, Misty," I whispered to myself while I stood there, wondering what was going to happen next.

"I'm sure that I left it here," I heard a woman's voice say. And then I heard the sound of someone turning the doorknob from outside. That's when I knew that person was coming in here.

Oh my God! Whoever it is, they're coming into my apartment. Shit! What am I gonna do? I panicked. Without hesitation, I turned around and ran back into my bedroom. Afraid to hide in my walk-in closet, I got down on the floor of my bedroom and pushed my overnight bag underneath my bed. As quietly as I could, I slid underneath my bed as well.

"I think I left the warrant documents in the kitchen," I heard the woman say. And that's when it hit me that she was on a call with her cell phone.

I heard her walk into the kitchen and then she stopped moving. "It's not in here," she told the caller. "Let me check the bedroom. It might be in there," she continued while her footsteps alerted me that she was coming in my direction. Boy, I was a nervous wreck.

Immediately after she entered into my bedroom, I was

able to get a look at her shoes and that's when I realized that the woman behind that voice was Detective Belle. She was right inside my bedroom. And the documents she was looking for had to be the search warrant and my arrest warrant. That had allowed the forensic team to go through my apartment and fuck it up. On a different day, I wouldn't be hiding underneath my bed. Instead, I would be cursing her ass out and showing her to the front door. But since I was a wanted lady, my desire to fuss her could only be a thought in my head, and that was as far as it would go.

"I got it," she told the caller. "It was lying on top of our suspect's dresser," she continued, and then she fell silent. A couple of seconds later, she said, "She was a person of interest, but now we have his remains, she's a suspect. Finding her before she tries to leave town takes precedence," she continued as she walked back out of my bedroom. She didn't utter another word until she got into the living area of my apartment. "If those stupid fucking agents hadn't let her get away, she would be in my custody right now. Speaking of which, we just learned that the mother was kidnapped forty-eight hours ago, so the DEA agents and my office assembled a team to try to locate her mother, since we just found out that she's still alive."

She made her way out of my apartment, and the next thing I heard was the front door closing. When I heard her locking the door from the outside of my apartment, I slid back from underneath my bed and then rushed over to my bedroom window. I peeped through my window blinds and watched Detective Belle as she walked back to her vehicle. "Lord, please let her get into the car and pull off. I can't afford to be arrested right now. I've got a lot of stuff I need to do, so please help me, God!" I prayed out loud.

I noticed that I always prayed to God when I fell into a trap. But it's not like I'm trying to use Him; it's just that I can't do these things on my own. And besides, if I get Him to handle it, things would end well.

After waiting for what seemed like forever, Detective Belle got back into her vehicle and drove away. Boy, was I happy to see that. Without any incident, I grabbed my bag and raced toward the front door of my apartment. On my way there, I passed by my lamp table and was side-tracked when my eyes glanced at two photos of my family in the picture frames. One of the pictures was of my mother and me when I was five years old. We were attending my preschool graduation. My mother really looked sober and proud of me. I swear, I would give anything to revisit that time in my life. It was a simple and drama-free life.

The next picture was of me, my mother, and my dad. This picture was taken while we were out together on one of our weekly family nights. We all looked happy too. I would pay anything to relive those days, but I can't. I will just be grateful that my mother was still alive, and maybe this situation would bring us closer, once we see each other again. Well, at least I hoped so.

Immediately after I realized that I couldn't go back in time, I once again snapped back into reality. "Come on, Misty, it's time to go," I said underneath my breath, and before I took another, I grabbed both pictures, tucked them underneath my right arm, and then I made my way back out of my apartment.

10
MY TO-DO LIST

It took me less time to get out of my apartment and return to Mrs. Mabel's apartment than it did when I left Mrs. Mabel's apartment to get into mine. Talk about speed. The moment after I closed and locked Mrs. Mabel's front door, I walked over to her couch and collapsed down on it, and then turned on her TV. "Fuck! Fuck! Fuck! That bitch said I'm now a freaking suspect in Terrell's murder! What the hell am I going to do now?" I began to sob. "When they catch me, they're going to lock my ass up without bond. And what will I do then?

"Why couldn't Terrell just leave me the hell alone? I told him on many occasions to go on with his life, but he wouldn't do it. So now I'm gonna have to go to jail because of him? This shit is unfair." I continued complaining while I sobbed. I swear, I wished that I had enforced my restraining order against that guy by calling the cops every time he reached out to me, then I wouldn't be in this jam. *Fuck!*

While I lay back on the couch, a news bulletin started broadcasting: "This just in, the Virginia Beach Police have released the name of the person whose dismembered remains were found two days ago inside the Webbers' Funeral Home. We're told that the body belonged to twenty-seven-year-old Terrell Mason. We understand that he lived in Virginia Beach and was the owner of a janitor business, which was thriving."

"He didn't own shit! He was a fucking drug dealer!" I blurted out.

"We spoke to the family not too long ago and they're saddened by this news and ask that we give them their privacy so that they can mourn the loss of their loved one. We reached out to the lead detectives of this murder investigation, but so far, we haven't heard back from them. We will keep you informed as this investigation continues. My name is Tonya Spaulden and you're watching *Ten on Your Side*."

I can't tell you how many times my stomach did somersaults. I just wished that everyone would shut up about Terrell. *Who cares if he's dead?* He was a piece of shit. He was disrespectful, a cheater, and he was abusive. So, why won't they air that? Why won't they talk about him being a drug dealer? He wasn't an owner of a janitorial business. He was a fucking swindler. And he didn't give a damn about anyone but himself, so kill that noise.

After the news report for Terrell ended, I wasn't interested in watching anything else, especially after almost running into Detective Belle and now hearing that Terrell's body had been identified. *What am I going to do now?*

* * *

I cried about my situation for the majority of the time Mrs. Mabel was gone. When she returned, I had managed to pull myself together by taking a shower and changing clothes. "Good evening, sweetheart," she greeted me when she came in the house. I was sitting on her couch and watching television.

"Hi, Mrs. Mabel," I greeted her back, giving her a warm smile.

"I see you changed your clothes." She noticed this after she had closed the front door and locked it. She walked farther into the apartment.

"You won't believe what I've done."

"It looks like you went into your apartment and got some clothes."

I smiled bashfully. "Yeah, that's exactly what I did."

"How does it look over there?" Her questions continued as she walked by me. I didn't realize she was putting her purse in her bedroom until she came back into the living room empty-handed.

"It's a mess. I started to stay in there and do a major cleanup, but I didn't want to take the risk of the cops coming and seeing me."

"What exactly did they do over there?" she asked as she took a seat on the love seat across from me.

"There's black dust everywhere. Doors, doorknobs, window seals, tables, and chairs, you name it."

"Why would they do all of that?"

"Mrs. Mabel, I haven't the slightest idea. Cops will tell you one thing and do another. They do it to keep everybody in the blind."

"So I hear that they found your ex-boyfriend."

"How do you know?" I asked her. I wanted to pick her brain to see exactly what she knew.

"The news came on while I was in the waiting area of my doctor's office. They showed his picture."

"Really?" I said, trying to act surprised.

"Yes. The news reporter said that they found his body and they have a few leads."

"I hope they find the person that did it." I wanted to make it look like I was concerned about Terrell and his family getting justice.

"I hope they do too. Because regardless what that guy did, no one deserves to die, especially the way he did."

"You're right," I agreed.

"You might wanna call his folks and send them your condolences."

Shocked by Mrs. Mabel's suggestion, I agreed with her gesture, but I knew I was never going to call Terrell's family. They would send the cops on my ass quicker than I could blink my eyes. In addition to them calling the cops on me, they'd tell me to shove my condolences up my ass, and rightfully so. They didn't care about how Terrell used to treat me. All they cared about was that the person that killed their loved one got what she deserved. Point-blank!

"Remember when the cops said that your life was in danger?"

"Yes, ma'am."

"Do you think that the person that killed your ex-boyfriend could be looking for you too?" she asked me. She gave me an expression of concern.

I thought for a second, because first of all, I'm the one that killed him, so if I tell her that, I'd be sealing my fate in a court of law. On the flip side, it was important that I be careful with my words because I didn't want her to think that by having me staying here in her place, she would also be putting her life in danger. So, what should I tell her? "Terrell had a lot of women. When he and I first started dating, an ex-girlfriend of his started stalking us. She threatened him bodily harm if he continued to see me. And she threatened me as well. Thank God she never went through with it, because I don't know what I would've done if she had. Oh, but just recently, I was told that Terrell owed a lot of money to some very bad people. So the only thing I can think of is that they went to him for payment, and when they realized that he didn't have it, they killed him," I said. Telling her this made-up story didn't take much to conjure up. I just hoped that the words I chose didn't scare her to the point that she wanted to get me away from her as quickly as possible.

"And you're not afraid for your safety?"

"No."

"And why not?"

"Because I don't know them. The only people he introduced me to are the people in his family."

"People in this world are so mean and cruel," she commented.

"Yes, they are, Mrs. Mabel. That's why I try to stay by myself."

"That's the way you gotta be sometimes. Can't trust people nowadays. You better learn from this situation with your ex-boyfriend and watch the company you keep," she warned me, and then she got up from her sofa and headed into the kitchen. "Want something to drink while I'm in here?"

"No, I'm good. Thank you, though," I said, watching her as she walked into the kitchen. Mrs. Mabel was a small woman in size, but she was a strong woman in wisdom and heart. You can't pull the wool over her eyes and tell her that it's cotton. And knowing this, I knew that I had to stay two steps ahead of her. While she grilled me with one question after the next, I wasn't sure if she was trying to catch me in a lie or she was trying to gain the facts about the saga concerning Terrell and my safety. Thankfully, the story I gave her sounded plausible and to her satisfaction, because if it hadn't, she'd probably send me packing.

11
A FEW HOURS LATER

Four hours passed and all I found myself doing was flying around Mrs. Mabel's apartment and watching television. Mrs. Mabel cooked an early dinner for us. The oven-baked salmon and steamed veggie medley hit the spot, considering I really hadn't had anything good to eat in the last two days. The food was delicious.

Once I filled my tummy, I got Mrs. Mabel to watch a couple of movies instead of watching shows with commercials running every seven to eight minutes. I felt like the less commercials we saw, the better my chances were that she wouldn't see any news reports concerning Terrell's murder case or anything with my name attached to it.

While the television was playing, I started thinking about my mother. To hear Detective Belle say that she wasn't dead gave me the happiest feeling in the world, which was why I cried after coming back into Mrs.

Mabel's apartment. And even though I saw a light at the end of that tunnel, I now had to find out where my mother was. I had no idea how I was going to do it, but I would find a way, even if it meant putting my own life on the line.

On her way to bed, Mrs. Mabel suggested that I sleep in the guest bedroom this evening. I thanked her, but insisted that I'd rather sleep on the sofa again. That way, I could hear what was going on outside. She told me she understood and went to bed. "Let me know if you need something," she said, and then she disappeared into her bedroom. I knew that it would be impossible for me to get a good night's rest because of everything I had going on. When I knew for sure that Mrs. Mabel had gone to sleep, I turned the TV station to the local news so I could stay informed of what was going on around the city. For the first couple of hours, there was no breaking news, so I grabbed a blanket from the hall closet and found a good spot on the sofa to snuggle into.

I hadn't realized it until I heard a noise that I had fallen asleep. At first, I thought it was Mrs. Mabel doing something in her bedroom, but when I muted the TV, I heard the shuffling sound again. After I listened for a minute or so, I realized that the sound was coming from outside, so I jumped into action. I powered off the television, and then I tiptoed to the window and peered through the blinds. I didn't see anything on the sidewalk or the grass that led up to this apartment building, so I crept to the front door and looked through the peephole. My heart sank into the pit of my stomach when I saw two men creeping into my apartment. I couldn't tell who it was because their backs were facing Mrs. Mabel's front door. One part of me wanted to open the door and let them know that I saw them, but then I realized that if I did say something, I could be putting myself in danger or at risk of being caught. So I stood there and watched as those two guys entered into my personal domain. I felt so helpless and defeated to have no say-so or be able to take action against something that concerned me. As I continued to look at my apartment door from Mrs. Mabel's apartment, my helplessness elevated to anger.

The feeling of hopelessness began to take over my entire body, and I felt like if I continued to stay there and did not do anything, then I might be allowing these guys to take things from my house that had sentimental value. And what they couldn't take, they could possibly destroy. I knocked on Mrs. Mabel's bedroom door and asked her if I could come in.

Swiftly she got up and opened her door in less than three seconds. She stood there with a puzzled expression on her face. "What's wrong? Is everything okay?" she asked me.

"No. I just saw two guys break into my apartment and now they're inside, probably stealing me blind."

"How do you know two guys are in your apartment?"

"Because I heard a booming sound while I was lying on the sofa. So I got up and looked out the window, and when I didn't see anything, I looked through your peephole, and that's when I saw them going into my apartment."

"Maybe it's the police," she suggested.

"The police are not going to break into my apartment. I heard them kicking my door, and then when I got up and looked at the peephole, they were going inside."

"Think we oughta call the police?"

"By the time they'd get here, those guys would probably be gone."

"So, what do you want to do?"

"If you could open the door and scare them, or let them know you see them, I'm sure they'll run away."

"I don't know, Misty. That sounds a bit dangerous. I mean, what if it's the men that killed your ex-boyfriend?" she asked me, her facial expression very grim-looking.

She went from this hard-ass lady that won't take anyone's shit to this meek and scared old woman. I guess that's when I told her that Terrell probably was murdered at the hands of some men he owed money to, I must have terrified her. *Damn! I really put my foot in my mouth.* Now I had to think of another way to get her on board so I could find out who was in my apartment.

"Look, I'll tell you what, we'll do it together, okay?" I tried compromising with her.

She hesitated and then said, "I don't know. I think it would be best to call the police."

"Never mind," I said, and stormed off.

"So, what are you going to do?" she asked in a whisper-like tone.

I ignored her because I didn't even know what I was going to do. So having her ask me irritated me, because all I needed her to do was open up her front door, yell to let them know what she knew—that they were inside my apartment—and that she was going to call the cops. And I really didn't know if this tactic could possibly scare them away.

"Hey, what are you going to do?" she repeated, but I ignored her again. And before I knew it, she was down on my heels.

I stood there for a moment, trying to figure out what I was going to do, and that's when she said, "Why don't you do it?"

I thought for a second and that's when that same idea popped into my head. And without further thought, I opened her door, slightly ajar, and yelled, "I know you're in there. Now you better leave before I call the cops."

I stood there and nothing happened. I couldn't tell you if they heard me and they were laying low to see if I was going to close the door. Or if while I was in the back of Mrs. Mabel's apartment, trying to get her to do what I was doing now, they had already left.

I continued to stand there while Mrs. Mabel stood behind me. She and I both stood still to see or hear what was going to happen next. And then a minute had passed and we heard a little crackle sound coming from my apartment. It startled me because I knew that there was still someone inside my apartment.

"Did you hear that?" Mrs. Mabel whispered.

"I heard you in there. Now this is your last warning. If you don't leave right now, I'm gonna call the cops," I threatened, and then I stepped backward just in case the people in my apartment wanted to wave their guns at Mrs. Mabel's apartment door.

"You heard her. We're going to call the cops if you don't leave right now," Mrs. Mabel blurted out. I couldn't believe that she opened her mouth. Just a few minutes ago, she didn't like the idea of opening her front door and making her presence known. Now she's all over the top of me, damn near breaking her neck to be heard. I looked back over my shoulder with a *now you wanna open your mouth* expression.

"Look, there they are!" she yelled, and startled the hell out of me.

I turned my attention back toward my apartment, and by the time I did, I could only see the backs of both men. I couldn't tell if they were white or black or young or old. I did manage to see that they hadn't had anything in their hands, so I felt a little better. "Did you get a chance to see their faces?" I asked her.

"I did."

"What did they look like?"

"Two young guys with dark hair."

"White or black?"

"White, I think," she said.

I pushed the front door closed and ran to a nearby window. I opened the blind and peered out between them and didn't see anything or anyone. "Fuck!" I spat. The frustration inside of me began to boil over.

"Watch your mouth, young lady," Mrs. Mabel chastised me.

"I'm sorry, Mrs. Mabel, but two guys were just in my apartment," I explained, trying to reason with her.

"They were probably some young punks that live in the neighborhood. They see the cops walking around this neighborhood, asking questions about you, and then running in and out of your apartment sends the message that you're not home. And if you're not home, your place is a breeding ground for robberies," she pointed out. But I wasn't trying to hear a word Mrs. Mabel was saying. It was bad enough that I had to deal with the fucking cops ransacking my place. Now here come more petty thieves. *Why don't these people just let me live in peace?*

Seething on the inside and dealing with the many

thoughts circulating in my head, I felt like I was about to have a nervous breakdown. *Tell me what's going to happen next? Ugh!*

Without saying anything, Mrs. Mabel opened her front door and then she walked out of the apartment. I was too distraught to find out what she was doing. I knew I needed to calm myself down so I wouldn't say or do anything that I might regret later.

"Those guys broke the lock on your door," she announced.

"They did what?" I asked her, even though I already heard what she said.

"I closed your door, but it wouldn't lock. The doorknob is slightly hanging off," she explained.

"You have got to be kidding me?!" I said, and then I removed myself from the arm of the couch, sat down on the cushion, and then buried my face into the palms of my hands.

"I'm gonna call the cops," she informed me, and reached for the cordless phone for her landline, which was on the end table beside her lamp.

I quickly looked up. "No, don't do that." I was totally against the idea of her calling the cops. What was she trying to do, get me arrested?

"Why not?"

"What are they going to do? I mean, it's not like they're gonna fix my door."

"I think they will."

"I don't," I said, and then I stood up on my feet. "When you closed my door, did it open back up?"

"No, it didn't. It closes, but it doesn't lock," she replied, giving me a strange look.

"Okay, well, it'll be all right. I'll just stay in the living room and listen out for anyone else who tries to go into my apartment."

"I don't think that would be wise. What if someone else goes in there and comes back out and starts shooting at you this time?"

"That's just a risk I'm gonna have to take," I told her. And I was not backing down.

"I'm sorry, but I can't let you do that. You'll be putting me at risk if someone fires their gun the next time."

"I understand, Mrs. Mabel," I said, because I really wanted her to be quiet. Just a couple of days ago, she was taking up for me when she saw the cops ransacking my apartment. But now, her constant worrying was straining my nerves. What I needed her to do was to be quiet until I figured out what to do next.

"Are you still against me calling the cops?" She was pressing this issue.

"Don't call 'em. I'll take care of it," I said with finality, and then I fell silent. I didn't want to talk to her anymore. I was done engaging with her.

"Well, if you don't need me anymore, then I'm gonna head back into my bedroom. I got another doctor's appointment tomorrow morning," she announced, and then she went back into her bedroom.

I wanted to say, "Good riddance, you old bitch!" but I had to remind myself that she did open her house to me. So I needed to be patient and play by her rules.

I really needed this lady to lay low here in her house. My safe house for now. But I was beginning to wonder what her deal was. All of a sudden, she wanted to talk to the cops? She didn't want to talk to them when they questioned her on two occasions. I could really see how flaky she was getting. Before too long, she was gonna want me to leave. And to be ready for it, I was gonna have to get my exit plan together. I was gonna need a new place to lay low.

It had been a few hours since those guys broke into my apartment, so I hadn't had one wink of sleep. I'd walked from the window and back to the couch over one hundred times, to say the least. And in that time, I heard movement in front of the building, but when I looked out the window, I could tell that the noise came from cats and dogs running around the Dumpster near the street. I also saw a couple of cars drive by the building. Surprisingly, I hadn't seen any cops in plain clothes ride by. And this was strange too. I figured now that I was a suspect in Terrell's murder, why wasn't some cop patrolling my neighborhood tonight? Or maybe they were and I just couldn't see them . . . food for thought.

Sleep finally caught up with me. It didn't stick with me long. I dozed off around five o'clock, and when Mrs. Mabel woke me up around eight, I realized that I slept for three hours. "I'm heading out," she told me as she headed toward the front door. "Let me know if you need something before I come back."

"Okay, thank you," I replied, and then I got up from the couch and headed to the bathroom. After I peed, I washed my face and brushed my teeth. When I came out of the bathroom, I walked over to the front window and peered between the blinds. A lot of my neighbors with cars were gone. Most of them were military, so I knew they were on the military base ten miles from here. I also didn't see an unmarked car parked across the street either.

Something was going on and I hated being in the dark about it.

While I was looking out of the window, I thought about my apartment. As bad as I wanted to leave here and sneak in there, so I could see how my place looked after those guys left late last night, I realized that I couldn't risk getting caught. So I left well enough alone. I'd have my chance to go back in there, but today was just not the day.

12

AMERICA'S MOST WANTED

As I thought about all the shit that happened last night, with the guys breaking into my apartment and Mrs. Mabel doing the switcheroo on me, it showed that it was only a matter of time before she was gonna get tired of me being in her apartment. I was gonna need to figure out something before it was too late.

I wasn't in the mood to eat anything, but I did, however, make myself a hot cup of tea. I added a little bit of honey to it and it was perfect. I found over the years that tea and two teaspoons of honey was a match made in heaven. It relaxed me too.

Once I had my hot cup of tea in hand, I headed back into the living room and powered on the television. I turned to the news on channel 10 to see if anything concerning Terrell's case was being reported, since Detective Belle mentioned to her caller that I was a suspect now. I needed specifics, so I waited thirty minutes, and nothing happened. Thirty minutes turned into an hour, and nothing happened. And one hour turned into two hours, but finally a reporter started her broadcast.

"Channel 10 has been following this story for a few days now. We first reported that during a routine fire inspection, the city's fire chief found a dismembered body in the crematory area of Webbers' Funeral Home. The body was identified and the deceased victim is Terrell Mason. Late last night, the Virginia Beach Police arrested a woman who, they believe, played a key role in this murder investigation. We're told the woman's name is April Roberts, she's thirty-four years old, and a bartender at a local gentlemen's club. Right now, there's no word on what charges Ms. Roberts is facing. But we will keep you updated as this investigation continues. I'm Mitch Leman and I'm reporting live for *Ten on Your Side*."

"No fucking way. This can't be. How the hell they find April?" I started off saying as my heart started beating uncontrollably. "She is going to throw me underneath the bus! There's no way she's going to take an L for the team, especially since she never got paid for it."

See the plan was for Tedo to pay her after we walked away with the shipment of Percocet and Vicodin. But since the heist fell apart, and Tedo is dead, she lost all the way around the board. So, once again, I knew she was not going to take this fight lying down. She was going to implicate me as soon as the cops pulled her into the interrogation room.

When the news report ended, I sat back on the sofa and thought about how my whole world was falling apart around me. The only good thing I had left in this world was when I heard Detective Belle mention that my mother was still alive. Knowing this lit a fire underneath me. And before anything bad happened to me, I had to make things right for my mother. She was the last blood relative that I had left. So that was what I would do.

Paranoid that there was a huge chance that Detective Belle told Agent Sims that I murdered Terrell, I had a sick feeling in my stomach. This whole time, I had played the I-don't-know game; and for them to find out different was going to give them a huge amount of playing field, so they could use me all they wanted.

Out of nowhere, and while I was sitting on Mrs. Mabel's sofa, I heard loud knocking from outside her front door.

Boom! Boom! Boom!

"Open up the door, bitch! We know you're in there!" I heard a woman say. Alarmed by it, I jumped to my feet, tiptoed to the front door, and looked through the peephole. I saw four women standing outside of my apartment. "Open this door, bitch, and come out here and face us!"

Realizing that Terrell's mother, two sisters, and his female cousin were standing outside my front door, and banging on it like their minds were going bad, started a whole new anxiety attack inside of me.

Standing there with their backs facing Mrs. Mabel's apartment didn't allow me to look into their eyes. I knew that they were mourning the loss of Terrell, but they needed to do that shit somewhere else. I didn't need that attention on my place. I just thanked God that Mrs. Mabel wasn't here. If she was, then shit would've really hit the fan. I could see her now, telling me to go outside and confront Terrell's family. I could also see her confronting them herself, talking about what kind of good person I was. And then that's when Terrell's mother and sisters would argue the fact I wasn't a good person. This whole thing could get ugly quick.

I stood there for at least five minutes, listening to them berating me like I was some fucking mass killer on the run. I thanked God that they didn't try to open my front door, because if they had, they would've definitely had access to my apartment. Shit would go downhill from there, I was sure.

Getting sick of hearing their mouths and the noise that they were making, I called 911 and explained to the operator about how loud and intrusive those women were and that they needed to be escorted from the property. Calling the cops today versus last night was a whole different ball game. Last night Mrs. Mabel's reason wasn't concrete enough for me. I figured since the guys had gotten away, why waste time calling the cops? How were they going to help the situation? They weren't going to be able to make any arrests because the guys had already left. Now today was different. These annoying chicks were causing a scene in front of my apartment. What was the point of it all? Since they hated my guts, then why don't they go about this differently?

"Everybody, this bitch that lives in this apartment had something to do with my brother's death," I heard one of his sisters yell.

"She sure did, and we ain't gonna let her get away with it either!" Terrell's mother yelled.

"She better turn herself in to the cops, because if she doesn't, I'm gonna beat her ass!" Terrell's other sister yelled.

"Could y'all take that somewhere else?" I heard a voice say. By looking through the peephole, I couldn't see who the person was, so I raced over to the window to see if I could get a better look. And sure enough, I saw my neighbor that lived on the opposite side of my apartment. He was an older white guy. I can't tell you how old he was, but I do know that he was a UPS driver. He was also a quiet guy. Don't know if he has a wife or kids because I barely ever saw him.

"And if we don't, what's going to happen?" Terrell's cousin challenged him.

"Yeah, what are you going to do? Call the police," Terrell's mother interjected.

"Listen, lady, you guys are disturbing the peace," he replied.

"The chick that lives in this apartment disturbed our peace when she murdered my brother."

"Yeah, what do you have to say about that?" Terrell's mother chimed in.

"Look, I'm sorry to hear about your brother. But the cops have been all over this apartment complex. They've been asking everyone if they'd seen that lady. And none of us have, so what you need to do is get behind the cops that are investigating your brother's case and take that stuff up with them. Hanging out in front of her apartment door isn't going to bring your brother back," he said, trying to find a soft spot in this debate so he could defuse this situation.

"We understand what you're saying, but you can't tell a person how to mourn a deceased family member," I heard Terrell's cousin say.

"You're absolutely right. But as a resident, I felt like I had to tell you guys that you're going about all of this the wrong way. That's all." His tone turned sympathetic.

"We appreciate what you're saying," Mrs. Mason mentioned.

"Oh, no problem, ma'am! Now y'all have a nice day," he said, and then he walked off. I watched him walk to his truck, get in, and drive off.

A few minutes later, Terrell's mother, sisters, and his cousin all walked back toward the parking area of the apartment complex. I watched them until they climbed into a black Cadillac SUV and sped off.

I literally had to wipe the sweat trickling down from my forehead. *Damn! Who would've thought that Terrell's family would come to my apartment and create a scene like that? Fuck!* I was so glad that Mrs. Mabel wasn't here! If she was—oh my God—things would've blown right up in my face. That *I'm an innocent person* would've gone right over Mrs. Mabel's head. I'm sure she would've gone to the extent of making me face Terrell's family while they were outside of my apartment. I could see Terrell's mother calling the cops and telling them where I was, and while the cops were en route to my apartment, I would've been fighting one, if not all, of them. And three-girls-on-one wouldn't have been a fair fight, but they would not have cared. Getting revenge for Terrell was all they would've focused on.

13

PROOF OF LIFE

I settled my nerves after Terrell's family left. I thanked God for my neighbor. If he hadn't checked them, those silly-ass hos would've still been standing outside of my apartment making threats. I also thanked God for Mrs. Mabel not being in here too. Things would've definitely gotten out of hand.

As I sat in Mrs. Mabel's apartment, I did feel somewhat safe. But then again, I didn't. I couldn't say it enough about how I was going to get myself out of this situation. I was stuck between a rock and a hard place. I was beginning to feel stifled in this apartment. In addition to that, I felt like I had no say-so about anything concerning me. Everything was good in the beginning when Mrs. Mabel opened her door to me. Now I was having regrets and wanted a way out. But if I left, then where was I going? I couldn't go to my grandmother's house. I couldn't go to my mother's house either. I no longer have a job, so I couldn't hang out there. So, what the hell was I going to do?

Now that the cops had April in custody, it was only a matter of time before they came looking for me. There was not a doubt in my mind that they were going to plaster my face all over the TV and Internet. And once that happened, I probably wouldn't be able to walk anywhere in public. Talk about losing your freedom.

To get my mind off the stresses in my life, I hopped in the shower and thought that it would help me relax, but it didn't. Instead, I found myself bawling my eyes out. Tears soaked my face, and no matter how much I tried to wipe my eyes with my bath cloth, tears kept coming.

Thinking about my mother being in the hands of Ahmad's mafia was causing me to have a panic attack. I knew my mother has probably shitted on herself by now. My mother wasn't a ride-or-die chick like me. I knew how to survive a little. But she didn't know how to do that at all. *I gotta get her out of this situation, and I mean now.*

Immediately after I took my shower, I dried off and put on another change of clothes. Upon my arrival back into the living room, I looked outside to see if any new cars had parked in the area. When I didn't see anything new, I sat down on the couch and sifted through the channels on TV. It didn't matter what channel I turned to, I just could not get into it. I turned the channel back to the news station so I could stay current with the news. What had been bothering me was that my mother's name hadn't been mentioned in the news. What was the cops' angle? Was it not important to broadcast? Someone needed to say something to the public, just in case someone saw her and knew where she was.

So, what the fuck is going on?

I swear, I wanted to call Agent Sims and Detective Belle so badly and curse their asses out. What kind of game were they playing? My mother's life was on the line, so why hadn't anyone publicized it yet? Was it because she was my mother and her life wasn't important? Or were they waiting for me to turn myself in and make them do something in exchange for my role in Terrell's murder? Better yet, they wanted me back to testify against Ahmad's family, and once I did that, they'd send out a team to rescue my mother?

Whatever was going on in Agent Sims's and Detective Belle's heads, it needed to stop. An innocent woman's life was on the line and she needed to be found. Point-blank. I knew one thing, if they didn't spring into action, then I would, and I was going to expose everyone in my path.

After traveling back and forth to the window and back to the sofa over five times, I saw Mrs. Mabel as she pulled up underneath her carport and got out of her car. While she was taking a couple of bags from the back seat of her car, I saw the little boy that came by the day before. He was approaching her with his box of chocolate candy bars. I watched him as he talked to her about the assortment of candy he had. She smiled at him the entire time as he talked about what he had. A few seconds later, she started walking toward this apartment, and the little boy was in tow. To prevent her from unlocking the front door on her own, I stood there and opened the door myself. "I see you're back," I commented as Mrs. Mabel approached the front door.

"Yes, I'm here. And I got a little salesman with me," she said as she walked into the apartment. After she walked by me, she looked back at the little boy and said, "Come on in here, baby. And I'm gonna get you that dollar after I put these groceries down."

The little boy walked into the apartment and looked up at me. "Did you eat your candy bar?" he asked me. And that's when it jogged my memory that I hadn't eaten my chocolate bar. It also dawned on me that I had no idea what I did with it after he handed it to me. But then it hit me that as soon as he gave it to me, I took it with me into my apartment during which time I packed up a couple of outfits and stuffed them into my overnight bag. Alarmed by the fact that it was still there, and that it wouldn't be a good idea if the cops came back to my apartment and found it, I asked the little boy to go and get it for me. "Sweetheart, if you go into my apartment and get my candy bar that I bought from you yesterday, I will buy one more from you," I said.

"Where is it?"

"When you go in there, go straight to a bedroom straight down the hallway and you should see it on my dresser, near the mirror, or on my bed," I instructed him.

"Okay," he said, and then he turned around and walked away from me.

"It's already unlocked, so just push it open," I told him. I watched the little boy as he pushed open my front door and stepped inside my apartment. "Leave the front door open and go down that hallway." I instructed him further while I continued to watch him.

"Where did he go?" Mrs. Mabel asked after she walked up behind me.

"I just sent him into my apartment to get something for me," I told her.

She handed me a dollar bill. "Give him this dollar when he comes back," she said.

"Sure," I replied.

In a flash, the little boy disappeared in my bedroom and came out two seconds later with my candy bar in his hand. I smiled because he didn't know how he had saved my life by doing what he had just done. I mean, if Detective Belle or Agent Sims would've gone back into my apartment and noticed that a candy bar was there now, but it wasn't there the first time they searched it, they would've known automatically that I had been there. Thank God for little boys like this cute thing walking back toward me.

When he walked up to me, he handed me the candy bar I bought from him yesterday, and then he handed me two more. Another bar for me, and one for Mrs. Mabel. "Two dollars, right?" I said, and then I handed him the money.

"Yep," he replied as he took the two single bills in his hand.

Immediately after he took the money, he thanked me and then he turned around to leave. I stopped him. "What is your name?" I asked him.

He looked back at me and said, "John."

I smiled. "Hi, John," I said.

"What's your name?"

"Suzie," I lied to him with the biggest smile I had. Once again, seeing this little boy getting his hustle on was so rewarding. I could see this young boy growing up to be a CEO of a Fortune 500 company. I hoped his parents saw the entrepreneurship in him because he had the potential to go straight to the top.

I closed and locked the front door after the little entrepreneur walked away from the apartment. I set all three candy bars on the counter as soon as I walked into the kitchen. "Have you eaten lunch?" Mrs. Mabel yelled from the back of the apartment.

"Are you gonna cook?" I yelled back.

"No, I bought a couple of tuna fish sandwiches from the deli down the street."

"Sounds good. I'll wait until you get in here so we can eat together," I insisted.

"I'm on my way now," she replied, and then she appeared around the corner. Armed with a smile, she walked into the kitchen, carrying a clear package with a new doorknob lock-and-key set. "I stopped by the hardware store and picked up this beauty," she said while she handed it to me.

"Cool. Thanks," I replied after I took it from her hands and looked it over. "How much did it cost?" I wanted to know. She was already allowing me to stay in her apartment, so buying me a new lock for my apartment was very thoughtful.

"It was a little over forty dollars," she told me. And before I could comment, her cell phone rang. "Where did I leave my phone?" she wondered aloud.

"It's in your bedroom. I'll get it," I told her, and then I headed to her bedroom. Midway to her bedroom, her doorbell rang. I stopped and turned toward her. She stood there in the entryway of the kitchen and looked back at me. "Are you expecting someone?" I whispered.

"No. I'm not," she whispered back. "Go to my bedroom and close my door. I will come get you when they're gone," she assured me.

"Okay," I said as my heart rate sped up.

Mrs. Mabel watched me until I walked into her bedroom and closed the door behind myself. I stood there on the other side of the door with my ear to it so I could hear whoever was at the front door. I was so freaking nervous; it sounded like I was breathing hard at one point, so I held my breath. When I couldn't hold my breath any longer, I started breathing as quietly as I could. "Who is it?" I heard her yell.

I couldn't hear the person on the other side of the door, but when Mrs. Mabel asked the person to repeat it, I heard a man's voice, but I couldn't decipher his words.

"How can I help you?" she continued, and that's when I cracked her bedroom door a little. It was slightly ajar so I could get a good look at who was at the front door, but at the same time, they wouldn't be able to see me.

"My name is Officer Kahn and this is Officer Pax, and we would like to ask you some questions," I heard the guy say to Mrs. Mabel.

I couldn't get a look at the guy talking at the front door. At this angle, all I could see was the police patch stitched to the arm of the uniform. "What kind of questions do you need answering?" Mrs. Mabel asked him.

Before the gentleman answered, he swayed his head to the right of Mrs. Mabel's shoulder so he could get a look inside of the apartment. "Are you looking for something?" Mrs. Mabel asked. It was apparent that she caught him looking over her shoulder.

"I'm just acting with precaution, ma'am," he replied.

"I should be the least of your worries," I replied sarcastically.

"Is there someone else in this apartment?" I heard the other person say. This alarmed me. And I felt that at any moment those cops could move Mrs. Mabel out of the way and rush back here with their quickness!

"No, I'm the only person here. And why do you ask?"

she questioned them. The cop that looked over her shoulder the first time did it again. This time I saw his face. "Oh my God, it's Ahmad," I said, barely audible.

Fear and anxiety consumed my body all at once. I immediately closed the door to Mrs. Mabel's room and locked it. Then I ran to the window and opened it. I punched the screen out of the window and watched it fall down on the ground. "Where are you going? You can't come in here," I heard Mrs. Mabel say, and then I heard a loud thud.

Confused and scared to death, I ran into Mrs. Mabel's walk-in closet and closed the door. Only residents of the apartment complex knew that we have a small storage space in the ceiling of our closet, so I climbed to the top shelf and eased the hatch back quietly.

"The door is locked. She's gotta be in here," I heard an unfamiliar voice say.

"Open it," I heard Ahmad instruct the other guy.

"Fuck! Fuck! Fuck!" I whispered, trying to pull myself carefully up into the ceiling.

Boom! The sound of the bedroom door after it slammed the wall behind it terrified me. "Fuck! She climbed out of the window!" I heard Ahmad roar. His voice boomed. Anyone would be terrified to be around this guy. "Go get her before she gets away. Kill her. I want her dead," Ahmad continued.

The other guy's footsteps went from walking to running, while Ahmad stayed behind. I thought one part of him must have had doubts that I climbed out of the window, because I heard him pushing around the stuff stored underneath Mrs. Mabel's bed. He walked to the closet next. I couldn't see what he was doing, but I heard him open the closet door, move the clothes hangers around, and then I heard him shut the closet door back.

When I heard Ahmad open another door and close it, I knew he was looking in the hall closet directly across from Mrs. Mabel's bedroom. After he closed that door, I heard the shower curtain move, so I knew he was in the bathroom.

I heard Ahmad making his way back out of the bathroom and I also heard the other guy with him panting. "She got away," the other guy said.

"How the fuck did we let her get away?!" Ahmad's voice boomed again.

"I told you we should've gotten her after we sent the kid to sell her the candy bar the first time," the other guy said.

"You know we couldn't get her. The feds were all over this place yesterday. Leaving when we did was the best course of action," I heard Ahmad say.

"You may be right, but the boss isn't gonna be happy when he calls today and we tell him that she got away."

"We'll tell him that the cops have been all over this place, and as soon as we get the chance, we'll have her in our hands," Ahmad explained.

"What about her mother and her boyfriend? What are we going to do with them?"

"Kill the boyfriend. And the mother, we're gonna use her as bait."

"What do you mean?"

"If we don't pick her up by day's end of tomorrow, we'll get word out to her that we'll trade her life for her mother's."

"How are we going to do that?"

"Just sit back and watch. Now let's get out of here."

"What we going to do about the old lady?" the other guy wanted to know.

"What kind of question is that? We're going to leave her here," Ahmad replied sarcastically, and then I heard them both as they left the apartment.

14

MY FLESH & BLOOD

Trying to piece everything I just heard together was becoming overwhelming. I mean, how fucking stupid did he think I was? To find out that Ahmad had that little boy come here to set me up was pretty clever, but I was two steps ahead of him. On the downside, the fact that Mrs. Mabel got caught up in this setup was pretty fucked up. Once again, I got someone shot and killed because of their affiliation with me. Granted, Mrs. Mabel was starting to get on my freaking nerves, but she helped me by giving me a place to lay low so the DEA and the local cops couldn't touch me. She was a rider. So, how can I just let this shit go? Besides that, what would the cops say if they came here and saw this lady dead? My fingerprints would be all over this place. I'd be their main and only suspect. *Now, how am I getting myself out of this one?*

Afraid to move an inch, I sat there in the small space above the closet. Thinking about how I was going to maneuver around this situation, I buried my face into the palms of my hands. Filled up with a bunch of sorrow, I let out a floodgate of tears. Why was all this shit coming at me like this? I was just a fucking pharmacy tech at a pharmacy with an aspiration to become a pharmacist, but look at how I screwed that up. It seemed like every time I tried to remedy my situation and move forward, I got caught up in some bullshit. It never failed.

After sitting around in this little-ass ceiling space for every bit of ten minutes, I figured the coast was clear, so I very carefully slid the ceiling square cover from the opening off to the side; then I carefully stepped down onto the top shelf. Once my foot was firmly placed on the top shelf, I put my other foot down and then I made my way down to the closet floor. Immediately after I planted both of my feet on the floor, I opened the closet door as quietly as I could, to prevent anyone from hearing it if they were still lingering around the apartment. Things seemed quiet, so I stepped out of the closet, tiptoed to the bedroom door, and peered around the corner.

When I realized that I was still in the clear, I looked down the hallway toward the front door and noticed the door was closed shut. Taking direction from my gut, I tiptoed down the hallway toward the front door. When I got halfway down the hall, that's when I saw Mrs. Mabel's lifeless body lying on the floor four feet away from the front door. I rushed over toward her, and right when I was just about to drop down on my knees to see if she was breathing, my gut spoke again. It told me how that would be a bad idea, especially if I got her blood on my hands. But as I stood there and watched her lying in her own blood, I thought about the fact that if I hadn't come here in the first place, then Mrs. Mabel would still be alive. I even thought about the fact that my mother's boyfriend, Carl, was about to be murdered because of me. Now, why was that? Why was I always putting all these people in harm's way? I knew my grandmother said that I wasn't going to get into heaven by way of suicide, but what if I wasn't supposed to go to heaven? With all the mess I caused, I deserved a one-way trip to hell. I guess I would soon find out.

Knowing that I needed to leave this apartment ASAP, I grabbed my duffel bag from the guest bedroom and started piling all of my stuff inside of it. I went into the bathroom, grabbed my bath cloth, and toothbrush. Next, I ran into Mrs. Mabel's bedroom with my duffel bag in hand and grabbed her purse, took her car keys and $74 she had inside of it, and stuffed them both down inside of my front pants pocket. From there, I ran into the kitchen and grabbed both deli sandwiches, because I knew that I was going to be hungry at any given moment. But then something happened and my peripheral vision caught it. I turned my complete focus around and that's when I saw three cops running toward Mrs. Mabel's apartment.

"What the fuck!" I said as fear engulfed me, and then I sprinted back to Mrs. Mabel's bedroom, where my duffel bag was. "No! No! No! They're gonna pin her murder on me. And then I'm gonna be booked on two counts of murder. I can't let this happen. No! No! No!" I whispered while my heart rate far exceeded sixty miles per hour.

The moment I walked into Mrs. Mabel's bedroom, I locked the bedroom door, grabbed my duffel bag from her bed, and then looked at the window. Realizing once again that I probably wouldn't be able to squeeze my body through it, much less my bag, I raced to the closet and climbed back up the shelves. At the top shelf, I shoved my duffel bag into the space first, and while I was pulling myself into the ceiling space, the cops kicked in the front door. "Virginia Beach Police," I heard one of them shout.

"Oh shit!" I heard another cop say.

"Is she alive?" I heard a third voice say.

"No. I'm dispatching homicide right now."

"Check the other rooms. We may not be alone," the first officer said. By then, I had climbed back into the ceiling space and closed the square peg back into its place. Feelings of regret, fear, and trepidation overwhelmed me as I heard cops emerge.

"Clear," one said from another room.

The cop that entered Mrs. Mabel's had to kick the door in first. I couldn't see what he was doing, but I heard him meticulously covering himself with every step he took. When he opened the closet door, he pushed and pulled the clothes hanging from their hangers. Once he saw that it was empty, he yelled to the other officers that his area was clear. "Whoever was here had to have jumped out of the window. So I'm gonna go outside and check the perimeter," he continued.

"Johns, have you dispatched the coroners?" I heard one of the officers ask.

"Yeah, they're en route now," another officer replied. Although all three of the cops were in the front room of the apartment, I could hear every word they uttered.

"Who could do this to an old lady?" one of the cops said.

"We got a lot of heartless people in the world," another cop replied.

"I'm gonna go back to the car to get the yellow tape," the other cop said.

"Make sure you keep the neighbors back an extra sixty feet."

"Will do."

It didn't take the local cops long to dispatch homicide detectives and the city coroners. They were all in Mrs. Mabel's apartment five minutes after they were called. It didn't surprise me when Detective Belle and her partner, Detective Caesar, appeared on the scene. I realized they were here after they entered into Mrs. Mabel's bedroom and asked the forensic specialist that was at the window dusting for prints if he had found any visible prints. He told them he had two sets of prints and this made them happy. "Think her murder is connected to the Misty Heiress case?" I heard Detective Caesar ask.

"There's a huge possibility," I heard Detective Belle reply.

"If that's the case, what do you think happened?" he wanted to know.

"I don't know. But we will have an answer by the end of the day," Belle said.

"Hey, you guys, I found prints in the second bathroom. Whoever was here used the toilet, the sink maybe to brush their teeth, and they also took a shower, because they left a bath cloth, so there's gonna be DNA all over it."

"Sounds good," Belle said.

"Yeah, that's awesome," I heard the other detective agree.

"Hey, Caesar, Belle," another person shouted.

"Yeah," Belle and Caesar said in unison.

"Got a lady outside saying that the lady who lived here had a female visitor," I heard the person say.

"Where is she?" Belle asked.

"She's right outside of the yellow tape," the guy replied.

"Come on, Caesar, let's hear what she has to say," I heard Belle say to Detective Caesar.

Hearing Detective Belle instruct her partner to follow her outside to speak with an eyewitness made my heart nearly jump out of my freaking chest. *Who in the hell knows that I am here?* No one saw me when I initially walked into Mrs. Mabel's apartment, so where did they get their information from? Had Mrs. Mabel had a chance to tell someone that I was here? And if she did, who could it be? And why would she do it? She knew I was trying to lay low. Was I missing something here?

Knowing that Detective Belle and Detective Caesar were on their way to speak with this so-called witness had me terrified. Not to mention, the fact that I left my bath cloth behind in the bathroom. And now that the cops had it, they would indeed pull my DNA from it. How in the hell did I forget to grab it?

For the duration of the evidence gathering, I heard different cop voices as the cops walked about Mrs. Mabel's apartment. I heard one guy say that whoever murdered Mrs. Mabel was a heartless person. I heard another guy say that it looked like a robbery. The same guy who had just spoken also said that he found a store receipt in the kitchen that indicated that Mrs. Mabel purchased two sandwiches, and from the time of the receipt, it was 12:05, which was less than thirty minutes ago. So, not only were the two sandwiches missing, they knew what time Mrs. Mabel was killed. I swear, all of this news was killing me on the inside. These cops weren't going to let up with this investigation. When they found out it was me, Detective Belle and Agent Sims were not going to sleep until they locked my ass up. I felt sick in the stomach and wanted to throw up all over this ceiling storage, but when I thought of them finding me and hauling me off to jail, I fought back the urge of regurgitating.

15

THE FIRST FORTY-EIGHT HOURS

It seemed like time was creeping by slowly. It felt like these guys had no intentions of leaving. Every time I heard one cop announce that they'd cleared one room, meaning they logged all the evidence, I'd hear another cop say that they found something else. It was like a fucking circus; everyone was juggling their own act with no intentions of leaving.

Detective Belle walked back into Mrs. Mabel's apartment with her partner, Caesar, in tow. She made an announcement and it sounded like she was making it in the living-room area. "I just spoke with one of the neighbors. Her name was Tina. She's an older woman. Looked to be in her late forties. She said that she knew Mrs. Mabel for a long time. She was like the neighborhood grandmother. She was a nice lady and everyone loved her, so it's hard to believe that someone would kill her. She also said that she spoke to Mrs. Mabel this morning and everything seemed fine. But when she saw two uniformed cops run away from this apartment, she felt something was wrong, because cops only run when they're in pursuit of someone. And you know what, guy?" Belle said.

"What?" a few cops said in unison.

"She's right. And you wanna know why?" Belle continued.

"Why?" the same cops said.

"Because within the last hour, there weren't any calls from dispatch for this area or any area within twenty miles. So tell me who were those two cops that the lady saw?"

"Was she sure that they were cops? I mean, they could've been security officers," I heard one of the guys say.

"We asked her that same question. And she said she knows what Virginia Beach Police uniforms look like. She also said that they were driving one of the city's police vehicles too," I heard Detective Caesar reply.

"Don't you think it's ironic that a murder was committed at the apartment next door and now we're investigating another one?" I heard someone ask. I couldn't make out the voice because there were over eight to ten people.

"There's a strong possibility. And also remember that we have the suspect April, who has agreed to testify in front of a grand jury and say Terrell Mason was already dead when she entered into the apartment next door. Now fast-forward to now, when Agent Sims and I tried to speak with this lady here, she wouldn't cooperate with us. It almost seemed like she had a bond with Misty Heiress, which was why she expressed her grievances with us for going through Misty's things in her apartment. So, what if someone from Terrell's family or a friend of his came by Misty's apartment to seek revenge and Mrs. Mabel got in their way?" Belle said.

"I can definitely see that," Detective Caesar commented.

"Me too," another voice said.

"Yeah, that's plausible," someone else said.

"Okay, so we may have a motive here. Now I'm gonna need you guys to comb through this place very thoroughly. Too many dead bodies are popping up. So let's get a handle on it and let's do it now," Belle demanded.

It took all those cops a total of five damn hours to collect all the evidence they needed. When they finally filed out of here, one by one, it felt like a ton of anxiety lifted from my shoulders. I let out a long sigh of relief and then I laid my head down on my duffel bag.

Thinking about everything I heard from the police got my mind racing. Okay, so they got one thing right, which was that the two guys that ran away from this apartment weren't real cops. But as far as who they think killed Mrs. Mabel, they were all wrong. Terrell's family or close friends had nothing to do with Mrs. Mabel's murder. But if they wanted to believe they did it, then so be it. My main priority was me. Not only was Ahmad, along with his henchman, looking for me, but Agent Sims and Detective Belle were too. So, as soon as they pulled my DNA from the towel and bath cloth I left behind, they're gonna think I murdered Mrs. Mabel and they'd have me on something like *America's Most Wanted*. Once that happened, I wouldn't be able to stay in this area. Finding somewhere to go was what I needed to concentrate on.

I had no idea where I was going to go. Nor did I know what I was going to do. I had no plans. All I had were the keys to Mrs. Mabel's car. So I figured that if I could use it to get away from here, I'd have a clearer mind to be able to come up with a good plan. "Okay, Misty, it's time to go. You gotta get out of here before someone else comes here," I whispered to myself.

After building up enough courage, I finally willed myself to climb back out of the ceiling space. On my way down, I made every step carefully. I wanted to be as quiet as a mouse. Getting caught was not an option for me. Once I had landed with my feet placed firmly on the floor, I slid the closet door back as quiet as I could. I stood still for a moment to see if I could hear any movement. After realizing that there was no more movement in the house, I stepped out of the closet and tiptoed over to the bedroom door. I peered around the corner of Mrs. Mabel's bedroom and into the hallway. I looked toward the front door, where her body had been, and it was gone. I was relieved to see that. I was even more relieved when I walked around the apartment and saw that I was alone. But the cops and forensic officers had left a lot of black dust and markers around the apartment to let someone know that they had been there. It was one of those crime scenes that you'd see in a movie. I stood there and looked down at the puddle of blood and felt so bad that Mrs. Mabel was murdered because of me. I mean, if she hadn't picked me up at the freaking grocery store and brought me into her home, she'd still be alive now. Probably watching her favorite shows. But no, the moment I stepped foot into this apartment, everything went downhill from there. I had a hand in creating this lady's demise. Now, how fucked up was that?

I knew that I wasn't going to be able to leave this apartment just like that. I also knew that in order for me to leave this place without being seen, I was gonna have to move strategically. That might entail leaving here with a wig on and sunglasses. I might also need to leave here when it got dark outside. More important, whenever I did decide to walk out of this apartment, no one, including the agents, cops, or Ahmad, could be able to see me. If they did, then I'd be fucked.

16

GETTING REVENGE

While I waited for the perfect time to leave, I kept my eyes fixed on the parking lot area of my neighborhood. It seemed like every time I saw a good chance for me to walk out of this place, I either saw one of my neighbors walking by or hanging out in the parking lot with someone else. I swear, I was about to pull my fucking hair out. It was becoming a little nerve-racking, to say the least.

After waiting in the living room for another hour or so, I finally saw my opportunity to leave. There were no cops around watching the apartment building, nor did I see any federal agents camped outside in their cars. This was my time, so I grabbed my duffel bag and raced toward the front door. Immediately after I opened the front door to leave, a Channel 10 news station van pulled up into the parking space next to Mrs. Mabel's car.

"Nooooooo! This can't be happening," I whined softly. One part of me wanted to rush toward Mrs. Mabel's car and get into it before this news crew set up. But then, the other part of me wanted to turn around and go back into Mrs. Mabel's apartment. "Shit! This can't be happening. Ugh!" I said once more, and then I sighed heavily.

The distance between Mrs. Mabel's car and the news station van from where I was standing was too close, and I knew that I wasn't going to make it in time before either the news reporter or the camera guy would see me.

"Damn! I just can't get a break!" I cursed, and then I turned back around. But instead of going back into Mrs. Mabel's apartment, I opened my front door and slid in there without anyone noticing it. I was pissed that I couldn't lock my front door after closing it. I did stick one of my kitchen table chairs underneath the doorknob, hoping to keep anyone from getting into my apartment. This was just a temporary fix, but it worked.

I dropped my duffel bag down on the floor and peered out the window of my living room. Trying to figure out what this reporter was about to say had me on edge. I mean, I knew it's her job, but damn, can't you just leave well enough alone? I was trying to get out of this place and they were keeping me hostage. I was not supposed to be in my apartment right now. What if the cops decided that they wanted to come back and reexamine some areas in my apartment? I'd be screwed up if that shit happened, because not only would they be able to sneak into my place from the back of the apartment building, they'd be able to come into my apartment without unlocking the door. Okay, so I pushed one of my kitchen chairs to hold the door back, but that wouldn't hold up against the pressure of a couple of cops. They'd be able to kick that door

in on the first try. Hopefully, that wouldn't happen. I
prayed to God that it wouldn't.

I stood there on pins and needles and my heart racing,
trying to figure out what was going to be said. Would the
news reporter mention what had happened in my apartment, or would she only cover the murder of Mrs. Mabel?
Lord knows, all eyes would be on this place as soon as
the camera started rolling.

A few of my neighbors started coming outside to see
what was going on. They began to huddle around one another in a circle. A couple of them looked in the direction
of my apartment, as well as Mrs. Mabel's apartment,
since they were connected. I wondered what they were
saying. The mere thought that I was a topic of their discussion caused me a serious amount of shame and embar-
rassment. This wasn't how my life was supposed to be.
So, how can I stop it? How can I take things back to
where they were? I swear, I don't know how much more
of this that I can take. Hopefully, not much more.

The camera started rolling when I saw the light illumi-
nating from it and that's when I knew this thing was for
real. I couldn't make out what the black woman was saying, because not only was her back facing the building,
she was too far away for me to hear anything. So I rushed
over to my television and turned it on. After it came on, I
turned to the news channel and there they were reporting
live outside.

"I'm standing in front of building 210 of Kings Grant
Apartments, where an elderly woman was murdered inside of her apartment. She was found dead from two fatal
gunshot wounds to her abdomen a little before one o'clock
today. I spoke with several neighbors, who say that she
was a beautiful and kind lady, so to hear that she was

murdered was both shocking and sad. The woman's identity will be released, once her family is notified. As of right now, investigators have no suspects or motive. Anyone with information is urged to call the crime line. I'm Christian Lundy, and I'm reporting for *Ten on Your Side*."

"Hey, I see a light in that apartment next door," someone a few feet away from the cameraman said.

This caught the eyes and ears of the reporter. "What are you talking about?" the reporter asked as she walked over toward the woman standing a couple feet away from her. The cameraman turned his camera directly at a full-figured black woman dressed in an oversized blouse and blue pants.

I watched the woman as she pointed toward my apartment. Caught off guard by this sudden change of events, I raced over to the window to see if my neighbor was actually pointing at my apartment. When I opened my blinds, just enough to see, I gasped for air at what happened next.

"What do you mean someone is in the apartment?" the news reporter questioned my neighbor as she damn near shoved her microphone in her face.

"That other apartment next to the one with the yellow crime tape. It belongs to the lady the police are looking for. That apartment has been dark for days, because no one has been there. But now it looks like someone is there. Yeah, see someone is looking out of the window." My neighbor continued as if she was a private investigator, solving a damn problem; that's when I let the blinds go and stepped back from the window.

"Did you get that, Jim?" I heard the news reporter say while the live report was airing.

"Yep, I'm still rolling," I heard him acknowledge.

"It has been alleged that a woman wanted by the local

police may, in fact, be hiding in her apartment. I have her neighbor here who just noticed movement in that apartment. My cameraman, Jim, and I are on our way up to this apartment to check things out." The news reporter continued to report, all while making her way up to my apartment. But I couldn't let her come up here and see me. If I did, then I'd be sealing my own fate. I was either gonna be captured by the DEA or by Ahmad and his crew. So the best thing for me to do was to get the hell out of here.

Without hesitation I powered off my television, grabbed my duffel bag, and ran over toward the front door. I removed the kitchen chair that secured the doorknob, snatched the front door open, and then made a run for it. Instead of running toward the front entrance of the complex, I made a run for the back of the apartment complex.

"Hey, wait. Stop!" I heard the news reporter yelling for me to stop. I ignored her and kept running. I was not about to let this lady put me on camera. But then I stumbled over a glass bottle and slipped and fell down on the ground. Pain shot through my ankle. "Fuck!" I said, gritting my teeth. And before I could stand back up, the news reporter had managed to catch up with me. The high voltage of light coming from the camera nearly blinded me. The news reporter leaned down toward me, almost shoving her microphone down my throat. "Hey, are you the woman that the police are looking for? Did you know anything about your neighbor's murder? And were you hiding inside of that apartment?" Her questions continued.

"Get that damn camera out of my face. I am innocent of all that shit the cops are trying to plant on me. And I saw who killed Mrs. Mabel!" I said after I finally stood up on my feet.

"Who was it?" the reporter asked me, keeping the microphone in my face.

"It was the mafia that kidnapped my mother and her boyfriend. Now tell the cops to go and do their jobs and try to find out where they are and leave me alone," I spat out, and then I ran off again with my duffel bag in hand.

"Well, there you have it, folks. The young woman from that apartment just sent Virginia Beach their first clue. Now let's see if they take it and use it. I'm Christian Lundy reporting for *Ten on Your Side.*"

After running three blocks, I felt like I was finally out of the woods. More important, I felt a little liberated. Not to the point that I just cleared my name, but to allow the world to see and hear me say who really killed Mrs. Mabel, and that Ahmad and his family had my mother, and the cops needed to do something about it.

I thought about finding a back way to enter into my mother's house, but I knew the cops and Agent Sims would come there looking for me, since I went back into my apartment after I felt that it would be safe to do so. If I went back into my place, there was a huge possibility that they'd come looking for me at my mom's house too. So I left well enough alone and decided to figure out another place to go. But before I did that, I hid behind the nearest tree and changed my shirt, since the entire viewing audience saw what I was wearing on TV. I even put on the wig I took from Mrs. Mabel's apartment. I didn't have a mirror on hand, but I knew that I had a good disguise. I just hoped that it kept me undetected until I could find another safe haven.

17

KISS MY ASS

Trying to figure out where I was going to hide out had become harder than I expected. I'd been walking for an hour and a half now. I was pissed off that I didn't get a chance to take Mrs. Mabel's car. The freaking news reporter snatched that option from me when she started running down behind me. *What am I going to do now?*

Luckily, it was dark out, because if it wasn't, the cops would probably have me in handcuffs right now. Speaking of cops, a total of three cops had already passed me. I can't tell you why they *weren't* looking out for me, but I can tell you that I was fortunate that they weren't.

I walked up Virginia Beach Boulevard and approached the traffic light at the corner of Newtown Road. At this intersection, I saw a truck that looked like my mother's boyfriend's son's truck. His name was Carl Jr. I wasn't sure how old he was, but I knew he was over the age of twenty-five.

I raced toward the truck before the light turned green. And by the time I approached the passenger side of the truck, I was disappointed to find out that the driver wasn't him. "Ugh!" I said, and let out a long sigh.

While I turned around to get back to the sidewalk, that's when it hit me that I should reach out to Carl Jr. If I could get him to help me get my mother back, everything I was doing would be worth it. But I figured that it would only work if he believed that his father was alive but in harm's way. So, as of right now, that's what it was going to be.

After walking a block and a half, I was able to flag down a taxicab. The driver was a black older woman. She was in her own world listening to her gospel music. The only words she uttered when I got in her car were "Good evening. And where are you going?"

I spoke back to her and requested to be taken to Norfolk. I told her that I didn't know the exact address, but I knew the name of the street. With that, she said okay and then we headed uptown.

The entire drive to Norfolk, I bounced words back and forth in my head, trying to figure out how I was going to approach him when I asked him for his help. I knew I had to be convincing, because this guy really didn't know me. He'd only seen me maybe twice, if not three times. And all of them were at Thanksgiving and Christmas get-togethers. I just hoped that he didn't turn me away or call the cops on me. If he did, then I was going to be screwed.

Approximately fifteen minutes later, the cabdriver had

gotten me to my destination. "We're on Thirty-fourth Street," she announced.

I sat up in the back seat, trying to eyeball the block. This street was a one-way street, so for all I knew, the cops could be watching his house. So I needed to be extra careful. "Could you drive all the way down and circle the block?" I asked her.

"Sure," she said.

Halfway down the block, I recognized Carl Jr.'s town house. It was located to the left side of the street. I also recognized his truck parked in the driveway. Only one light was on in his house, and that light was coming from his bedroom. That gave me hope that he was, in fact, inside the house.

When the taxi driver made a left turn to circle back around to get back on Thirty-fourth Street, I stopped her. "You know what? Just pull the car over. I'm gonna get out right here," I instructed the woman.

She pulled her cab over to the side of the road. Immediately after I paid her from the money I took from Mrs. Mabel's purse, I got out of the car and walked onto the sidewalk. I saw an entryway alongside an old house, which would give me a way to hop the fence to get to Carl Jr.'s house. Thankfully, there were no dogs in sight, barking and alarming neighbors that something or someone was coming.

I climbed an old, raggedy metal fence that separated Carl Jr.'s backyard from the other land owned by the homeowners that lived around him. The backyard of his home was completely black. This was good for me, being in the dark and everything. I climbed onto the back porch and knocked on his door, as lightly as I could. I just hoped that I was doing it loud enough for him to hear.

The first four tries hadn't worked, so I was forced to knock harder. After doing it another four times, I finally got Carl Jr.'s attention. As soon as he walked to the back door, I heard him shouting, asking who was at his door. I told him who I was, and almost at that instant, he opened the door. He stood on the other side of the screen door, with his cell phone against his ear, and just looked at me. "Can I come in?" I asked him.

"Hey, Mom, let me call you back," he said, and then I watched him as he disconnected his call. A couple of seconds later, he unlocked the screen door and pushed it open. "Hey, you're Misty, right?" he said after he opened the door.

"Yes."

"Come in," he insisted, and quickly moved out of the way.

I stood to the side of him after I crossed the threshold. "Would you please close your door?" I asked. He saw the alarmed look I had on my face.

"Yeah, sure," he said, and immediately closed the door. "I just saw you on TV. But your hair wasn't like that."

Hearing him tell me that he saw me on TV instantly caused me to have an anxiety attack. I placed my right hand over my heart while I leaned against the nearby wall.

"Are you okay?" he asked as he placed his hand across my right shoulder.

"I need to take a seat."

"Let's go into the living room," he said, and then he led me toward the front area of his house.

I took a seat on the couch only a few feet away from the entrance of the kitchen and then I took Mrs. Mabel's wig from my head. "Thank you for letting me in. 'Cause I really had nowhere else to go."

"Don't worry about it. It's cool," he replied.

"I take it you and your mother were talking about me being on the news?" I questioned him, even though I already had the answer to my question. As he explained how he was shocked to see me lying on the ground and telling the news reporter what I said, I began to size him up. He wasn't that tall. Maybe five-eight and 150 pounds. He had the body frame of Floyd Mayweather, but was average-looking in the face. So far, he seemed like a good guy, but time would tell.

"You know, the cops came by here two days ago. They were asking me when I last talked to my father. And I told them that he and I talked on the same day he was supposed to come by here and stay for a while. But he never showed up."

"Did they tell you what happened to your dad and my mother?" I asked him.

"They didn't tell me that they were kidnapped. I heard that come out of your mouth when you were on the news. But they told me that they were missing."

"Who told you that? The cops or the federal agents?"

"Federal agents are on this?"

I let out a long sigh. "It's complicated."

"So, is it true? The mafia has them?"

"Yes," I said regretfully.

"But why?"

"Is there someone else in here?" I asked him. I wanted to make sure that if someone is here, then I needed to choose my words carefully.

"No, my girlfriend is at work."

"Do you guys have kids?" I pressed the issue.

"No. It's just me and her."

I hesitated for a moment and then I said, "The guy I was working for at a local pharmacy was dealing illegal prescription drugs right underneath my nose. According to the DEA, my boss had been dealing since before I got there. After two months of working there, I kind of figured that he was dealing. I needed a job, so I turned my head and continued to mind my own business. Unfortunately, someone robbed the pharmacy, so the cops had to get in on it. One thing led to another, and before I knew it, the DEA agents wanted me to wear a wire, but I declined. So, one day, my boss saw me talking to the cops outside the pharmacy and thought that I was snitching on him. And it didn't help clear my name, because a few days later he got arrested.

"Word got back to his family and everything went downhill from there. I guess when it got hard for them to find me, they started looking for anyone close to my family. I'm sorry that they got my mother and your father. But, just so you know, we can get them back. But I'm gonna need your help to do it," I explained to him.

"As much as I want to help you, I'm not into that life. I got locked up shooting a nigga that stole a grand from me when I was nineteen years old. Did ten years upstate. Had to fight niggas almost every day to prove my manhood. I'm thirty-two years old now, so I'm not interested in anything that would put me back in that situation. But I do have someone that would love to help you out," Carl Jr. said.

"Who?"

"My baby brother, Rich. When I called him and told him what you said on TV, he became angry and started threatening to do something to the mafia guys that took our father."

"Can you get him to come here so I can talk to him?"

"Yeah, I'll get him on the phone now," he told me, and then he started pressing buttons on his iPhone. A couple seconds later, I could hear the other line ringing from where I was sitting. That's how loud his cell phone volume was. "Junior, what's up?" I heard the other guy say.

"Yo, come to my crib now. Got something I want you to see."

"A'ight, I'm on my way," I heard the other guy say, and then Carl Jr. disconnected their call.

"He's on his way."

"Yeah, I heard him. How long do you think it'll take him?"

"You in a rush?" Carl Jr. asked sarcastically.

"No. I was just asking."

"He's not too far from here. Give him about thirty minutes and he'll be here," Carl Jr. said, and then he started walking toward the kitchen. "Thirsty?"

"I'll take a bottle of water, if you got it."

"Bottle of water coming right up," he said as he opened the refrigerator door. After he grabbed a bottle of water and a bottle of Heineken from the side door, he walked back into the living room. He handed the bottle of water to me, but kept the bottle of beer for himself.

"Thank you," I said after I took the water from his hand.

"You're welcome," he said, and then he sat in the chair directly across from me. "Tell me why you were running from the news reporter?" he asked after taking a sip from his bottle.

"Because I didn't want to be on TV."

"How did you fall?"

"I tripped over a bottle."

"Is it true that you killed your ex-boyfriend?"

"What made you ask me that?" That question came out of thin air. Was it a trick question?

"The guy's family went on TV and said that you killed him."

"That's a lie. I didn't do shit. They need to talk to all of his side bitches!" I spat. I was getting frustrated by his implication, even though I was lying. *I'm the real victim here, not that piece of shit–ass nigga, Terrell. He fucked up my life. Not the other way around!*

"I'm sorry if I offended you," he apologized.

"It's okay. It's just I went through a lot of shit behind that guy. I regret the day I met his ass. He didn't give a fuck about anyone but himself. And people like him don't get far in life. To be honest with you, I'm glad somebody got rid of his ass!" I roared. Just the mere thought of that bastard got me in an uproar. Not only that, but the fact that April had ratted me out and would testify against me when the cops finally caught me had me on edge too.

"I'm sorry if I made you upset."

"Don't apologize. I'm good," I tried to assure him, and then I took another sip of my bottled water. "Tell me about your brother," I said, changing the subject.

"What do you wanna know about him?"

"How old is he? How close are you two? Is he a street cat? Or is he a hothead? You know general questions."

"Well, he's twenty-four years old. He did a three-year

bid upstate for selling dope. Now he's out and right back in the streets selling drugs. And as far as him being hot-headed, he would definitely snap out and put a bullet in somebody's ass if he feels like someone's disrespecting him."

"Think he'll help me get our parents back?"

"Oh, most definitely."

"Does he drive?"

"He has his driver's license, but he doesn't have a car. He drives his girlfriend's around, most of the time, especially when she's at work."

"Are you gonna talk to him first? I mean, I would rather for you to break the ice when he gets here."

"Sure. I can do that," he said. "But can I ask you something?"

I braced myself for this question; I swear, I didn't know what he was going to ask me.

"How well did you know my dad?"

"Well, I didn't see him much when I stopped by my mother's place. He'd either be at work or in the bedroom, watching TV."

"Did you like him?"

"Yes, I thought he was a cool guy. He didn't talk much, but I knew he loved my mother."

"Good, I'm glad," he replied, and then he said, "Did you know that your mother was turning into an alcoholic?"

"Where did you hear that from?" I asked sarcastically. I wasn't liking where this conversation was going.

"My dad would stop by and tell me how much he loved your mother, but her drinking was kinda pushing him into leaving her."

"Okay, and what does my mother's drinking have to do with them both getting kidnapped?"

"It has nothing to do with it. I was just sharing a concern that my father had concerning your mother, being as though my father used to be an alcoholic. He's concerned that he may relapse."

I sat there and thought for a moment. I didn't want to continue down this road that Carl Jr. and I were going. I mean, I understood his concern for his father, but him relapsing wouldn't be a problem if he was dead. Too bad he didn't know. "Look, I understand how you feel. And I'm sorry for snapping at you. It's just that I wanna get my mama back safe and sound. She doesn't need this shit in her life."

"What about my father? He's there with her and he had nothing to do with none of it," Carl Jr. interjected.

"Well, that's what I meant. Both of them need to come home," I recanted, even though I didn't mean a word of it.

"Do you think that they're going to be all right? Are those guys really bad people?"

"I don't know. It's really hard to tell." I lied once again, knowing full well that his father could be dead.

"What do you mean?"

"Those guys don't want your dad and my mother. They want me. So I believe that they're willing to exchange their lives for mine," I said. I swear, those words literally tumbled from my mouth like a leaky faucet.

"And how do you know that?"

"Because I know. Remember I used to work for those guys."

"Don't you think that it would be better if you let the cops handle it? I mean, you talking about exchanging your life for their lives, like it's that easy. Don't you care about living too?"

"Of course, I do. But when I think about what my mother could be going through right now, it puts me in the mind frame to think more about her than myself."

"You're talking about my father too, right? I mean, because every time you bring your mother up, you never add my father to the equation. Do you know something that I don't?"

"I'm sorry if I keep doing that. It's just that I got a lot of stuff on my mind," I told him after I took another sip from my bottle of water.

Carl Jr. kept our conversation going with one question after the next. At one point, it felt like I was going through an interrogation. But I knew he just needed the questions concerning his father answered. So I did my best to answer his questions as delicately as I could.

18

IN KILLING MODE

Carl Jr. was right. It took his baby brother, Rich, less than thirty minutes. I must admit that this guy was a character. He walked through the front door with another guy in tow. As soon as he saw me, he smiled. "So, is she that something you needed to show me?" he asked after looking at me from head to toe.

"Yes, this is Misty, and, Misty, this is my brother, Rich."

Rich walked over to where I was sitting and extended his left hand. "Nice to meet you," he said as we shook hands. The guy that was with him stood by the front door.

"Same here," I told him when he let my hand loose.

I stared at Rich for a brief moment while he stood before me. I had to admit that this little fellow was kind of cute. He looked like the actor Larenz Tate. In fact, he had the look and the height. It was crazy weird. But I went with it.

"Are you the lady from the news?" he asked.

"I was about to ask her the same question," the big guy by the front door said.

"Yeah, and that's why I'm here," I began to say.

"Yeah, she said she knows where her mom and our dad is," Carl Jr. spoke up.

"Ain't that what she said on the news?" Rich said as he looked at Carl Jr.

"Yes, I did, but it's more complicated than that," I began to explain.

"Hey, wait, what's your name again?" Rich asked me.

"Misty."

"Oh shit! You're the girl that supposed to killed that nigga Terrell," Rich added.

Instantly my insides were engulfed with a ball of nerves mixed with anxiety and fear. Hearing Rich say that I was the girl that killed Terrell paralyzed me. How am I supposed to act after hearing this? Stay here and defend myself? Or run out of here and never look back? I needed some help trying to figure this thing out. Finally, a thought popped in my head. "Look, I don't know where you got that information from, but I didn't have shit to do with that nigga getting killed."

"That ain't what April said." Rich pressed this issue as he stood a few feet away from me. For a minute, he looked like he was about to interrogate me. My heart rate sped up at an increasing amount. I wasn't sure how I was supposed to react to his statement, so I just sat and looked at Carl Jr., hoping he'd step in and help me.

"You worked at the pharmacy down on Church Street, right?"

"I used to."

"Yeah, your cousin Jillian got with my homeboy Tedo and tried to rob that spot, but got shot up and killed by the cops," Rich added.

"That's not how that happened."

"Explain it to me," he insisted.

"When my cousin and Tedo came down there to rob it, the owner of the store's family had come there, and so they had a shoot-out with Tedo and the other guy that was with him."

"You didn't tell me that a robbery took place," Carl Jr. interjected.

"That's because you didn't ask me."

"That was because I didn't know."

"Look, we can sit here all day and go back and forth about who robbed who, and who got shot. I lost my cousin Jillian and my grandmother behind those guys. And now they got my mother and y'all father, so are you going to help me get them back, or what?" I replied sarcastically. I needed these fucking idiots to realize that it's not about what happened; it was about where we were now and how did we start from there.

"Answer this one question," Rich said.

"What is it?" I asked him, but at the same time, I dreaded what he was about to say. *You never know where stuff is going to go with this fucking guy.*

"Are you working with the cops or federal agents? Because that's what's going around on the streets."

"No, I am not. I mean, if I were working with them, do you think I'd be running from the fucking cameraman and that dumb bitch of a news reporter? Do you think I'd be here asking for y'all help? If anyone is snitching, it's that April chick. She's the one telling the police that I murdered Terrell, and her and Tedo chopped his body up," I said further.

Rich stood there and looked at me like he could see through me. He did this for the next sixty seconds, and then he finally said something. "If I find out that you're lying to me, I'm gonna kill you dead. Now do we have an understanding? Because I don't fuck with snitches. Snitches are rats. And I don't like rats. They are nasty and filthy!"

"I get your point," I told him, but deep inside of me, I became fearful and petrified of this guy. He might have been a small guy in stature, but his heart was cold and vicious. I wanted no part of it.

"I'm gonna only do this because my father got caught up in this shit. So tell me who we're dealing with?"

"I really don't know how many there are, because most of the family lives in DC, but I do know they have an Indian restaurant near the JANAF Shopping Yard. They open at eleven o'clock in the morning and close at ten o'clock at night. I figure if you follow one of them home, you'll find out where our mom and dad are."

"Think we could rob those motherfuckers?" Rich wanted to know.

"I don't think that would be a good idea. The first time my cousin and Tedo tried to do it, the whole thing fell apart."

"That's because they didn't know what the fuck they were doing. If me and my crew run up on them, we're gonna come out on top."

"I'm sure y'all are good at what you do, but all I'm interested in doing is getting my mother back," I expressed.

"Well, I'm interested in getting compensated for my

work. So, if you want to get your mama back, then you're gonna have to do it my way," he said. I watched his body language while he was looking at me, and from there, I knew that he meant what he just said.

I sat there for a moment and mulled over the pros and the cons of his proposition. On one hand, I wanted no part of his robbery scheme. Getting involved with another robbery would take me on a slippery slope. On the other hand, this was the only way I was going to get my mother back. And I couldn't leave her like this. I got her into this mess, and now I had to figure out how I was going to get her out. "I'm willing to do it your way," I finally told him.

"I knew you would see it my way," he said confidently.

"So, when are you trying to make a move?" I asked him.

"It's too late to do it tonight, so if everything goes right tomorrow, we can do it then."

"So, what am I going to do until then?" I asked both him and Carl Jr.

"What do you mean?" Rich asked.

"I don't have anywhere to stay. Remember, I was running from my apartment when the news reporter was following me."

"If it was up to me, then I would let you stay. But my girlfriend isn't gonna have it," Carl Jr. spoke first. So I looked at Rich next.

"Look, I be at the trap all night long. So, if you don't mind watching a nigga hustling, then you can come with me," Rich offered.

Before I opened my mouth to give him an answer, everyone in the living room heard someone on the other side of the front door trying to come in. Rich and I both looked at Carl Jr. He stood up from the chair and told Rich's homeboy to move to the side so his girlfriend could come walk into the house without the guy blocking her way.

As soon as she unlocked the front door and pushed it open, I zoomed in on her at first sight. She was pretty, like La La Anthony, and petite, like Jada Pinkett Smith. She was definitely an eye catcher. "Hi." I smiled and spoke to her first.

"Hi," she spoke back as she took off her jacket and hung it up on a coatrack next to the front door. She hung the straps of her purse there too.

"Why you home so early? I thought you had to work late tonight," Carl Jr. asked her.

"I got Tammy to come in and take over my shift," she replied, looking at him. And then she looked around the entire room.

"What's good, Sabrina?" Rich smiled at her.

"Everything is good. What's going on in here?" she wanted to know as she closed the door and locked it.

"We're just in here reminiscing about old times," Carl Jr. lied.

I don't know how he came up with that lie that quick. I did know that if she believed it, then he was bad, man.

"And who is she?" She continued to hurl her questions in the air.

"I'm Misty," I said, making the introduction.

"Wait, isn't she your father's girlfriend's daughter?"

"Yes, I am," I answered before anyone in the room could.

"You were on the news tonight too, right?"

I hesitated for a second and then I said, "Yeah, I was."

"So, what brings you here?" She wasn't letting up. She was going to ask me as many questions as she wanted to, and if I decided that I didn't want to answer them, then I could definitely see her throwing me out of her house.

"She came here to let us know where our daddy is," Carl Jr. spoke up.

"Well, where is he?" she asked Carl Jr.

"Some mafia guys," he replied.

"And how do you guys know that?" she asked, this time looking directly at me.

"The same guys got her mama," Carl Jr. answered.

"I'm not talking to you. I'm talking to her. So let her answer," the girlfriend replied impatiently. The way she looked at me, I knew she wasn't liking me at all.

"Because I used to work for those guys and I heard things," I told her in a nice and respectful manner. As badly as I wanted to curse her ass out, I didn't. I knew that it wouldn't be the greatest idea, considering that I was at everyone's mercy. I needed shelter. And I needed a team of street dudes to help me rescue my mother, even if it meant that I would have to trade my life for hers. Doing it alone wasn't an option.

Sabrina took a seat on the couch next to me. But she was on the far left side of me. "Do you know why those guys got your mother and their father?" She directed more questions to me.

"If I get into that, we'll be here for the rest of the night," I responded, because I really was not interested in repeating everything, I had just told the guys.

"I got all night," she told me.

"Come on, Sabrina, we don't have time for that," Carl Jr. interjected.

"Why not? I wanna know if she's bringing drama to my household. Now, am I wrong for that?"

I stood up to my feet. "I'm sorry. I swear, bringing drama to this house was the last thing on my mind. I just came here to tell the guys I know where their father was. That's it."

"You could've called them and told them that," she continued.

"I didn't have their number," I said, and started making my way toward the front door. "Are you ready?" I asked Rich.

"Yep, let's go," he said, and then he pointed to his homeboy and told him to open the door.

"Me and you are going to have a heart-to-heart," I heard her warn Carl Jr. while we were walking out of the house.

"Look, I'm not going to be arguing with you tonight. I'm not in the mood."

"I don't wanna argue either. But you're gonna tell me why she was in our house. Remember, you just got out of jail not too long ago." She didn't back down.

I didn't hear Carl Jr.'s rebuttal; Rich had closed the front door behind us. But after we got into the car, I made mention of it. "Is she always like that?" I asked Rich.

"Yeah, she's got a lot of mouth. I couldn't deal with her shit. I would've kicked her ass out of my house a long time ago," Rich commented after he climbed into the passenger-side seat, while his homeboy climbed into the driver's seat. After he put the key into the ignition, he put the gear in Drive and sped off down the one-way street.

"So that's his house?" I asked after him while I looked

at my surroundings. It had just hit me that we left using the front door. I looked over my shoulders and through the back window to see if we were being followed.

"It's my dad's house. But he let me and my brother stay there after he started dating and moved into your mom's crib. The house is paid for. All we gotta pay are the taxes, utilities, and the cable bill."

"If your dad left the house to you and Carl Jr., then why aren't you there?"

"Because I hustle and sell drugs. And I can't disrespect my pops by bringing that shit to his crib. He worked hard for that spot, so I'm gonna treat it like he does. You understand?"

"I sure do," I replied, still looking over my shoulders with every left and right turn the big guy made.

"So let me ask you something," Rich said.

"What's up?"

"What were you going to do if me or my brother would not have helped you?"

"That's a good question. But I don't know what I would've done."

"So, is it true that your cousin and Tedo would've struck gold if they would've gotten away free and clear?"

"What do you mean?" I asked him.

"How much would they have made if they got away with all those pills?"

"I don't know. Maybe a couple of hundred grand," I lied. I figured if I told him that the street value of that robbery would've been over a million dollars, he'd probably go into this thing thinking he could get something close to that. I didn't need that headache. I mean, he already told me that if I didn't help him with this robbery, then he wasn't going to help me get my mother back. He was a fucking moron, and I hoped he didn't bite off more than he could chew. Whether he knew it or not, I was going to devise my own plan for my mother after he got me inside. After that, he and his crew would be on their own.

Rich got excited and turned around in the seat and faced me. "You gotta be shittin' me! Two hundred grand? And Tedo and that other nigga fucked that up? Shit! If it was me, I would've come out of that spot with every pill they had, and I wouldn't have left any witnesses. Everybody in that joint would've gotten spread."

"Yeah, right," I mumbled. Listening to this fool hype himself up like he's Scarface was a joke.

"Where did you say that restaurant was?" Rich changed the direction of the conversation.

"It's right around the corner from JANAF," I told him.

"Come on, Mike, let's head down there," Rich instructed his big friend.

"I'm on it, boss," Rich's flunky said.

Mike made his way onto Princess Anne Road and then he took it all the way up to the intersection of Military Highway. After he made a right turn, he drove another two miles and there we parked fifty feet away from the Indian restaurant. "Pull into that parking lot over there," Rich instructed Mike as he pointed to a parking lot in front of the restaurant.

While Mike headed into the parking lot, I looked at the parking lot of the restaurant and noticed that there were only a few cars parked in front of it. It was close to closing time, so I knew that a couple of those cars were patrons.

"Do any of those cars look familiar?" Rich asked me.

"Those cars that are parked in front of the restaurant belong to customers. The family that owns the restaurant park their cars on the side of the building," I told him, and then I turned my focus on every angle around the vicinity. I knew the DEA agents were watching this place, so I had to make sure they weren't tucked somewhere in the background, watching the car I was in.

I think I looked over my shoulders at least twenty times just to make sure. I knew one thing, for sure, if the agents were watching this car too, they were doing a helluva job. I couldn't find their cars nowhere in sight.

"Do they have a lot of traffic going in there?"

"Yeah, every time I went there to eat, they were always packed with customers."

"Do you know how many family members work there?"

"It varies. Sometimes seven. Other times ten."

"Think they sell the pills there too?"

"I don't know."

"What'cha think, Mike? Think they sell their pills wholesale out of there?" Rich asked him.

"I know I would, especially if I had a legit restaurant."

"Yeah, me too. Having that restaurant is a nice cover-up," Rich added.

"I think so too," Mike agreed.

"A'ight, so this is what we're going to do. We're gonna sit out here and wait for those motherfuckers to come out of there so we can see how many of them work the late shift. Then we're gonna follow them to their crib so we can find out where they live. After we accomplish that, we'll put our plan together," he said with finality.

At this point, there was really nothing else to say to Rich. Listening to his plan made me believe that he was more concerned about robbing those guys than trying to rescue our parents. In his conversation, he said absolutely nothing about how he planned to save his father. All Rich saw right now was how he was going to make off with a bunch of money so he could go and fuck it up to buy weed, bottles of champagne, and stripper bitches. That was it. This further gave me the drive to come up with my own plan. My mother was all I had left, and I would do anything to make sure she didn't suffer for my mistakes.

19

MY LIFE FOR YOURS

Rich made Mike and me sit out in the parking lot for over an hour while we waited for those people to come out of the restaurant and get into their cars. Five people, in all, came outside. Rich seemed excited about it. "I thought you said about seven to ten people work there?" Rich asked me.

"They do."

"Well, it looks like five people just came out of there."

"Maybe someone left right before we got here," I tried to rationalize.

"If I'm gonna rob this place, I'm gonna need the right numbers," he said, sounding like he was getting agitated.

"Things change all the time. So, why don't you plan to run into seven guys instead of five. I mean, it's better to plan for more than the other way around?" I responded sarcastically.

"Look, I don't need you telling me how to do my shit! So sit back and only speak when I ask you a question," he shot back.

I could tell that this guy wasn't woman-friendly at all. He was a fucking bully. And the longer I was around this nigga, I knew things were going to get a little heated. It was time for me to make an exit plan. This Rich guy was worse than I had expected.

"Come on, let's go," Rich instructed Mike.

Mike backed out of the parking spot and followed two cars to Highway 264, which was only one mile away. As soon as they approached the ramp, one car took the ramp, while the other one decided to take the far left to travel north of the ramp. Mike looked at Rich for direction. "Which one do you want me to follow?" he wanted to know.

"Follow the guy who's traveling alone."

"Why not follow the other car? There are four people in there, so you know that they're going home," I wondered aloud.

"Because that car had a woman in it, and no mafia-type family is going to have their women around anything illegal. They need her to cook, clean, and take care of the kids. That guy who's alone is going somewhere he didn't want that woman to see."

"If you say so," I said, and let out a long sigh.

Mike followed the guy who was in the car alone. He managed to tail the guy for three miles down South Military Highway without being detected. While he kept his eye on the guy in the car in front of us, I kept my eyes on everything around me. For all I knew, the agents could be following the guy in front of us too. Or even worse, they could be following us because we're following him.

Well, after looking over my shoulders at least two dozen times, it looked as though no one was following us or the guy in front of us either. I felt relieved.

The guy driving ahead of us finally ended up taking us to a house in the Greenbrier, off Volvo Parkway. A lot of doctors, lawyers, and hedge fund executives lived in this waterfront community. The homes in this area ran you from $750,000 to $1,250,000. A golf club and boat lifts were all inclusive.

Rich and I watched the guy drive his vehicle into the garage. A few seconds later, the garage door closed. Mike parked the car at the corner of the guy's block, so his home was in full view. "That's a big-ass house he lives in, huh?" Rich said.

"Damn right. That shit is huge. I know it's gotta be worth one million," Mike commented.

"If he lives in a house like that, they gotta be worth double that," Rich pointed out.

"Think they may have drugs in there?" Mike said aloud, giving me or Rich a chance to answer him.

"They might. You can never tell with people like that. I mean, they ain't street people like us. You know that we'll hide drugs anywhere," Rich spoke up.

"You damn right. It's called survival of the fittest," Mike commented.

"Think we should go and check the layout? Maybe walk around the back of the house. See if there is another way to get in when we start making our plans?" I suggested.

"No. That's too risky. We know where the guy lives, so we'll come back," Rich replied.

"But what if it's too late? What if this is the last night that our family will take their last breath? What if they are trying to get in touch with us now so we can pay their ransom?" I asked, tossing out every scenario.

"Look, homegirl, I know you miss your mama, because I miss my pops, but we can't go into those people's house like we run shit. We gotta come up with a plan. Because when I go in there, I'm coming out with everything I want, because I'm not going back."

"But what about my mother and your father? It seems like all you care about is robbing these people. When you talk about these people, the first thing that comes out of your mouth is that you want to rob them. Saving our parents from them is the furthest thing from your mind." This guy was truly annoying me. And from his facial expression, I was sure he was about to let me have it. So I braced myself and listened to what he had to say.

He turned around in his seat and gritted on me really hard. I wouldn't be surprised if his blood was boiling. "First of all, you don't know me. All you know was that Carl Sr. is my daddy. So, homegirl, when you step to me, come at me with some facts and some respect. Because if you don't, I'll show you a side of me that you'll never want to see again. Got it?"

"Yeah, got it," I replied nonchalantly. Because in reality, I couldn't care less about what he was talking about. Okay, he might be a street thug, and I was sure he had beaten up a lot of people and maybe even shot someone, but I couldn't focus on that right now. My main focus was to get my mother back. But since he made it clear that we were not doing any surveillance work tonight, I could do nothing but roll with it and pray that my mother would be all right until I could rescue her.

"Let's get out of here," Rich instructed.

"I'm on it," Mike said, and sped off.

* * *

En route to Rich's trap house, we stopped at the 7-Eleven located at the corner of Military Highway and Indian River Road. After Mike pulled into a parking space, he and Rich went into the store. Mind you, neither one of them asked me if I wanted something while they were in there, so I was really pissed off about that. But nothing prepared me for when I looked around to the left side of the car and noticed a government agent's car parked three cars over from the car I was in. The car was a dark gray Ford sedan with tinted windows. I couldn't see into the car, but I saw a silhouette of a man sitting in the driver's seat of the vehicle. With my heart racing at an uncontrollable speed, I turned my head slowly to the left. Every few seconds, I'd look through the front windshield of the car, hoping that these dudes would hurry up and get in the car so we could leave.

"Please come on," I said, even though I knew they couldn't hear me.

After a few more minutes, Mike came and got into the car first. Rich came and got into the car one minute later, carrying a pack of Oreo cookies, a six-pack of Bud Light, and four lottery tickets.

"I gonna win tonight, nigga!" Rich said cheerfully.

"You say that shit every time you buy tickets," Mike joked.

"Nigga, laugh all you want. When I do win, don't come smiling in my face, talking about 'Man, what's up? You gon' look out for me.' 'Cause I'm gon' tell you to haul ass!" Rich joked back.

While all of this was going on, I noticed the agent looking over at this car. Mike noticed it too when he backed out of his parking space. "See narcos watching us?" he asked Rich.

Rich turned around slowly and got a glimpse of the agent looking at us. Luckily for me, I couldn't be seen in the back seat. So my only hope was that these guys weren't carrying a gun or drugs, because if they were, they'd get arrested and I'd be hauled into the DEA office with a set of shiny handcuffs.

"Can you see how many in the car?" Rich asked both Mike and myself.

"It only looks like one," I said, and as soon as I said it, another agent emerged from the 7-Eleven. I didn't recognize the face. And as bad as I wanted to let out a sigh of relief, I knew I couldn't. I wasn't out of the woods yet.

"See that one coming out of the store?" Rich mentioned.

"Yeah, I see 'em," Mike replied while he backed the car in reverse.

"Have you ever seen him before?"

"Nah, I don't know who he is," Mike told him.

"Think he know us?" Rich sounded worried.

"I don't know, dude. But let's get out of here before they start fucking with us," Mike insisted, and then he continued to make his way out of the 7-Eleven parking lot.

While he drove away with caution, I watched the car with the agents inside while they were in view. The farther Mike drove away from them, the more relieved I became knowing that they weren't following us. Rich seemed more relieved than I was. "Thought I was gonna have to blast those niggas!" Rich announced.

"Me too," Mike agreed.

"Damn right! I won't let them niggas take me down,

especially after Hitler just hit me off with that pill package."

"You got that shit on you now?" Mike wanted to know.

"Yeah, where else is it gon' be? The nigga stopped by the spot and gave it to me right before you got there."

"What he want back from that joint he gave you?"

"A grand."

"Damn! That's it?"

"You damn right! That nigga knows what time it is. He knows I be putting in that work. And I ain't never been short when I gave him his dough," Rich bragged.

"Remember he gave you that bad shit two weeks ago. Yo, Rich, you acted like you was about to kill that nigga!" Mike joked.

"Yeah, I almost gave that nigga the business when he did that shit. But when he kept telling me he was sorry that he didn't know and took the price down, I couldn't do nothing but let 'em slide. I did tell 'em not to play with me like that again, because having that bad dope can fuck up your clientele. The worst thing that could happen to you in the hood is to be known for having bad dope. And you know that I ain't trying to have that shit lingering over my head. And that's why he made shit right between us. He knows I'm that nigga!" Rich boasted proudly.

"He didn't want you to pull that strap out either," Mike continued to joke.

"Nah! He sure didn't." Rich chuckled.

I sat in the background and listened to these idiots talk about how much respect they got in the hood and how ruthless they were. And that cats in the streets know they be hustling hard. Those two even talked about how many hos they were fucking. Rich acted like he had the most women chasing him to give him the pussy, and Mike complained about how much his girlfriend was getting on his nerves. The way this borderline fat boy looked, he had no room to talk about how his girlfriend stressed him out. In my opinion, he needed to constantly remind her about how good he had it. Because if I was the only chick left in the world, I still wouldn't fuck him. No way!

Rich was also boasting about how well a chick named Precious sucked his dick. I mean, he was really rooting for this woman, telling Mike that hands down Precious sucked his dick better than any of the chicks he ever had. The downside to her working her magic on him was that she worked all the time. "Man, a couple nights I called her and told her that I wanted to see her. But she told me that she was at work. So I told her to tell her boss that she had a family emergency and that she had to leave, and she told me that the only way she'd do it is if I pay her for the hours she's gonna lose. So I told her ass, hell nah! I don't pay for pussy. Then she said, 'Okay, I gotta get back to work,' and then she hung up."

"She hung up on you?"

"Yeah, that ho hung up on me."

"And what'cha do?"

"I didn't do shit! After she hung up, I called the next bitch!" Rich bragged. "And guess what?"

"What?"

"When I told the ho I wanted to see her, she said a'ight and brought her big-booty ass over to the spot. And I fucked the shit out of her ass too. I took my frustrations of that first chick out on the one that came through and let a nigga like me bust two nuts. I punished her ass!"

Listening to Rich tell his story about how he treated the women he slept with immediately made me think about how Terrell used to treat me. And the more Rich bragged about how disrespectful he was to the women in his life, it brought back bad memories of the horrible things Terrell did to me.

I remembered the first signs that he was cheating on me. He went from laying his cell phone around wherever he felt like it, and would answer all his calls in front of me, to either turning his cell phone off completely or he'd leave it in his car while we were chilling in my apartment. I didn't say anything about it at first. I didn't want to be that jealous girlfriend all guys run from. But then he started being blatant about it, by going outside to talk on his phone and not answering his phone at long hours of the day when I called him. And from there, it got messier. One night he and I had just come from the movies. On our way to my apartment, he decided to stop at the BP to get gas. When he got out of the car to go inside the store to pay for it, he forgot that he had his cell phone on his lap, so it fell down on the floor. I started to tell him that he dropped his cell phone, but then I thought, how would I find out who he's cheating with, if I didn't have the evidence? It was now or never.

As soon as he stepped foot into the store, I snatched his phone from the floor. When I pressed the Home button, the screen lit up and I was freaking devastated to see that this nigga had activated the thumbprint function so I couldn't get into his phone. There was no doubt in my mind that this nigga was cheating on me. I was so upset that I couldn't log in to his phone.

But let me tell you how God works.

While I was sitting there with his phone in my hand, the damn thing started to ring. My heart did a nosedive into the pit of my stomach when the name Simone was displayed on the screen of his phone. I didn't hesitate to answer the call. Simone and I had a very quick conversation about Terrell, because when he realized that he didn't have his cell phone on him, I saw him race out of the store and start running toward his car. Before he was able to open the car door and snatch his phone from my ear, Simone told me that they had been screwing around with each other for a couple of months. She told me where they met, how often they saw each other, and she even told me that they were talking about getting married. I swear, my whole world was turned upside down when she told me that. I remember Terrell yelling at me, asking me why I answered his phone. And how fucked up I was for doing it. I mean, he really turned that thing around on me like I was the one who had cheated. He was a piece of work.

From there, my insecurity level plummeted and I began to question if I was pretty enough to be with him. At the end of those thoughts, my answer was always no. To prevent myself from wallowing in the unhappy life I had with Terrell, I decided that it was time to take myself from that toxic relationship some months later. What was unfortunate was that when he noticed that I had officially left him, he started stalking and became physically aggressive toward me. I wished that things hadn't gone the way they did, because if he would've just left me alone, he'd be alive today.

20
TRAP HOUSE

Mike finally pulled into the neighborhood where he and Rich sold drugs. "Home, sweet home!" Rich commented after pulling up on the block where his trap house was located. We were on Bland Street in the Norview area of Norfolk. Like on all the blocks in the hood, you had to have a few cats on the corner watching out for the narcos when drugs are being sold on that street. They were called the lookouts. When we passed them, I knew the drug spot was only yards away from the corner.

"Time to make the donuts," Rich commented after Mike brought the car to a complete stop. After Rich closed the passenger-side door, Mike got out of the car next and I followed suit. I gave this old-ass brick duplex a look and was instantly grossed out with how it looked. Trash cluttered the small parking area. The smell of urine dominated the amount of trash we had to walk through to get to the front door.

Rich walked ahead of Mike and me, so he entered into the house first. I walked into the house second and Mike followed me. "Make sure you lock that door," Rich told him.

"I'm on it," Mike assured him.

"You can sit right here." Rich pointed toward a love seat that looked really dingy and grimy. I'm talking juice stains, pizza sauce stains, other food stains; you know it, it was there. I started to protest because how filthy the sofa looked, but I knew I wasn't in any position to win this fight. He didn't need me; I needed him. So I zipped my mouth and kept my thoughts to myself. The television had already been turned on, when we walked through the door, so I just sat there and started watching it.

"Want some juice or something?" Rich asked me while he walked toward the kitchen.

"No, I'm good," I told him. But in reality, I was kind of thirsty. I just didn't want anything from his house. It looked like a hoarder was living here. Shit was all over the place.

"You sure? We got Patrón," Mike said as he walked behind Rich.

"Yeah, I'm sure."

"You hungry? 'Cause we can put a frozen pizza in the oven." Mike was pressing the issue.

"Yo, nigga, leave her alone. She'll let us know if she wants something," Rich interjected before I could even open my mouth to answer Mike's question.

"Yeah, a'ight," Mike replied, brushing Rich off by shaking his head.

I watched Rich and Mike both as they were in the

kitchen. Rich took a small aluminum foil–wrapped item from his front pants pocket. The package item was about the size of the palm of his hand. After he had it in his hand, he placed it on the table and took a seat down on one of the kitchen chairs. "Mike, hand me that scale from the drawer," Rich instructed Mike.

Mike grabbed a digital scale from the drawer next to the stove and handed it to Rich. After Rich took the scale, he placed it down on the table in front of him. There was a plate, clear sandwich bags, and razor blades already on the table. When Rich dumped out the contents inside the aluminum onto the plate, I instantly recognized it. This negro was selling crack cocaine.

"That shit looks like a missile," Mike commented after he took a seat across from Rich.

"Yeah, I'm only gonna cut up twenty blocks," Rich told Mike as his razor cut the first rock.

Mike chuckled. "That shit looks like ten block."

"I bet'cha I get twenty for it."

"What'cha wanna bet?" Mike challenged Rich.

"Nigga, I'm not betting you for real! Look, if they don't wanna give me twenty, then I'm gonna tell 'em to get out of my damn face and haul ass!"

Mike continued to chuckle. "Man, you're a funny-ass dude!"

We hadn't been in Rich's trap house a good ten minutes before people started knocking on the door. Mike got up from the kitchen chair to answer the front door. "Who is it?" he asked.

"It's Ray-Ray. I gotta sixty sell," I heard the guy say from the other side of the front door.

"A'ight, hold up," Mike said, and then he walked back to the kitchen. The guy Ray-Ray stood at the front door and waited for Mike to come back. The moment Mike approached Rich, he dropped the money down on the table.

"Who that at the door?" Rich asked.

"Ray-Ray. Somebody out there wanna spend that whole sixty dollars."

While Mike was conducting the exchange with Rich, this Ray-Ray character stood at the front door and started eyeing me up and down. I couldn't get a good look at him because it was night out. But I heard him as he began to flirt with me. "How you doing?" he asked.

"I'm fine," I replied nonchalantly.

"Got a man?" he asked me.

"Yes, I do," I lied.

"Well, can we at least be friends?"

Before I got a chance to answer him, Mike interrupted the conversation. "Ray-Ray, cut it out. She doesn't want your crackhead ass."

Ray-Ray chuckled. "Come on, man, why you cock-blocking? I was about to ask her if I could take her out."

Mike handed him the drugs. "Take this shit and get out of here."

"Mike, I thought you were my boy?" Ray-Ray laughed and then he ran off.

After Mike closed the front door, he looked at me and said, "The day in the life of a crackhead."

I didn't respond. I just shook my head with disgust.

Mike headed back into the kitchen. He sat back down at the table and started having small talk with Rich. They talked about how much money Rich was going to make once he sold all the crack cocaine. They also talked about how they could change the way they distributed their drugs too—only allowing one drug runner to come to the house. This way, they could eliminate a lot of foot traffic. Mike agreed.

Once all the dope was cut up and packaged, Mike rolled up a blunt filled with some strong-smelling weed. Immediately after he rolled it up, he lit it, took the first drag from it, and then passed it to Rich. Ten seconds later, Mike released the smoke from his nose. "Now that's some good shit right here," Mike commented.

"Yeah, this shit is a missile," Rich agreed after he blew the smoke from his mouth.

As Rich passed the blunt back to Mike, someone knocked on the front door again. Mike stood up from the kitchen chair and walked back to the front door. "Who is it?" he asked.

"It's Monty and Jason," I heard a guy say.

Mike opened the front door and in came two thug-looking cats. They were both dressed in blue jeans, Michael Jordan sneakers, and hoodies. They spoke to me as they walked by me. I spoke back and turned my attention toward the television.

They didn't notice it, but I started watching them both from the corner of my eye. And when they entered into the kitchen, I was able to get a full view of them. Both were fairly decent-looking guys. They were around the same height, so one didn't stand out more than the other, expect that one wore a Caesar haircut and the other one red-colored dreadlocks. They even possessed that bad-boy exterior. Rich called out the guys' names and they appeared before him in the kitchen. "What's good, Monty?" Rich asked the guy with the Caesar haircut as he shook his hand. The guy with the red dreadlocks walked into the kitchen behind his friend. Rich shook his hand second.

"Jason, when you gon' take that bright-ass color out'cha head? You know your ass is hot. Every policeman in Norfolk know who your ass is," Rich joked.

"That's why I wear my hoodie all the time," Jason told him.

"It's too late now," Rich replied.

"Nigga, never mind about my hair, pass me that damn blunt," Jason continued, and reached for the blunt. Rich handed it to him.

Mike, Rich, and Monty made small talk as they watched Jason take a long puff from the blunt. As soon as he took the blunt away from his mouth, he passed it to Monty. And then Monty passed it to Mike. They started a rotation while they joked with one another. They started talking about the drought of cocaine they were experiencing and how it was important not to run out of product. Then the conversation's topic changed, and I was the topic.

"Yo, who that chick in there with?" Jason asked Rich and Mike.

"Ask him," I heard Mike say.

"That's your girl, Rich?" Jason pressed the issue.

"Nah, nigga, she's my meal ticket to some Arab cats with a lot of fucking money," Rich told him after he took another puff from the blunt and passed it on to Mike.

"What'cha gonna do, rob 'em?" Monty asked.

"You damn right! I'm tired of these out-of-town cats coming to my city and taking money out my pockets. It's time that they start paying restitution," Rich expressed.

"Yeah, bro, I'm wit'cha on that," Jason agreed.

"Yeah, me too," Monty agreed.

"Need any help? Because you know me and Monty got yo back," Jason offered.

"Say no more," Rich told him after he blew more marijuana smoke from his mouth.

"So, when you trying to do this?" Monty asked.

"I gotta check out a few things first. I'll know by tomorrow night," I heard Rich say.

"What's her name?" Jason repeated his earlier question.

"Misty," Rich told him.

"She got a man?" Jason wouldn't let up.

"Ask her," Rich insisted.

Seconds later, Jason came walking toward me. "Hi, Misty," he said.

I dreaded looking in his direction, but I did it anyway. "Hello," I replied.

"Hey, wait, did that nigga just say her name was Misty?" Monty interjected. When he did that, I knew he knew something about either the pharmacy robbery gone bad, or he knew what I did to Terrell, which was something I would continue to deny doing.

"Yeah," I heard Rich say.

"Yo, is that the chick that supposed to have killed that nigga Terrell?" Monty wouldn't let up.

"What'cha watching?" he asked as he took a seat on the chair next to me.

There was a commercial running, so I gave him a pass. *"Family Feud,"* I replied quickly, because I wanted to hear what the guys were talking about in the kitchen, especially since they were talking about me.

"Yeah, that's her," Rich confirmed Monty's question.

"Got a man?" Jason asked.

"Yes," I lied. I said it as quietly as I could, so I could hear the dialogue between Rich and the new guy Monty.

"Well, the next time you see him, tell him his services are no longer needed because I'm gonna take you from him?" he commented.

"I know a couple of niggas looking for her," I heard Monty say to them. And instantly I became panicked. All I could think about was how that guy Monty was going to put the word out that he knew where I was and collect on the bounty, once he delivered on the goods, which was me. "That bitch April told the police that that chick in there murdered that nigga, and that April and Tedo cut up his body and then they got rid of it. The same niggas got two chicks in jail that's gonna murk that bitch April. And they said that if Tedo hadn't gotten shot in that shoot-out, he would've gotten dealt with too."

"Did you hear me?" Jason asked me. He knew I wasn't listening to him, but he had no idea why.

"No, I'm sorry. My mind just drifted off for a minute," I told him. But inside my head, I did more than that. The words that had come out of Monty's mouth not only affected me emotionally, but they affected me mentally. It was hard sitting here, trying to answer this guy's questions. Whether he knew it or not, my life was on the line, and for the moment, his friend Monty had my life in his hands.

While Jason continued to badger me about where I lived, if I had kids, and what high school I went to, I continued to eavesdrop on the conversation Rich and Monty had about me. Before their talk ended, Rich began to whisper his plans to Monty. But I still managed to hear him tell Monty, in so many words, that he would agree to hand me over to the guys, but only after he used me for bait to rob those Arab cats and get his father back. I was floored when I heard Rich whisper that shit to him. He acted like I was nothing, a disposable piece of trash. To hear it come out of his mouth really put things into perspective for me. I knew that I was in here alone, and Rich had no intention of helping me to get my mother back, and he was going to throw me away to the pack of wolves, once this whole thing was over.

"What's up my dude? You got homegirl handcuffed in here," Monty said jokingly as he walked into the front room where Jason and I were.

Jason looked up at Monty. "Come on now, Monty, you know how I do," Jason said confidently.

"You better leave her alone. I heard she be murking niggas!" Monty commented.

"I be doing what?" I asked him, giving him a hard stare. As bad as I wanted to let sleeping dogs lie, I knew that he was trying to ruffle my feathers. If I didn't stand my ground, then he was going to tumble all over me.

"We know what you did to that nigga Terrell," he replied as he stood with his back against the wall by the entryway of the kitchen.

At this very moment, I was sitting on the couch, and Jason sat a few inches away, but my attention was directed toward Monty. I wasn't feeling this asshole at all. The fact that he was trying to throw me underneath the bus was an uncomfortable space to be in. I wanted to curse him out and storm out the front door, but then where would I go? I had nobody. The last person that had my back was Mrs. Mabel, but now she was dead. *So, what do I do? Sit here and take these dudes' mess?* "Listen, dude, you don't know shit about me," I told him.

"So you're denying that you murked that nigga Terrell?" He continued to stand there.

"Who wants to know?" I asked him defiantly.

"I wanna know. All these niggas wanna know too." Monty pointed to Rich, Mike, and Jason.

"Wanna know what?" Jason interjected.

"She's the one that murdered that nigga Terrell," Monty told Jason.

Jason looked at me. "Yo, word!" Jason said, as if he needed me to confirm what Monty had just said.

"Look, I haven't done anything. So I wish you would leave me alone," I told him, and then I looked at Rich, who was sitting in the chair by now.

"Come on, Monty. Leave her alone, dude!" Mike stood up and defended me.

It felt good to have someone in this freaking house take up for me. I saw Rich wasn't going to do it, so to hell with him. And whether he knew it or not, I was brewing up a plan for his grimy ass. And what was going to be so satisfying to me was that he wasn't going to see it coming. *Fucking asshole!*

"Nah, fuck that, Mike! That nigga Terrell was good people."

"I didn't know him like that," Mike spoke up.

"It don't matter. I know him. Him and his cousins lived on my block. His cousins helped me when these dudes tried to rob me at this New Year's Eve party last year," Monty explained.

"So, what'cha gon' do? Rat me out to them? Tell them where I am?" I spat out. This guy was starting to rub me the wrong way. I had tried to keep my mouth closed this whole time, but this dude Monty had plucked my last nerve.

"If it was up to me, I'd call 'em now. But Rich told me not to. So you better tell him thank you," Monty continued, gritting his teeth at me. This guy had never seen me before, but he acted like he hated my guts. He was having some serious issues.

"Is this the moment when I tell Rich thanks?" I gritted back at him. I wasn't backing down. I was tired of being Ms. Nice Girl. I figured if I kept my mouth closed, I wouldn't start up any drama. But this guy made that very hard to do. So, where do I go from this point now?

"Nah, bitch, this is the moment when you tell me to take out my dick so you can give me a blow job," Monty snapped. He took a couple of steps toward me too. Jason stood up and told him to chill out.

"Stop, man. Just chill out." Jason tried to reason with him.

"Yeah, dude, leave it alone," Mike agreed.

"Oh, I see what you niggas trying to do. Y'all trying to fuck her, that's why you're being nice to her. Making her feel like you gon' save her," Monty suggested. He was getting more agitated by the second. He even turned around to face Rich while he was still sitting at the kitchen table. "Rich, you hear these niggas taking her side?" Monty said to him.

Rich started chuckling. "Monty, you bugging out, dude. Just chill out, like Jason said. Everything is going to be a'ight," Rich said in hopes of calming Monty down.

Monty hesitated for a moment and then said, "Yeah, a'ight. I'm gonna leave it alone for now." But then he turned around toward me and said, "You're a lucky bitch! But I guarantee that that luck is gonna run out really quick."

"Yeah, whatever!" I told him. Because at this point, I knew he wasn't going to do a thing to me. And as of right now, Rich wasn't going to let anything happen to me because I was his meal ticket. But that's all going down the drain, and I couldn't wait to see Rich's face when it did.

21

I'M A MAD WOMAN

Monty and Jason left about twenty minutes after all that shit hit the fan. I swear, no one has talked to me like that since I was with Terrell. See what happened to him? I tell you what, things would eventually turn around in my favor. Just wait and see.

Rich ended up going outside to sell the drugs he'd just packaged up. Mike stayed in the front room with me and watched television. During a commercial, he sparked up a conversation with me. His icebreaker was asking me if I needed something, since I hadn't said much after Jason and Monty left. "I need to use the bathroom," I told him.

"It's upstairs on the left side," he told me as he pointed toward the staircase.

"Thanks," I replied, and stood up from the couch. I had to walk by Mike to go upstairs, so I stepped by him and headed up the flight of steps. I was up at the top of the staircase within eight seconds. When I entered into the bathroom, I was repulsed when I saw drips of piss on the toilet bowl seat. I wasn't going to sit down on that thing. It was fucking disgusting. So, how was I going to relieve myself? I looked around the bathroom, thinking about how this small-ass box looked worse than a restroom at a gas station. After realizing that the only safe place I could empty out my bladder would be the sink, that's what I did. I figured, why not? The motherfuckers in this house didn't like me anyway, so pissing in their bathroom sink was a great start to plans I had stored away for them.

After I urinated in the bathroom sink, I threw the toilet tissue into the toilet and didn't flush it. I washed my hands, but didn't rinse the sink out, so you could clearly see yellow drops of my pee around the sink bowl. I wanted those bastards to see what I did, even though I planned to deny it. The reward for me was knowing that I had one up on those assholes. Fucking idiots.

I walked back downstairs and sat in the same spot I was before I went upstairs. It seemed like as soon as I sat down and got comfy, fate reared its ugly face. An emergency broadcast from *Ten on Your Side* flashed across the television, with my image: "This just in, authorities are looking for Misty Heiress."

"Oh shit! That's you!" Mike blurted out after seeing my face on the news.

"She is a murder suspect in the killings of Terrell Mason and Mrs. Mabel Davis. She is a Virginia Beach resident and a former employee at Rx-Pharmacy Depot. She is believed to be armed and dangerous. If you've seen this woman or know where she is, please contact your local Virginia Beach Police at once," the newswoman reported.

"I'm not armed and dangerous!" I spat. I was about to spaz out. *Really, I'm armed and dangerous? And I didn't kill Mrs. Mabel. Ahmad and his accomplice killed her.*

"Her last sighting was earlier today when my colleague Christian Lundy witnessed her running away from her apartment. No one has seen her since then, so again, if you have any information on her whereabouts, please contact Virginia Beach Police. Remember, she is armed and dangerous. I'm Belinda Givens, reporting for *Ten on Your Side.*"

"Damn, girl, you're gangsta-ass shit!" Mike sat there in awe.

"I didn't kill that lady. Those Arab guys did it. And I'm not armed and dangerous. I don't have a fucking gun on me. Ugh!" I protested.

"It's bad when the police put your picture up on TV," Mike expressed.

"No shit! I can't believe that they're trying to pin that murder on me. And then to say that I'm armed and dangerous! That's some bullshit right there," I said with frustration.

"You know you can't be out on the streets now. If somebody sees you, they gon' call the police," Mike assured me.

"I think I'll take my chances with the cops than with those guys that know Terrell. Monty made it perfectly clear that those guys want to seek revenge on me," I mentioned.

"Don't worry about Monty right now. Rich told him that he couldn't fuck with you," he replied.

"Don't leave out the part where Rich told him that he couldn't mess with me until *after* he robs those Arab dudes and gets his father back."

"Nah, he didn't say that," Mike said, trying to lie.

"Listen, Mike, I know Rich is your boy and all. And I know you aren't trying to rat him out, but I heard him. I mean, he didn't even add my mother to the equation. So, why shouldn't I be worried about that? Rich don't give a damn about me. His main agenda is to rob those Arab guys, walk away with as much money and drugs as he can, and get his father back before the heist is over," I explained.

"Look, I'm not trying to get into all the politics with you about what Rich said, but I will tell you that Monty isn't the type of dude that would let stuff go. He's a hothead. And he has no conscience. When he say he's going to do something, take his word for it," Mike warned me.

"What kind of guy talks to a woman like that? He acted like I did something to him," I pointed out.

"It doesn't matter with Monty. He's one of those guys that would die for something he believes in. So just watch your back and what you say from now on."

"Yeah, all right," I said, and turned my focus back to the television.

A few seconds later, I looked back at Mike and said, "Please don't tell anyone that I was just on the news."

"Sure, no problem," he said, and then we both turned our focus back on the television.

Seconds turned into minutes, and minutes turned into hours. About three hours into my stay at this nasty-ass house, I found myself becoming drowsy. Before I even realized it, I had fallen asleep. Startled by the front door slamming, I jumped out of my sleep. When I opened my eyes, Monty started walking toward me. "I'm back," he announced, with a bottle of liquor in his right hand.

I looked around the room and noticed that Mike was nowhere in sight. I looked back at Monty and sat straight up in the chair. "Please leave me alone," I begged him, dreading what was about to happen.

Monty stood in front of me and took another swig from the liquor bottle. "You know that you are one lucky-ass bitch!" he commented after he swallowed the alcohol in his mouth.

"Look, I don't wanna start up another argument with you," I told him.

He laughed. "You think I wanna argue with you? I'm standing right here because you owe me."

Puzzled, I said, "Owe you for what?"

"For not telling Terrell's cousins where you at. I saw those niggas about an hour ago and I could've told them where you were hiding, but I didn't. So you owe me. And I'm ready to collect," he continued, and took another swig from the bottle. After he swallowed the alcohol, he unzipped his jeans with his left hand, then pulled out his dick. "Suck it," he continued, looking down at me like I was his slave.

"You better get your little-ass dick out of my face," I said calmly. In my mind, I had decided that if this dumb-ass motherfucker didn't get his penis out of my face, I was going to show him where to put it.

"What'cha gon' do if I don't?" Monty tested me while taking another swig from the bottle.

"I'm telling you right now, you better get that thing out of my face," I warned him again. I was two seconds from ripping the head of his penis from the shaft. I pictured blood gushing out of him like a waterfall while he squirmed around like a little bitch.

"Why the fuck you taking so long? Lick it," he instructed me, and started gyrating his penis in my face.

Without giving it a second thought, I grabbed his dick in my hand and tried to rip it from his groin. Monty screamed like a little bitch and dropped the liquor bottle on the floor in front of us. Vodka splattered everywhere after the bottle shattered. Some of it got into my eyes, but that didn't stop me from unleashing the beast on this disrespectful bastard. "I told you to get this shit out of my face, but you didn't. Now you wanna scream like a lil bitch! Man up, you stupid piece of shit!" I mocked him while I gritted my teeth.

Rich and Mike heard all the commotion in the house and ran in from outside. Rich came in the front door first and Mike followed. When I saw them rushing toward us, I let Monty's dick go and stood up from the couch. I figured whatever was going to happen next, I was going to be ready for it. I was tired of these losers treating me like shit.

While Monty rocked back and forth on the floor, with his hand covering his dick, Rich rushed to him, towering over Monty, asking what just happened. Mike stood a few feet away from the whole thing and watched as an onlooker.

"That bitch tried to rip my dick off me!" Monty shouted as he continued to rock back and forth. He was holding on to his penis for dear life.

"What the fuck is wrong with you?" Rich yelled at me.

"That nasty motherfucker took his dick out and told me to suck it. And I told him to get out of my face, and he wouldn't listen. So I did what I had to do!" I roared. I was ready to go head-to-head with Rich for even taking this asshole's side. He was the one out of line. *Now I'm the bad one?*

Rich got in my face. "Do you know what that nigga would do to your stupid ass?" He continued to yell and curse.

"What about what I just did to him?" I snapped.

"What, you think this is a joke!" Rich screamed at me.

"Why the fuck are you screaming at me? I was sitting in here, minding my own business, and then he comes in here and demands that I suck his dick! Was that not fucked up?" I continued to scream at him while I stood my ground.

With no warning, Rich lunged at me and smacked me with the back of his hand. The force from the sudden blow knocked me back and I collapsed on the couch. After I landed on my back, I held my face with my hand. "Are you out of your fucking mind?!" I screamed at Rich.

"Shut the fuck up, bitch!" Rich roared while holding his arm up in the air like he was ready to strike me again.

One part of me wanted to stand up and charge him with all the strength and force I had inside of me, but then I thought about how badly things could go if I did. But at the same time, I didn't deserve any of this treatment I was getting. What was I supposed to do? So I sat up on the couch, holding the palm of my hand against my face.

Meanwhile, Monty had gotten a grip on himself and was finally able to deal with the pain I inflicted on him. He climbed onto the couch near me. Immediately after that, he gave me the stare of death. "You feeling better, man?" Rich went to his aid after hitting me in the face.

I sat there and watched both of these assholes as Mike

stood away from us, but at the same time, I surveyed what had just happened. I really wanted him to be the adult in the room and tell those two bastards that what they did to me was wrong. But he didn't open his mouth—not one time.

"Yo, I swear, I wanna kill that bitch right now," Monty said through clenched teeth. I could see the veins bulging through the skin near his temple.

"Don't worry about her right now. She'll get dealt with," Rich assured him.

"What the fuck you mean, I'm gonna 'get dealt with'?" I spat out at him, even though I already knew what that comment meant.

"Bitch, just know that you're on borrowed time," Rich replied menacingly.

"Be a man and say what you gotta say!" I yelled at him.

Within a flash, Rich made a dash toward me; Mike must've known what was about to happen because he slid between us before Rich got within a couple of inches of me. "Move, Mike!" Rich roared at him. Mike's back was facing me while he shielded me from Rich.

"Come on, Rich, we got things to do, so let's keep this ship moving." Mike was trying to calm the situation.

"Nah, fuck that! She keeps running her mouth, and I need to make her close it for good." Rich kept ranting while trying to push his way by Mike. Thankfully, Mike wasn't allowing that to happen. Not only was he bigger than all the guys there, but for some reason, he acted like he wanted to protect me. He didn't say it out of his mouth, but his actions showed it.

"Rich, man, come on, dawg. You're better than that," Mike continued, trying to hold Rich back.

"Move out the way, Mike," Rich warned him.

"Nah, fuck that bitch!" I heard Monty say, and then he lunged at me with full force. *Bam! Bam! Bop! Bop! Bam!* Monty's blows hit my face, one after the other. I tried to shield my face with my arms, but it didn't work. "You fucking bitch! I told you I was going to fuck you up!" He continued to hit me with one fist after the other. I tried desperately to cover my face, but it wasn't working out. At one point, I tried to get up from the couch, but I couldn't. Monty was hitting me so fast and so hard. "Bitch! I'm gon' kill your ass today!" He gritted his teeth.

Realizing that I was getting my ass wiped, Mike turned away from Rich. "Come on now, Monty!" Then he bear-hugged Monty and lifted him up in the air. This gave me only half of a second to hop off the couch and make a run for the front door. Unfortunately for me, Rich caught up with me before I could make it to the front door. He grabbed me by my hair and snatched me backward. "Bitch, you ain't going nowhere!" he growled at me.

I lost my balance and collapsed onto the floor. I started kicking Rich and screaming like my mind was going bad. "Get the fuck away from me! Leave me alone!"

"Damn, Rich, man . . . ," I heard Mike say, and then I heard a gunshot. *Pop!*

Next came a loud thud. *Boom!* It seemed like everything from that point went in slow motion. Rich stood up and turned around to face Mike and Monty. I stopped kicking and screaming and looked in the same direction as Rich. I blinked my eyes so I could be clear about what had just happened. Then I looked and saw that Mike had collapsed on the floor, while Monty was standing over him with a revolver in his hand. My heart rate went from twenty miles per hour to 150; fear had engulfed my entire body. All I could do was sit there on the floor. My body felt paralyzed, while Rich rushed over to Mike's side. "Yo, Monty, look what the fuck you just did!" Rich snapped.

Monty continued to stand there with the gun in his hand. "I told him to get off me," Monty said, trying to justify his actions.

"Man, give me that fucking gun!" Rich said, and took Monty's pistol from his hand.

I watched Mike in disbelief as he covered his stomach, where Monty had shot him. "He's gonna die if y'all don't take him to the hospital," I pleaded to them as Mike tried to speak. No one could understand him.

"Shut the fuck up, bitch! This was all your fault!" Monty roared.

"That shit wasn't my fault!" I roared back at him.

"Look, both of y'all shut the fuck up! We gotta get him to the emergency room before he dies! Help me get him off the floor," Rich said.

"Who's taking him to the hospital?" Monty wanted to know.

"Nigga, you're taking him. You the one shot him," Rich replied pointedly.

"But I'm driving my girl's car and she's gonna know something happened if he leaves a lot of blood in her car," Monty expressed.

"Man, I ain't trying to hear that shit! You're taking him to the hospital. Let's hurry up and get him out of the house and put him into the car," Rich told Monty.

Monty let out a long sigh; then he helped Rich pick Mike up from the floor. Mike whimpered like he was in a lot of pain. I felt so sorry for him. To see him in this situation made me feel so bad for him, especially since he was taking up for me. He tried to do everything in his power to prevent Monty and Rich from attacking me. And even though he couldn't hold them back like he intended, I still appreciated his gesture, because he didn't have to do it.

I watched Monty and Rich as they carried Mike out of the house. As they struggled with his body, I noticed Mike's cell phone had fallen out—I assumed from the back pocket of his pants. Getting my hands on that phone would give me an edge on them.

22

DANGER IS NEAR

As soon as they walked outside, I scrambled over to where Mike's cell phone was and snatched it up from the floor. I shoved it down into my pants pocket. It only took Rich and Monty a few minutes to put Mike into Monty's girlfriend's car, because Rich was back in the house with me less than a minute later.

"Get yo ass up and clean that blood off the floor!" Rich demanded.

"Why I gotta get it up?" I protested.

"Because you started this shit!" Rich argued.

On any other occasion, I would've cursed Rich out and told him to kiss my ass. But I couldn't do it now. I mean, he and Monty just beat my ass for running my mouth a few minutes ago, while Mike tried to defend me. So, do you think that I am going to run my mouth while I am alone in this fucking house? Hell no!

"What the fuck are you waiting for? Get up and wipe that blood up from the floor before I jump on your ass this time. Unlike Monty, I'll make you suck my dick, with the barrel of my gun to your fucking head. I dare you to do anything other than put it in your mouth, because if you don't, I'll splatter your brains all over this mother-fucker!" he roared while giving me the look of death. It was an expression of evilness and I wanted no part of it. Hearing this guy say out loud that he'd shoot me in my head sent a lightning bolt of horror through me. I was in a complete state of fear. The amount of torment I would endure could be unimaginable. What should I do?

I stood up slowly while Rich changed out of his jacket and shirt. He grabbed a white T-shirt from a package of T-shirts he had in the closet by the front door and changed into it. After he pulled it down on himself, he looked at me and said, "Why the fuck you just standing there?"

"I need some cleaning stuff and a rag or something," I told him.

"Go in the kitchen. There's some dishwashing liquid in there. Use the dishrag hanging from the faucet," he instructed.

Taking Rich's instructions, I headed into the kitchen and grabbed the dishwashing liquid from the counter and the cloth rag tied around the faucet nozzle. I also grabbed a gallon-sized pot from the stove and filled it halfway up with water. Thankfully, Mike bled out on the ceramic floor. If it had been a rug or carpet, then there's no way I would've been able to clean it up.

"You know, I thought you were a nice guy," I said to Rich after I got down on my knees to clean up Mike's blood.

By this time, Rich had taken a seat on the couch across

from me and had started counting money he had taken out of his pocket. "What makes you think I'm not one?" he replied without taking his eyes off his money.

"You and Monty beat me up like I was wrong for what I did," I began to explain. "Do you know how much my face hurts right now? And as bad as I want to look in a mirror, I know I'm going to cry, once I see all the bruises," I continued talking while dampening the floor with the water from the pot.

"You should've kept your mouth closed when I told you to."

"Rich, he pulled his dick out in my face and told me to suck it. And I was supposed to sit back and not say anything? Was I supposed to let him disrespect me like that?" I pressed the issue.

"I'm gonna need you to shut up."

"Why won't you just answer my question? I mean, don't you think I deserve an answer? Do it for your dad and my mom, because we're technically brother and sister," I reminded him, hoping he would catch the bait.

"You mentioning my father isn't going to work with me. I'm gonna let you in on a secret," he started off, looking straight at me. "I don't like my father. He was a piece of shit when he was married to my mother. He cheated on her. When he was an alcoholic, he beat on her. He even beat up my brother. My brother forgave him, but I didn't. So to hear you say do it for my father makes me wanna jump on you right now and beat the daylights out of you. So you'll know how my dad used to do me when I was a kid. That motherfucker was a mean-ass dude. I remember when I was a child, I used to hope that he would get in a car accident and die so he wouldn't come home and put his hands on me and my mama. He was a fucked-up nigga.

So I hope that those Arab dudes kill him slow when they start chipping away at his life. See, I can't say too much about your mama because I really don't know her. But if she's anything like my dad, I wish death on her ass too."

"So you don't care if they kill my mother?" I questioned him.

"Why should I? She ain't my mama! My mama is dead! So stop with the questions before I spaz out on your ass again," Rich said with finality. And to oblige his wishes, I closed my mouth and continued to clean up Mike's blood.

Who would've known that Rich felt this way about his father? I swear, I wished that I had known this before his brother introduced me. I wouldn't have left the house with Rich, much less gotten into the car with him and Mike and come to this freaking trap house. I sure fucked up this time.

Thankfully, it only took me a few minutes to clean up Mike's blood; the sight of it gave me a queasy feeling in my stomach. Not to mention, there was a lot of it. I only hoped that Monty's dumb ass got Mike to the hospital in time so an emergency physician could operate on Mike. Mike was a good guy and didn't deserve getting shot. As much as Rich wanted to blame this whole incident on me, it wasn't my fault that Monty shot Mike. Mike made the judgment call to come to my rescue because he saw how these barbaric-ass niggas tried to hurt me. My only hope for him was that he came out of this all right. It would break my heart if he died.

After I cleaned up the rest of the blood, I took the pot and the rag back into the kitchen. I emptied the bloody water into the sink and then I set the pot on the stove with the nasty dishrag inside of it. I dreaded going back into the front room where Rich was, but I had no other choice, so I headed back in there and took a seat on the sofa.

While I sat there and watched the television, another breaking-news segment popped on TV. There was no doubt in my mind that it would be about me. It was all bad timing. If they were going to broadcast my face up there again, then Rich would see it, and I didn't want that to happen.

"This just in, authorities were called to the Ghent area of Norfolk by a resident walking their dog. It has been told by homicide detectives that a man's body was dumped alongside the curb on Twenty-first Street. It appears that he was shot in the head twice, execution style. No word if this was a mob hit. The identity of this victim will remain anonymous until the family has been notified. There has been speculation that this murder could be linked to the other murders we've been reporting on these last couple of days. Police said that if anyone knows what happened to this man or who murdered him, please contact your local Virginia Beach Police at once. My name is Tonya Spaulden, reporting for *Ten on Your Side*."

Before the camera was taken off the news reporter, Rich's cell phone started ringing. I watched Rich as he answered the call. "Yo, what's up?" he said to the caller. I couldn't hear what the caller was saying, so I waited for Rich to speak again, giving me some indication as to who was talking to him.

"I just saw it on TV," he spoke again, and then fell silent. "Nah, I ain't going. You go," he continued. And when he uttered the words "I ain't going. You go," I knew he was talking to his brother. Surprisingly, he didn't say anything else. He disconnected the call and then placed his cell phone alongside him, so he could continue to count his money.

"Was that your brother?" I asked him.

"Yeah," he replied.

"So that was your father that they found?"

"Yep."

"Did he say anything about my mother?"

"Nope."

"So, how do you feel?"

"What's with the fucking questions? You're my therapist now?" he snapped, giving me the evil eye.

"No, I'm not."

"Well, so you know, since my dad is dead, I'm no longer doing a rescue mission. I'm just running up in the spot and robbing those cats."

Rich telling me that he was no longer doing a rescue mission was old news. I heard him mention it to Mike. So, why try to break the news to me now? Fucking loser!

"So my mother is shit out of luck, huh?" I boldly asked.

"Unless you go in there and rescue her yourself."

"You know what? That's some bullshit! How am I gonna walk in the Arab's spot and take my mama without a gun? Do you know what they'll do to me and my mother?"

"That's not my concern."

"You're a grimy-ass nigga! I don't know why I let you and your brother talk me into coming here with you. Not only have I gotten my ass wiped by two niggas, now I gotta deal with the fact that you aren't going to help me get my mama back."

"Call me *grimy* again and see what happens!" he dared me.

"Yeah, whatever," I said. I could tell that he was getting agitated really quickly, so I left him alone and turned my attention back toward the television.

For the next hour or so, Rich and I didn't say a word to each other. When the crackheads knocked on the front door to buy drugs from him, he served them, they gave him the money, and then the deal was done. He did this for the next ten times without incident. One of the crackheads gave him a hard time about the size of the drugs, so he cursed them out and told them to leave before he whipped their asses. Instead of leaving, they took the micro-sized drug, paid him the money, and then left. Rich couldn't care less if they bought the drug or not. He knew he would sell it because the product was good. And that's all he kept telling them.

While he took care of his business, I told him I had to use the bathroom. When he gave me the green light to go, I went upstairs. When I got into the bathroom, I closed the door and locked it. Rich didn't know that I had Mike's cell phone. And I wasn't going to tell him either. This cell phone was going to be my ticket out of here if I came up with a strategic plan to get out of here and rescue my mother in the process.

Immediately after I entered the bathroom, I turned the bathroom sink water on so Rich wouldn't hear me when I started talking on the phone. Before I got on the phone, I looked at my face in the mirror. When I saw the bruises on my face, I got filled up with tears. The purple and blue bruises around my eyes and around my mouth made me very sad. I didn't deserve this beating. I didn't do anything to warrant this treatment. So, why did they do this to me? To scare me into a submissive state of mind? If that's what their intentions were, then they were sadly mistaken, because it would *not* happen. Whether they knew it or not, I was a very strong woman and I would show them just that when all of this shit was over.

Standing there with the phone in my hand, I knew I had to call people that would help me execute my plan to help me get my mother. And I knew that I would only have one opportunity to do it. There can't be any fuckups, because people's lives were hanging in the balance. The most important life would be my mother's, so timing was key and I planned on using it wisely.

The first person I knew I had to call was Agent Sims. I knew his cell phone number by heart, so I knew I wanted to call him first. Whatever I needed to tell him could only be in a one-minute phone call. I figured calling him and telling him that I had nothing to do with Ms. Mabel's death would be a good place to start. I could also tell him that I was with Rich, who was Carl Sr.'s son, and that he planned to rob and kill the Arabs to avenge his father's murder. Most important, tell him that I'd call him back when I had more information.

After taking a deep breath and then exhaling, I dialed Agent Sims's number and pressed the Send button. "Agent Sims," he said.

"This is Misty and I only have thirty seconds to talk, so be quiet and listen to what I gotta say."

"Where are you? We thought that you were dead," he said.

"Well, I'm not, and just so you know, I'm calling from a burner phone, so you won't be able to track it."

"Can you tell me where you are so I can come and get you?"

"Shut up before I hang up the phone," I threatened him.

"Okay, I'm listening."

"Look, I had nothing to do with Mrs. Mabel's death. Ahmad and another guy did it. I saw them when they shot her."

"We know that, and that's why we want to bring you in."

"I am not gonna tell you where I am, so please shut the fuck up," I hissed, letting him know that I meant business. "Now, I know that you guys found Carl's body, and one of his sons wants to seek revenge. He's preparing to go after them by robbing them and avenging his father's death. So stay on guard and I will call you back with more information when I get it." I then hurried and disconnected the call. My heart rate raced at an uncontrollable speed. I tried to calm my nerves, but my heart wouldn't let me. So I just went with the flow and kept the train moving.

My next call was to Ahmad. I just hoped that he hadn't changed his cell phone number, because if he had, then I was fucked. And my plan would only be a half-sided one, meaning I got Agent Sims on board, but Ahmad wouldn't be. I crossed my fingers after I dialed the number and pressed the Send button.

"Hello," I heard Ahmad say. But I was too afraid to respond. Hearing his voice struck me like lightning. I could open my mouth, but no words would come out. "Hello," he said again. I knew he was wondering who was calling him, and I wanted him to know that it was me, but I could not speak. What was wrong with me? I had it all planned in my head, what I was going to say to him, but nothing happened. "Who's there?" he asked.

"I saw what you did," I finally said. But I kept my volume at a whisper.

"Who is this?" he wondered aloud.

"I saw you when you killed that lady, you fucking jerk-off! You're a fucking coward," I ranted, but I kept it in a whisper.

"Where did you go?" he asked me. His voice sounded menacing. I could tell that if I had been in front of him, he'd probably break my neck with his bare hands.

"Don't worry about where I went. Just know that the man you killed, and left his body on the side of the road, his sons want to kill you. They want to make you pay for what you did to their father. And they say they're going to rob you of every dime you have. And if you have drugs, they are going to take that too."

"Send them over."

"Oh, don't worry, they're coming for you. They will find you too," I warned him.

"You do know I still have your mother?" he told me.

"Yes, I do."

"You do want to see her again, right?"

"Of course, I do. What kind of question is that?"

"Well, you're gonna have to make a trade."

"What kind of trade?"

"Your life for hers."

"Let's do it," I said without hesitation.

"You do know I'm gonna kill you slow, right?"

"Okay what you do to me, to let my mother go, so we can even the score."

"When?"

"I'll call you back with that information. But before I call you back, I need proof of life. Where is she? I need to hear her voice," I told him.

"Hold on a minute," he said, and then I heard complete silence. No movement. No talking. Nothing. But then a couple of seconds later, I heard someone fidgeting with the phone. "Hello," I heard a tiny voice say.

Just like that, it felt like fireworks exploded inside of me. For the moment, I began to feel excited, because I knew my mother was on the other end of the line. "Mom, is that you?" I said anxiously.

"Yes, baby, it's me. Where are you?" she wanted to know. But before I could answer that question, Ahmad took the phone away from her. "That's enough. You know she's alive. Let's make the trade now," he said with finality.

"I will call you back with that information."

"Don't take too long, because as you know, the DEA is closely watching my family. And if they decide to intervene in this thing between you and me, then I'm going to kill her, and no one will ever find me. Understood?"

"Yeah, I understand. But you better keep your word, or I'm gonna have my mother's boyfriend's son and his friends kill some of the innocent people in your family. Now, do you understand where I am coming from?"

"I don't like threats, Ms. Misty."

"I don't like them either. So stay by the phone and I'll call you back by noon tomorrow."

"I'll be waiting," he assured me.

Knock! Knock! Knock! Startled, I fumbled with the cell phone in my hand and almost dropped it. "Yo, what'cha doing in there?" I heard Rich ask from the other side of the bathroom door.

"I'm using the bathroom," I replied as I powered the phone off and shoved it down into the back pocket of my pants.

"Hurry up. I gotta pee," he told me.

"Okay, I'm coming," I told him, and then I flushed the toilet like I had just used it. I turned on the faucet water too, to pretend like I was washing my hands. I turned the faucet off and then I opened the door. Rich was front and center when I laid eyes on him.

"Can you get the fuck out of my way?" he said impatiently.

"Sure. No problem," I replied, and moved out of his way.

While he handled his business in the bathroom, I headed back downstairs. When I stepped foot back in the front room, I looked at the front door. Something inside of me wanted to leave this place and not look back. But then I figured that if I left, I wouldn't have the backup I needed to help me get my mother back. Ahmad would kill both my mother and myself if I came for her alone, and I couldn't have that. Not now. Not ever.

23

WALKING TWO STEPS AHEAD

I was shocked when Monty brought his dumb ass back to the house. Rich was standing at the front door serving one of his crackhead customers when Monty pulled up in his girlfriend's car. "What's going on with Mike? Is he going to be all right?" Rich didn't hesitate to ask Monty after he stepped foot in the house.

"I don't know. When I got to the emergency room, I helped him out of the car and walked him inside. When the nurse saw him bleeding, she got him a wheelchair and wheeled him back behind the double doors," Monty explained.

"Was he still breathing?"

"Yeah, he was breathing. He was talking too. So I told him to hold on and that he was going to be all right," Monty continued.

"As soon as the cops find out he's been shot, you know

they will show up and start asking him a whole bunch of questions."

"You think he's gonna snitch on me?" Monty sounded worried.

"Hell nah! What kind of nigga you think Mike is? That nigga is legit! I trust him with my life. Because he's that type of dude!" Rich told Monty.

"Well, he sure didn't act that way when he was takin' up for that bitch right there." Monty pointed at me.

"There you go with that bullshit again," I commented. This guy had only been in the house for two minutes and he was talking about me already.

"Shut the fuck up! Ain't nobody talking to you." He gritted his teeth at me. His horns were flaring up again. Now, how would I handle this nigga if he decided he wanted to fight on me again? I couldn't take too many beatings.

"Calm down, Monty. Let it go, man. We got other shit to do," Rich spoke up. "You know they found my pops." He changed the subject.

"Who found him?" Monty changed his tone.

"The police. The cats that got her mom killed my pops and dumped his body on the side of the road on Twenty-first Street."

"You talked to the police?"

"Nah! But it was on the news. My brother called me and told me that the cops stopped by his place and told him."

"Yo, dawg, that's messed up. That shit makes me so mad that I want to go out there and kill those motherfuckers on sight," Monty expressed.

"Me too. But we'll get them, so don't even worry."

"Have you thought about when you're trying to go to their spot?"

"I want to do it tomorrow night."

"Since we ain't got Mike, want me to bring in two more dudes? I could get Jason and my homeboy Paul to come with us."

"I only need you and one more person, but hit 'em both up. Let 'em know what we're trying to do and tell 'em we gonna do it tomorrow night."

"A'ight. I'ma call 'em now," Monty said, and then he pulled out his cell phone. He took a walk outside of the house and returned less than one minute later. Immediately after he closed the front door, he looked at Rich and said, "They're in."

"Good," Rich said as he walked back into the kitchen. I watched him open the refrigerator and pull out a bottle of beer. "Want one?" he asked Monty.

"Nah, I'm good. I wanna talk about this job we getting ready to do," Monty said as he walked into the kitchen behind Rich. He stood at the entryway of the kitchen and gave Rich his undivided attention.

"I want to rob the restaurant first. And before we leave, I wanna kill everybody in there except for one person, because that person will take us to their big house not too far from the restaurant."

"Which house was that?"

"It's a big-ass house down on Military Highway. That shit is big as hell. I know that gotta have a ton of money and drugs in that spot."

"Well, you know I'm down. But what'cha gon' do with her?" Monty asked Rich after he looked back at me.

"She's going too."

"What, we gon' leave her in the car? 'Cause she might

be a distraction when we go up in the restaurant," Monty pointed out.

"Nah, she ain't gonna be a distraction. She wanna get her mama out of there, so I'ma let her do it."

"So you mean to tell me that you're gonna help that bitch get her mama back?" Monty questioned Rich, sounding and looking like he had a bad taste in his mouth.

"I'm not helping her do shit. When she goes inside their spot, she's on her own, 'cause I'm not giving her a burner and I'm not gonna watch her back. Like I said, when she goes in there, she's on her own."

"Sounds good to me," Monty said, and then he started rubbing his hands together like he was about to eat a delicious piece of cake.

I swear, it took everything within me not to curse both of these niggas out. These two dudes were the most grimy and selfish niggas I knew. All they cared about was themselves.

I don't know how I made it through the night. When I woke up the next morning, I noticed that I had fallen asleep on the couch and that I was all alone. That was until I heard the toilet flush inside the bathroom upstairs. Not too long after, I got up and headed upstairs so I could use the bathroom myself. It only took me a matter of minutes to unload all the pee I had inside my bladder. As I exited the bathroom, it shocked me to run into a female companion of Rich's. Surprisingly, she was a very pretty girl. She was about my height, but a tad bit smaller in weight. She kind of resembled the singer Keri Hilson. She smiled and said good morning; I said good morning too. And before we could exchange any more dialogue,

Rich walked into the hallway, where we were standing. "She seems nice," Kim said.

"Don't let her fool you. She's a real bitch when she wants to be," Rich replied.

"I'm sure everybody can be that way," I responded defiantly, and then I headed back downstairs.

He chuckled. "I told you," he told her, and then I heard him walking down the staircase behind me.

I immediately started saying a quiet prayer, hoping he wasn't following me to start up drama. All I needed was to stick around just a little bit longer so that I could get the details of Rich's plans to rob Ahmad and the rest of his family. With his plans, I could come up with my own so I could rescue my mother in the process. That was it.

As soon as I made my way back downstairs, I sat on the couch, where I had slept just a few minutes ago. Rich, on the other hand, went into the kitchen, grabbed a container of orange juice, and started drinking out of it. When he was done, he put the container back into the refrigerator and headed back upstairs.

A few minutes later, I heard him and the girl arguing from one of the bedrooms. "I'm not leaving here until you give me my money!" I heard her shout.

"I told you, I'm not giving you no more money."

"Yes, the fuck you are. You promised me," she added.

"Well, I lied," I heard him say.

"You know what, you ain't shit! You just like all the rest of them niggas!" she spat out at him.

"Yeah, I heard that before."

"Oh, so you think this shit is funny? I'ma call my cousin Reggie and he gon' fuck you up," she threatened him.

"Look, I ain't trying to hear all that bullshit! Get your

shoes and your bag and get the hell out," I heard Rich snap. Seconds later, I heard a tad bit of scuffling.

"Get off of me."

"I'ma get off of you when you get out of my house."

"You think this is a house? This is a dump. A fucking trap house!" she shouted. I could tell that she was very angry with the way Rich was treating her. But how did she think he was going to treat her? He didn't hide the fact that he was a disrespectful-ass loser. The whole world knew this. So why was she getting upset? He played her. Now she needed to get over it and keep it moving.

Rich and the girl argued for the next three minutes, if not more, and when he got tired of going back and forth with her, he ended up escorting her downstairs. When they entered into the front room, she looked at me and said, "Oh, I get it now. You're trying to get rid of me so you can fuck her."

"Oh no, ma'am. Trust me, it's not that type of party," I told her.

But she didn't believe me. She continued to rant about how she knew that I was going to suck his dick, and how she knew that I was going to let him fuck me in my ass. But the kicker was when she said that while I was sucking his dick, he would be tasting my pussy. All I could do was shake my head. She was one delusional chick. Whether she knew it or not, I wouldn't fuck or suck Rich's dick for all the money in the world. Too bad, she wouldn't believe it.

"She seemed really nice," I said sarcastically after he closed the front door and locked it.

"Yep, just the marrying type," he shot back, giving me just a tad more sarcasm as he walked right by me.

"Don't forget to send me the invite," I managed to say while he headed back upstairs. I thought he would have a rebuttal, but he didn't.

While he was upstairs, doing God knows what, my stomach started growling like there was no tomorrow. I had a few dollars in my pocket, but going to the store wasn't an option. I either would need Rich to make a trip for me, or he needed to get someone to bring food to me. Or if he had something in the refrigerator for me to eat, that would be better. And the only way I would know that would be to ask Rich. "Rich, do you have anything in here that I could eat?" I yelled from the front room.

"There's some Frosted Flakes and milk in the refrigerator," he yelled back.

"Can I get some?"

"I don't give a fuck!" he shouted.

Instead of continuing the dialogue with this guy, I stood up from the couch and went into the kitchen. As I entered, I got an eyeful of dirty dishes in the sink, with mildew and old food stuck to the dishes. I saw a couple of roaches skittering around on the countertop, and when I opened the refrigerator and saw old and expired food inside of it, I immediately lost my appetite. There was no way in the world I was going to eat anything coming out of this kitchen. This place was a hazard to eat from, so I backed myself out of the kitchen and headed back into the front room. I figured I had been hungry for a few hours, so waiting another couple of hours wouldn't hurt me.

After I sat down on the couch, I powered the TV back on. I sifted through the channels to see if I could find something good to watch, but it seemed like every program I ran across, I had already seen it. So I settled for *48 Hours* on the ID channel. The show was about a missing twelve-year-old girl that went to school one morning and never came home. As the show was coming to an end, the investigators found out that the little girl's uncle on her mother's side had something to do with her disappearance. In fact, he had picked her up from school, took her out for ice cream, and then raped her in a hotel room. And to prevent her from telling what he had done, he strangled her until the last breath in her body. What a sick individual, that man was. She was such a beautiful and innocent little girl. And while I sat there, I wondered why people could kill other people so easily? Especially little innocent children that only wanted to do little kid things. If that guy had left her alone, she wouldn't be dead. The same thing goes for my grandmother, my cousin, Mrs. Mabel, and Carl Sr. We live in a cruel world, and there was nothing we can do about it.

Five minutes into another TV show on the ID Channel, someone knocked on the front door. Rich rushed down the staircase and answered the door. When he realized that Monty was on the other side of the door, he opened it and let him in. "What's good, dawg?" Monty said as they both did the handshake to the body dap.

"Trying to figure out how we gon' do that job tonight," Rich replied after he closed the front door shut.

"Trust me, it can't be that hard. Remember, we've done a whole lot of robberies, so it can't be any different from all the other ones."

"Yeah, you're right," Rich agreed.

Monty sat down on the sofa across from me, while Rich stood up and leaned against the wall next to the entryway of the kitchen. "Have you figured out what time we going?" Monty wanted to know.

"Yeah. We gonna go to the restaurant they own first. They close at ten o'clock tonight. So I want to run in there, right before they close. This way, we can wait until all the customers leave and then we got 'em."

"Think they gonna have a lot of money in that joint?" Monty wanted clarity.

"They got to. It's the weekend."

"What if they don't?"

"Don't worry, they will. After we hit their restaurant, we gon' kidnap one of the family members and make them take us to their house. They're bound to have a lot of money there. Cats from outta the country don't put all their money in the bank. They stash that shit in their houses. But what's even better about the situation is that these motherfuckers sell drugs. So they gotta have a lot of dough stashed away in their crib. What drug dealers you know put that money in the bank?" Rich asked.

"Nobody I know."

"My answer exactly."

"Sounds like we gon' be rolling in some serious cash later on tonight."

"You damn right!" Rich commented while he rubbed his hands together.

I tried to pretend that I wasn't listening to their conversation by not taking my eyes away from the television. Monty brought my name up in their discussion. "Misty, your face looks like shit!" he said like he was mocking me.

"If women-beating niggas like you would keep their hands to themselves, we wouldn't be having this conversation."

"Oh, so now I'm a woman beater?"

"I'm a woman, and you're a beater, and when you put

those two things together, you come up with a woman beater," I stated, and then I turned my focus back toward the TV.

"See, this is why I need to get her in a room by myself. I would straighten her ass out. She'd be a model citizen, when I got through with her."

"Come on, Monty, let's chill out. We got bigger shit going on. So let's stay focused," Rich instructed. And thank God Monty listened, because I wouldn't be able to handle another attack, especially the way they beat me the other night. All I could do right now was pray that God would be with me as I went through this journey tonight and then have my mother back in a safe place. That was all I cared about at this point. Nothing else.

24
STRAIGHT BULLSHIT

I don't know where the time went. It went from sunlight to sundown in a matter of minutes, it seemed like. I was both nervous and anxious at the same time. While Rich and Monty relished the idea of robbing the Arabs for their drugs and money from their stash, I was thinking about how I was going to get my mother back and into a safe place. She was my main priority while I still had breath in my body.

An hour before we left the house, Rich and Monty and the two guys that Monty had recruited were all sitting at the kitchen table. They were suiting up and filling up the clips for their handguns for tonight's robbery. I also listened to Rich give them last-minute instructions and plan B directions, just in case things went south. The two guys Monty brought into the fold were Jason and Paul. I knew Jason from the first night at the trap house, but this Paul fellow, he seemed like a hothead with no limits as to how far he would go. His entire conversation consisted of him bragging about how he was going to kill everyone in sight. And that included kids. He even boasted about how many bodies he laid to rest in the past two years. He talked so much that it was becoming unbearable to listen to him. Rich interrupted him, thank God, by announcing what the overall goal was. And how much time they had to do it. His plan seemed solid. But with any heist, something always seemed to go wrong. I just hoped they were ready for it, because it would happen.

When it was time to leave, everybody, including myself, grabbed our things and headed out the front door. I climbed in the back seat with Paul and Jason while Monty and Rich climbed into the front seat. Monty was the driver and Rich rode shotgun. "Y'all niggas ready to get this money?" Rich said with excitement.

"You damn right!" Monty said.

"Sure 'nuff," I heard Jason say.

"Been ready," Paul said.

Pretty much everybody in the car was ready to rob Ahmad and his family for every dime they could find. I could hear the greed in their voices. These guys meant business. And there were no ifs, ands, or buts about it.

"Think we might run into some pretty women while we're there?" Monty asked Rich.

"What'cha trying to get married?" Rich joked.

"Nah, dawg, I just wanna fuck one of them chicks while their husband watches," Monty replied.

"Damn, nigga, that's some cold shit right there," Jason commented.

"Call it what you want. I just wanna show 'em how Americans fuck their bitches," Monty explained.

Everybody in the car laughed, like Monty had told the funniest joke in the world. Jason and Paul thought it was really funny. "Yo, dude, you say some crazy shit out of your mouth," Jason told him.

"Yeah, man, you's a funny nigga!" Paul commented.

"It ain't like I try to be funny. I just be saying some real shit," Monty explained to them.

"Look, ain't nobody fucking nobody's wife. We're going in there for two reasons. One is to rob them of all their drugs and their money. And two, to leave no witnesses. Understood?" Rich said.

"Yeah," Paul said.

"You got it, boss," Jason said.

"You always gotta take the fun out of stuff," Monty replied jokingly.

"Look, Monty, I ain't got time for all that crazy shit. I just want to go in there, do what we got to do, and get out."

"A'ight, say no more," Monty said, and then he changed the subject. "I wonder how Mike is doing."

"I talked to his girl last night."

"What she say?"

"She said he was doing good. So I asked her if the police had been by there to talk to him yet and she told me no. So I told her, when they do come, to get Mike to tell them that some dude in a black hoodie tried to rob him and shot him," Rich explained.

"What did she say?"

"She said okay."

"Did she say when he was getting out?" Monty asked.

"She said she doesn't know yet."

Monty paused for a moment and then he said, "I feel so bad I shot that nigga."

"You should," Rich said candidly.

"I'ma look out for him after we do this job," Monty suggested.

"I think it would only be right," Rich agreed.

"Say no more," Monty concluded, giving Rich the sign that he was going to look out for Mike when he was paid for his part in the upcoming robbery.

For the rest of the ride, the guys talked about what chicks they fucked, what local dudes were snitching, and how much time the cats they knew were doing in prison. Their conversation topics were dumb and meaningless. The fact that they seemed entertained by it was completely absurd. I swear, if we didn't hurry up and get to this restaurant, I was going to go fucking crazy in this car.

"Why are you always quiet?" Jason sparked up a conversation with me.

"Because there's really nothing to talk about," I answered.

"There's a lot of stuff we could talk about," he insisted.

"Well, I guess it may be that way for you, but for me, I can only ask to trade for one thing."

"She's blowing you off, dude," Monty interjected.

"Nigga, mind your business," Jason replied.

"I think you better listen to Monty," Paul spoke up.

"Nigga, you need to mind your business too," Jason told Paul.

Paul and Monty both started chuckling. "Remember, chicks that help you rob the next man ain't to be trusted," Monty announced to everyone in the car.

"Yeah, and remember that these are the same people

that kidnapped my mama and Rich's daddy too. They don't mean shit to me."

"She got a point there," Jason commented.

"Nigga, you just agreeing with her because you want to fuck her," Monty pointed out.

"Why can't he be agreeing with me because I'm telling the truth and I'm stating facts?"

"Bitch, don't talk to me. I don't fuck wit you like that," Monty hissed at me.

"Damn, dude, you really don't like her, huh?" Paul chimed in.

"She talks too much," Monty told him.

"I only talk when I need to," I interjected. Monty was really starting to get on my damn nerves again. I was trying to hold back, but he was trying my patience.

"Sound like you might have to leave her alone, dude," Paul chimed in once more.

"Yo, dawg, why don't you just chill out. I've got too much shit going on in my head to be listening to y'all going back and forth with each other. Try to figure out how we gon' walk away with all this money we about to get," Rich spoke up.

I was happy that he did speak up, but I was more shocked than anything. I was even more shocked that Monty didn't say anything back to Rich. I guess he figured that he didn't want to get on Rich's bad side. At least while we were on our way to the restaurant. Whatever his reasoning was, it worked out for all parties involved.

We pulled up to the Indian restaurant a little after nine o'clock. It was Rich's idea to send Monty, Paul, and Jason into the restaurant to get a table and also to check out the scenery. Rich and I sat in the car and waited for the place to close.

Rich didn't know this, but I was also watching the scenery out here. Knowing that the DEA are actively investigating Ahmad and his family, I knew I had to look over my shoulders just to make sure that the DEA agents weren't watching Rich and me on this very night. So far, everything looked cool; I just didn't know how long it would stay this way.

"I wonder how many people are in there?" Rich blurted out.

"Well, I see four cars, so it can't be any more than ten to fifteen people in there, and that's including the staff."

"I hope you're right," he said, and then he fell silent.

I let out a long sigh and said, "I sure hope I get to see my mother tonight. I swear, I miss her so much. I can't believe that I've been able to hold myself together this long."

I thought Rich would comment about my desire to see my mother, but he didn't. Once again, he made me painfully aware that he couldn't care less about whether or not I rescued my mother. This was a reminder that I was on my own.

One by one, the customers started leaving the restaurant. During the departure of the last white couple, Rich and I entered the restaurant and were greeted by an Arab woman dressed in hijab, covering her entire hair and her neck. "Sorry, but we are closed," she told me. I could tell that she was a woman, in her mid- to late forties.

"Can we get takeout?" Rich chimed in.

"No, I'm sorry it's too late. Our cook has already started cleaning the kitchen."

"Do you have anything that's already cooked? I would take that," I asked her.

"No, I'm sorry. You're gonna have to come back tomorrow when we open at eleven." She stood firm.

Without any warning, Rich pulled out his gun and pointed it directly at the woman. She gasped. "If you scream, I'm gonna kill you," he threatened her.

"You can have anything you want," she told him.

"Where's everybody?" Rich asked her.

"They're all in the kitchen," she replied nervously, her voice was cracking.

While Rich had the woman in front of us cornered, Paul, Jason, and Monty went into the kitchen, where all the other staff members were. I heard a lot of commotion coming from the kitchen. Loud screaming, someone dropping pots and pans, and I even heard two gunshots sound off. *Pop! Pop!*

I rushed into the kitchen area to see if my mother was back there or hidden in a back office. When I entered into the kitchen, Monty had one Arab dude lying on the floor in front of him, but I could tell that he was dead. The puddle of blood around the area of his chest painted that picture very clear.

Paul and Jason had another older lady and two middle-aged guys facing the wall near the freezer. Monty had Jason grilling them about where they were hiding the money. The woman spoke up and told them that the money they made today was in the back office. She even volunteered to take him back there and give it to him if she promised not to kill anyone else and leave. Monty wasn't going for it and started cursing the lady out.

"You don't call no shots, lady! We do!" Monty's voice boomed.

"What about the drugs? We want them too," Rich said from behind me. I had no idea he was behind me until he opened his mouth and spoke. The woman that he held his gun on had come into the kitchen with him. She looked scared shitless.

"We have no drugs here. My cousin owned the pharmacy until it was closed down a few days ago," the woman that Monty had his gun pointed at said.

"How much money do you have here?" Rich asked the same woman.

"Whatever we made today. Every time we close out the register at night, we make our drops to the bank the very next morning," the woman continued.

"Monty, take her back to that office and get all the dough they got. Jason, take everybody else to the buffet room. Paul, you follow me." Rich was laying out the instructions.

"Wait!" I shouted to get everyone's attention. "What about my mother? Ahmad kidnapped my mother and her boyfriend a couple days ago. And I am looking for her. Now, can anyone tell me where she is? Where has Ahmad put her? Where does he have her hiding?" I continued. I desperately needed at least one of them to have the answer to my question.

Everyone looked back and forth at each other. "No, we don't know where," one of the guys facing the wall said.

"We don't know anything about that," the woman standing next to Rich chimed in.

I stood there, hopeless. "Are you sure? Please tell me," I begged them all. "I promise I won't tell the cops on you. I just want my mother. That's it."

"No, I'm sorry. We don't know anything," the woman standing by Monty replied.

"Tell me, where is Ahmad? Where does he live?" I pressed the issue. I couldn't let up. Someone was going to answer my questions.

"We don't know," the chef said.

"You're lying. You do know where he is!" I yelled at him. I was losing my patience with these fucking people.

"Look, fuck all that! They said that they don't know where your mama is. So let it go," Rich interjected.

"That's really fucked up. I bet'cha if your mama had been kidnapped by one of these motherfuckers, I bet you'd kill these people on sight," I argued.

"You damn right I would. But you ain't me. They said they don't know where homeboy is or your mama, so let's move on," Rich stated, and then he turned his focus back toward the staff of the restaurant. "I gave everybody instructions, now let's get to it," Rich concluded, and then he headed out of the kitchen.

Instead of following Rich to the buffet area, I followed Monty and that woman to the back office. When we got back there, she walked straight to a desk in the corner. She walked around it and pulled the top left drawer and grabbed a stack of bills. After she handed the bills to Monty, he noticed that there was a safe in the far left corner of the office. "Why the fuck didn't you tell me that there was a safe in here?" he wanted to know. He was not a happy camper.

"No money in there," the Arab woman told him.

"Don't fucking lie to me. Open it up!" he roared. While the woman crawled down onto the floor to open the safe, I started searching through important documents that would list any and all real estate properties owned by Ahmad's family. I figured by doing so, I would find a possible location of where they could be hiding my mother.

"I told you there was no money in here," I heard the woman say.

"What's all that paperwork in there?" Monty asked her.

My back was facing them both at this point. I was more focused on trying to find something that would help me find out where my mother was.

I heard the woman rattling pieces of paper. "It's just our stock accounts," she said.

By this time, I had turned around and was now facing them both. Monty had snatched the documents out of the woman's hand and had started looking them over. "Are those bank statements?" I asked him, hoping he'd say yes. This way, I'd find out that there was a house address on the statement, and that would be where my mother was.

"Nah, it says Fisher Investments. Looks like they got stocks and bonds," Monty told me.

"What does the home address say on it?" I asked him, and began to walk in his direction.

"It says 7113 Wisconsin Avenue, Bethesda, Maryland," he read.

"That's probably where the head mafia family lives," I replied.

"Might be. But it ain't got no money attached to it, so it does me no good," he said, and then he flung the papers across the desk. "I know y'all got more money somewhere else. Now tell me where it is, or I'm going to kill everyone in here," Monty threatened her.

"My husband has money at our house."

"How much?"

"Maybe thirty-five to forty thousand dollars."

"Well, let's go," he continued, and then he grabbed her by the arm and escorted her to the buffet area, which was where everyone else was. I followed.

"What'cha find?" Rich asked as soon as Monty, myself, and the woman reappeared.

"Looks like a grand, if that. But after she gave it to me, she said that she and her husband got money at their crib," Monty stated.

"How much?" Rich wanted to know.

"She said that they got about forty thousand."

"What we waiting for? Let's get out of this place," Rich instructed us.

"What are we going to do about these people?" Monty asked.

"Kill everybody but the chick that's riding with us to her house," Rich said, and he said it like he had no respect for humanity.

Before I could digest what Rich had just said, every one of the restaurant workers started whining and crying. "No, please don't kill us," one woman begged.

"Sir, please don't kill us. We promise that we won't call the police. Just let us go." I watched the chef plead for his life.

"Yes, we promise not to call the police. We have children. Please . . ." Another one of the workers started sobbing.

"All y'all just shut the fuck up!" Rich shouted.

The woman that we were taking with us started crying too. "I told you that I will give you all the money at our home if you don't kill my family. I won't do it if you kill them," she challenged Monty.

Monty smacked her hard. *Pop!* The woman stumbled,

almost losing her balance. "Don't you ever tell me what you're going to do. Me and that man over there, we're in charge, and we get the last word around here," Monty explained to the woman while pointing at Rich.

"You keep your hands off my wife!" a man roared from the floor. Rich had everyone lying flat on the floor with their faces turned to the right side. At this angle, the guy was able to see his wife getting smacked by Monty.

Monty walked over to the man and kicked him in his leg. "What'cha just say to me?" Monty tested him. Everybody in the room had heard the man; Monty heard him too. I think he wanted the man to repeat himself, to prove a point.

"Don't touch my wife anymore," the same guy said.

After he made it clear to Monty that he wanted him to keep his hands off his wife, Monty felt disrespected by the guy and made an example of him. Without saying another word, Monty drew his pistol and shot the guy in his head, execution style. *Boom!* Blood spewed from the man's head like a running faucet. Both of the Arab women cried out. "Noooo!" the guy's wife screamed, and ran to her husband's side. "Wake up, Faheem! Wake up!" She wept as she tried to lift his head up from the floor.

"Get that bitch under control!" Rich roared.

Monty snatched her up from the floor. "Shut that crying shit up!" Monty lashed out at her.

"Get your hands off her," the other guy yelled from the floor. He attempted to get up, but Paul aimed his gun at him and shot him twice. Blood started oozing from his head.

The only person left alive on the floor was the other Arab woman. She cried the entire time while members of her family were being killed right before her. Rich instructed everyone to exit the restaurant and that we would head over to the house where the money was. But before anyone could leave the room, Paul asked what they were going to do with the lady that was still alive on the floor. Rich looked at Paul and told him to kill her. So that's what Paul did. He shot her in her head at point-blank range. *Boom!*

25

LIVE BY THE GUN

I can't believe that I was one step closer to finally seeing my mother. I didn't care that I would only get to spend a few minutes with her before I traded my life for hers. All I wanted to do was see her one last time. Look into her eyes and tell her how much I loved her and how I appreciated everything she has done for me, even if I hadn't projected it that way. She was still my mother, and I loved her.

"Make sure we ain't being followed," Rich said.

"I don't see anybody following us," Monty assured him after turning his body around and looking out the back window. He even looked into the passenger-side window.

"Please don't kill me," the woman begged.

"Nobody is gonna kill you, just as long as you do what we tell you to do," Monty told her.

"You promise?" the woman asked. She needed some assurance. And I didn't blame her. She was riding in a car with a bunch of misfits—the same misfits that beat me for no reason; the same misfits that just murdered her husband and their son. So, why should she believe them?

"Look, I said we weren't going to kill you. Now shut the fuck up before we change our minds," Monty told her. But it was all a lie. Before we went into the restaurant, Monty and Rich had already planned to kill everybody in there. "Leave no witnesses," they said. So, what had changed from then to now? *Nothing.* They were heartless criminals and there were no changes in that.

"How much do we walk away with?" Rich wanted to know.

"So far, I'm close to a grand," Monty said happily.

"That's it?" Rich commented.

"Yeah."

"I thought we had about two to three grand," Rich said.

"I thought so too. But what can I say? There were more ones and fives than anything else," Monty explained.

"So we killed four people for one grand?" Rich questioned Monty. I could tell that he was getting extremely aggravated. The tone in his voice went from excitement to anger.

"You're saying it like that's a bad thing."

"Because it is. I don't kill people for that kind of money, unless they stole something from me or disrespected me. And in this case, neither one of them has happened," Rich said.

"You acting like we're done. We got one more spot to rob and then we're good. You are with the lady, and she said that the house we're going to has most of their money in it."

"What if she's lying?" Rich questioned Monty again.

"She knows that if she's lying, we're going to kill her, so I believe her."

"You better be right," Rich warned Monty as he drove in the direction of the house we went to the night before.

It seemed like the closer we got to the house, the more fearful I became. I knew I was with four street niggas with guns, but for some reason, I didn't feel protected. I didn't think that they were ready to go head-to-head with these men from the Middle East. I just really thought that they were out of their league. But we would see because there was no turning back. Not for me anyway.

"How much longer do we have to get there?" Monty's friend Paul asked.

"What, you gotta be somewhere?" Rich asked sarcastically.

"Nah, it's just that this lady keeps farting back here. I keep telling her to stop, but she won't," Paul told Rich.

"I'm sorry. I'm just so nervous," she spoke up.

"Look, I don't care how nervous you are, just stop doing it before I get mad with you and do something mean to you," Paul cautioned her.

"Okay, I will stop," she promised him, and then she fell silent.

As much as I wanted to feel sorry for this lady, I couldn't. I couldn't, because her family had kidnapped my mother and held her hostage. They even cut off her hand and sent it inside of a package and had it delivered to the hospital where I was. *How gross and heartless is that? You don't cut off a person's loved one's body part and send it to them. That's not cool. No matter how you look at it.*

"Yo, dawg, we got one thousand and sixteen dollars," Monty told Rich after he completed the money count.

Rich shook his head in a manner to express how frustrated he was becoming. After doing it for about five seconds, he said, "I'm telling you right now, we better come out of the house with at least the forty grand she promised to give us, because if I don't, I might be the only nigga walking out of there when it's time to leave." Rich expressed his anger to everyone in the car.

The entire car went silent. *I would pay a million dollars to read the minds of Jason, Paul, and Monty.* There was no doubt in my mind that these dudes were thinking shit about Rich. It wouldn't surprise me if they were saying to themselves that they'd kill Rich before he'd have a chance to kill them. That was what I would be thinking.

During the drive, I noticed that Monty had been getting a lot of text messages. It had become so annoying that Rich had to say something about it. "Yo, dawg, who the fuck is texting you like that?" he asked.

"Some niggas I know from around the way."

"Well, tell them niggas you working."

"They already know. They just wanna see where we gon' be done so they can come back and pick up homegirl," Monty explained.

I knew that the homegirl he was talking about was me. So I felt that I needed to address the situation. I mean, damn, he just killed three fucking people and I knew he was plotting my demise. How heartless could he be? "I know you're talking about me," I got the gumption to say.

"You fucking right I was talking about you," he didn't hesitate to say.

"You're one grimy-ass nigga! All you fucking care about is seeing people die. What kind of life is that? And how do you sleep at night?"

"I sleep very well, thank you. And I'm gon' sleep even better after Terrell's cousin do your ass in after I hand you over to them."

"You think it's gonna be that easy, huh?" I was really getting tired of this guy running his fucking mouth. He talked more than a freaking woman, more than a nagging-ass chick during her menstrual cycle. I just wished that someone would help me put this asshole out of his misery.

"Bitch, I'll end your fucking life now. Keep running your fucking mouth!"

"Do you think Rich is going to let you do something to me? I'm his cash cow right now," I defended my position. I knew the reason I was still alive was because Rich needed me to help him score money and the drugs that Ahmad's family had. So, whether he knew it or not, I had a little more time to burn. That time would be used to find my mother, and not for him to call Terrell's family and have them come and drag me to hell.

"I wish both of y'all shut the fuck up. I'm tired of hearing your mouths. I just wanna hear myself think for a minute," Rich interjected.

"She came at me," Monty tried to explain.

"Monty, just leave it alone. Let's take care of this business. After we get what we came for, then I don't give a damn what y'all do," Rich told him.

Hearing Rich tell Monty that he didn't care what he did after they robbed the house gave me an instant headache. Anxiety in my stomach started rumbling like a volcano. Just for that moment, I couldn't think straight. I wanted to think of a way that I'd be able to escape Monty's grasp after leaving that house, but I couldn't put two and two together. I couldn't even think about when my birthday was. I was a complete mess. *God, please help me.*

26

DIE BY THE GUN

When we arrived at the house, Rich pressed the garage opener that was clipped onto the sun visor. After the garage opened, Rich drove the truck inside of it and then closed the garage door behind us. "How many people are here?" was Rich's first question.

"Just my mother-in-law and my two children," the woman answered.

"Where will they be in the house?" Rich threw another question at her.

"My children should be in their bedroom asleep. And my mother-in-law should be in her bedroom as well," she said carefully.

"You said that the money was in a safe, so where is the safe?"

"It's in my husband's and my bedroom closet."

"Okay, now are you sure no other adults are in this house?"

"No, only my mother-in-law," she assured him.

"All right. Now, when we go in there, don't start yelling and screaming, because I will blow your fucking head off your shoulders if you do. Now, do you understand?" Rich threatened her.

"Yes, I understand," she told him.

"Okay, now I want you to stay close to me, because I'm gonna be walking behind you, so don't try no funny shit."

"I won't."

"Strap up and let's get this dough," Rich instructed the guys, and one by one, everyone filed out of the SUV and followed him and the woman into the house through the garage entrance.

We entered into the kitchen of the house, and no one was in sight. "Walk slow," Rich coached her.

"Okay," she whispered as she guided Rich, myself, Monty, and the other two guys through the kitchen.

"Where is your bedroom?" Rich started acting anxious.

"It's upstairs," she replied in a whimpering fashion.

"I don't wanna hear that whining shit, so cut it out before I get angry," Rich told her.

"Okay," she said, trying to suppress her sobbing as she continued to lead the way.

Upon approaching the staircase, Rich instructed the guys to go in different areas of the house. "Jason, I want you to go and check around the rooms down here, just to make sure no one else is here," Rich told him.

"A'ight," Jason said, and then he walked away.

"Paul, I need you to stay by the front door and make sure no one comes in here without any of us knowing," Rich told him.

"Got it," Paul replied, and walked off toward the front room.

"Monty, you come with me so we can get this money," Rich told him.

"Let's do it," Monty said eagerly.

"What about me?" I asked.

"Your job is done. We're here, so I don't give a damn what you do. Go kill yourself if you want to," Rich commented, and then he headed upstairs with Monty and the woman in tow.

"Oh, so my job is done, huh? We shall see about that," I mumbled to myself.

After Monty and Rich disappeared around the corner, when they reached the top step, I found a corner in the kitchen and started texting Ahmad. I needed to let him know that he had a nemesis here. **Come to the house near Military Hwy. Bring my mama with you. If you don't these guys said they will kill everyone in this house.**

OK, he replied.

As I looked at his text message, it gave me an uneasy feeling, even though he had only typed the word *OK*. I knew what kind of man Ahmad was. He was a calculating and dangerous man. I was sure that when he came, he was going to have an entourage consisting of his family with him. Rich and Monty had no idea what they were going to be up against. I just hoped that they were ready.

"Bingo," I heard Rich say from the kitchen. I also heard Monty laughing, giving off a sound like he was the Joker. It sounded evil and frightening.

"How much do you think it is?" I heard Monty ask.

"These straps are ten thousand each, so it looks like we got forty grand."

"You shitting me! I've never seen that much money in my life," Monty commented.

"Well, here it is. *Forty grand,*" Rich emphasized.

"How much is my cut?" Monty wanted to know.

"Take this ten grand and do whatever you want to do with it," Rich insisted.

"What about Jason and Paul?"

"What about 'em?"

"What? Wait. I gotta share my money with them?"

"I thought you knew that."

"Nah, I didn't."

"Well, now you do."

"Come on now, Rich, you know that's not fair. Me and Jason put in a lot of work. We killed those people back at that restaurant. You didn't have to do a thing."

"Nah, I didn't. But remember, this was my job. I put y'all niggas onto this. If it wasn't for me, you wouldn't have that ten grand in your hand right now."

"Yeah, I know, but let's be fair about it. I mean, you can at least give up another ten grand and let Jason and Paul split it."

"That's not gonna happen. I'm keeping this thirty grand because I set up this sting and I gotta share it with Mike when he gets out of the hospital."

"Rich, you know that's a bullshit-ass excuse, right?" Monty protested.

"Look, dawg, I'm not gonna stand here and go back and forth with you about this money. I'm keeping this thirty grand and that's the end of it. Now, if you don't like it, then do something about it. And if you ain't gonna do shit about it, then just shut the fuck up because you're beginning to sound like a bitch!" Rich scolded him.

"Yeah, a'ight," I heard Monty say, and then I didn't hear him utter another word. But I did hear someone else.

"Sania, is that you?" I heard an older, Middle Eastern woman's voice say. I rushed to the staircase because I knew this was not going to end well.

"Yes, Mama, now go to bed," Sania instructed her.

"What do you mean, 'go to bed'? Are you okay? You sound upset." The woman pressed the issue as she slowly made her way into the bedroom where Monty and Rich were.

Oh my God, lady, please go back in your room like the woman told you, I thought as anxiety ricocheted throughout my body.

"I'm not going back into my room until you tell me what's wrong with you."

The next thing I heard was Rich telling the woman to back up. "Who are you? What are you doing in this house?" I heard the woman ask boldly. I was shocked to hear her stand up against Rich and Monty.

"Mama, stop it. I will handle it. Please go back into your room," Sania pleaded with her.

"Put that gun away before I call the cops," the woman threatened Rich.

"Mama, please go back in your room," Sania asked once again. They all were in the hallway upstairs, so I could see everything they were doing.

"No, she's not going anywhere. Monty, grab her and take her downstairs," Rich hissed.

When Monty reached for her, he grabbed her hard and tried to pull her close to him, but when she jerked her body backward, she used all her weight and that caused her to fall backward down the stairs. "Mama!" Sania yelled as she ran down the staircase behind her mother.

I stood there and watched in horror as the woman tumbled down the steps toward me. I immediately got out of the way.

The woman finally landed at the bottom of the staircase, and when I looked down at her, I noticed how she wasn't breathing. I looked up the staircase at Rich and told them both that this lady was dead.

Immediately after I announced it, I saw Sania rushing toward us. "Oh my God! You broke her neck." Sania started crying hysterically.

Taking another look at this lady, I realized that Sania was right; her mother-in-law's neck was broken. I could see a huge bone sticking out the side of her neck.

Rich and Monty ran downstairs and looked at her themselves. But when they bent down toward her, Sania snapped on them. "Get away from her, you fucking killers! You killed my husband, my uncle, my cousin, and now my mother-in-law. You're fucking monsters!" She was going crazy, swinging at them and trying to fight them.

After she took the second swing at Monty, Monty lunged back and threw a punch so hard at Sania that when it connected to her face, she flew backward and landed on her back about three feet from where her mother-in-law was lying. Monty hit her really hard. "You know you gotta off her, right?" Rich said.

"Yeah," Monty replied, and pulled his gun from the waist of his pants and let off two shots. One hit her stomach and the other one hit her in the chest. I stood there and watched these innocent women get the lives sucked out of them, and it was all for nothing. Okay, their family

27

WE GOT COMPANY

I heard a car pull up in the driveway of the house, so I stood up from the little girl's bed and looked out of the window. I noticed that it was a dark-colored car. But I couldn't tell the make and model of it. "Is that my daddy?" The little girl looked back at me and asked.

"I don't know, sweetheart," I told her, and then I stood back away from the curtain. I figured that it had to be Ahmad because I texted him to meet me here. When he texted me and told me that he was in the car parked outside in the driveway, I was tempted to let the guys downstairs know that he was here. But then I figured that it wouldn't be in my best interest to do so. Rich had instructed Paul to be the lookout person at the front door, so I let him do his job.

We're in the house, I texted him back.

I saw him slowly emerge from the back seat of the driver's side. And while he was doing that, I noticed that there were two other people in the car. The person in the passenger-side seat looked like a woman. From what I could see, the body of the woman was full-figured, like my mother was. I couldn't see her face, so I prayed to God that it was her.

The person sitting in the driver's-side seat was probably one of the mafia hit men that Agent Sims was investigating. "I see somebody coming to the front door," I heard Paul say.

From there, all I heard were footsteps scurrying around downstairs. "How many is it?" I heard Rich ask.

"I just see one, dude," Paul told him.

"Does he have anything in his hands?" Rich kept the questions coming.

"Nah. He just walking with his hands on his sides. So, do you want me to answer the door if he knocks on it?"

"Fuck nah! We don't live in here, so we ain't answering nobody's door."

"But what if he doesn't go away?" Paul sounded worried.

"Nigga, are you all right? Because you sure are acting like a bitch right now!" Rich roared. Paul was irritating the heck out of Rich, and I enjoyed every minute of it. Before Paul could say another word, Ahmad rang the doorbell.

"What are we going to do, stand here and listen to that dude ring the doorbell?" Monty interjected.

"We ain't gonna open the door and let him in."

"We don't even know who it is. It could be a family member, so if we don't answer the door, he may call the cops," Monty suggested.

"And that's why we're going out the back door and

leaving this motherfucker," I heard Rich say, and then I heard footsteps. I assumed that they were heading toward the back door of the house. I knew that it would be a bad idea to get caught in the house alone if Rich and the rest of them were able to get away, and especially without any fighting power. So I grabbed Hamina's hand and told her that we were going to take a walk.

Without giving me any problems, she allowed me to hold on to her hand and walk her downstairs. While we were walking down the staircase, the doorbell chimer continued to ring. "That's probably my daddy," Hamina said with excitement. And as soon as we made it down to the last step, she tried to run toward the front door. I held on to her tightly and pulled her back. "No, we're not going that way, we're going this way." I showed her by pointing in the direction of the kitchen, and when she looked in that direction, she saw her mother's and her grandmother's lifeless bodies on the floor. She took off running.

"Mommy . . . Nana." Hamina started whining. I looked into her pretty little eyes and saw how they were quickly filling up with tears. Damn, I couldn't believe that I fucked up and allowed this little girl to see her dead mama and grandmother. *Ugh!*

"Come on, baby girl, everything is going to be all right." I tried to console her, but it wasn't working. I could tell that she really wanted her daddy now.

"My daddy is at the front door and he wants to come in the house," she told me. She knew in her heart that something wasn't right and she made me aware of it. "I want my daddy!" she started screaming, walking midway through the kitchen.

As she began to resist me, I started hearing gunshots.

Pop! Pop! Pop! Boom! Pop! Pop! This startled Hamina and we scrambled down to the floor. We hid underneath the kitchen table. With the tablecloth in place, no one would be able to see us, but we were able to see them. Truthfully speaking, we could only see their legs and their feet. Nothing more.

After hearing the popping sounds from the gunfire, Hamina and I saw two sets of feet scramble back to the kitchen. "Be quiet, okay," I whispered in her ear.

"Okay," Hamina whispered back in my ear as the tears continued to fall from her eyes. My heart went out to her. She was a sweet little butterfly and it bothered me that I couldn't stop her from crying. She wasn't supposed to see the lifeless bodies of her mother and her grandmother lying on the floor. Rich had already warned me that if she got a look at him, he was going to murder her in an instant. So I hoped and prayed that I could keep her alive, at least while I was here.

"Yo, what the fuck just happened?" I heard Monty panting.

"Did you see those two dudes shooting at us?" Rich asked him. He sounded out of breath, along with Monty. "I think they got Jason and Paul," he continued as he huffed and puffed. "Did you get a chance to bust a shot at him?"

"I think I did," Monty replied, but I could tell that it was a lie. And I knew Rich could tell too.

"Turn the kitchen light off," Rich told Monty.

"A'ight," he said, and flipped off the light switch that was near the sliding door to the patio, which was how they had run back into the house.

They stood there quietly. And so did the little girl and I. But that didn't last long, because a few seconds later, we heard movement coming from upstairs. I knew it had to be the other little girl that was in her bed asleep after the other little girl and I walked out of that bedroom. "Nana, where are you?" I heard the little voice call out.

The one that was with me couldn't hold her tongue. She shot out from underneath the kitchen table and sprinted toward the staircase to see her sister. "Bella, I'm coming," she said.

My heart went out to her when she ran away from me; I knew her life was about to be over. Rich and Monty both ran in her direction. "Get her, and I'll get the little girl upstairs," Rich instructed Monty.

"What are we gonna do with them?" Monty wanted to know.

"We're gonna use them to get out of the house," Rich told him, and then I heard footsteps running up the staircase.

"Who are you? And where is Nana?" I heard the little girl from upstairs ask.

"Get off me! Don't touch me!" the little girl down here demanded.

"Get off of her!" Bella, the little girl upstairs, said.

"Shut up before I kill you!" Monty's voice boomed. And then I heard a gurgling sound. I knew then that Monty was choking Hamina.

Thank God Rich heard it and demanded that he stop it. "What the fuck is wrong with you? We gotta keep her alive until we get out of here!" Rich roared.

"She wouldn't shut the fuck up!" Monty tried defending his actions.

"Touch her again and I'm gonna kill you myself," Rich warned him.

I couldn't see Monty's facial expression, but I knew he

wasn't too happy about Rich's threat. I thought he would have a rebuttal for Rich, but, surprisingly, he didn't. I knew the relationship between these two was gonna fall apart, and I didn't want to be around when it happened.

Meanwhile, they had to figure out a way to get out of this home without being shot. Their ace in the hole was keeping those two little girls alive. I just hoped neither one of them got killed in the process.

"Come on, let's go," I heard Rich say to the little girl named Bella.

"I know we got them, but how are we going to let the guy outside know that we have them?" Monty wanted to know.

"We're going to yell outside the window. Trust me, they'll hear me," Rich assured Monty.

As soon as they both had the girls in hand, they escorted them toward the front door. Rich cracked the door open just enough so that the guy outside could hear what he had to say. The lights in the house were still out, but the light from the street slightly lit the foyer area around the front door. This allowed me to see their every move.

"Hey, whoever you are, I just want to let you know that I have your wife and kids. So, if you try to shoot us again, we will kill the rest of your family!" Rich yelled outside.

No one returned any dialogue, so Rich repeated himself again. "Whoever you are, I just want you to know that I have your wife and your kids. So if you try to shoot us again, I will personally kill the rest of your family *slowly*. Don't try anything now, because I am a man of my word," Rich continued, and then he closed the door.

"Think they're gonna go forward?" Monty asked him.

"For the sake of these little girls, they better," Rich said with finality.

"So, what are we gonna do now? How are we going to get out of here?" Monty's questions kept coming one after another.

"We're going to leave out of here with that truck in the garage," Rich told Monty, and then he turned around and led the way to the door that opened to the garage. Monty followed him with Bella in tow. "Monty, I want you to drive, and I'll sit in the back seat with the girls," Rich said.

"What if they don't see the kids and shoot me while I'm trying to get away?"

"Don't worry. They won't try to shoot the truck. Get inside the driver's seat now, or I'm gonna do it, and when I do, I'm gonna leave you here," Rich warned him once again, and then he stormed off into the garage.

Monty heeded Rich's demand and followed him into the garage. Knowing that Monty and Rich were about to bail out of here and use the truck in the garage to do it, I knew that if I didn't leave with them, my chances of rescuing my mother wouldn't happen. That is, unless I got in the truck with them and derailed their escape before they could get off the block. This way, I could possibly get them to hand over my mother in exchange for the little girls. Who knows? I might not be able to trade my life at all.

While they were getting into the truck, I climbed from underneath the table and ran toward the doorway that led to the garage. "Don't leave me," I said loud enough for them to hear.

"Where the fuck was you?" Rich asked me before he closed the back door of the truck.

"I was looking around all the rooms for my mama," I lied.

"Get in the front seat," Rich told me.

"Nah, let that bitch stay here. She was ghost the whole time we was popping these pistols at them cats around the back of the house."

"Nigga, fuck you!" I said, gritting my teeth at Monty. I was fuming on the inside of my body. This guy had no knowledge of how bad I wanted him dead. He would find out tonight after I turned his ass over to these cats.

"I ought to smack you in your face, you dumb bitch!" Monty hissed. I could tell that he was seconds away from hitting me. Thankfully, Rich wasn't in the mood to watch Monty beat me up. He was more focused on getting out of this house and he wasn't going to let Monty interfere with it.

"Monty, shut the fuck up and close the damn door. I'm ready to get out of here!" Rich's voice boomed.

Seeing the urgency, I jumped into the front passenger-side seat and shut the door behind me. I watched Monty as he started up the truck and revved the engine. "Hit the gas and back out of here!" Rich shouted.

"Do you want me to open the garage?" he asked Rich.

"Just let it up a little bit and then flood the gas, just in case they start shooting."

"What about the car that's parked in the driveway? I'm gon' run into that when I back up," Monty expressed.

"I don't give a fuck about that car! Back into it!" Rich roared.

"I want my mommy," Hamina said.

"Yes, I want my mommy too," Bella whined.

"Shut up! I don't wanna hear shit else out of y'all!" Rich snapped.

Both little girls started crying. "Can you get them to shut up?" Monty shouted at the girls. He thought that he was going to shut them up by yelling at them, but it only made things worse. Both girls started sobbing uncontrollably. And Rich couldn't handle it, so he slapped both girls down on the floor.

One of the girls screamed at the top of her voice, scaring me and Monty both. Shocked that he could be so violent to a child, I stood up and screamed, "Stop it!"

I guess he was surprised by my audacity; Rich immediately let go of the girl. "God help me," I said quietly, sitting back in my seat. I couldn't wait to get away from these assholes.

Instead of opening the garage door first, Monty put the truck in reverse and sped backward through the door.

Boom!

The garage door burst open. We sped backward until we hit the car that was parked behind us.

Boom!

That was the sound that I heard when Monty slammed the truck back into the car. I quickly got a moment to see if my mother was still in the car, but when I looked a second time and saw that it was a man in the car instead of a woman, I knew that Ahmad was playing games with me. He wasn't really trying to get me to trade my life for my mother's. He tried to pull the wool over my eyes so I could hand him *me* on a silver platter. I thought of the intuition that I had to get in the truck when I had the chance. If I had stayed in the house, Ahmad would've found me and killed me right on the spot.

Immediately after I realized that my mother wasn't in the car, I got back down on the floor while Monty pushed that car back with the force from the truck. I couldn't believe it, Monty was really able to get the car out of the way.

I guess Ahmad and the other guys that were with him realized that the only way they were going to prevent the truck from leaving the house was by shooting out the tires. That was exactly what they did.

Boom! Boom! Boom!

One by one, the guys successfully shot both of the back tires. But that didn't stop Monty from putting the truck into Drive and attempting to barrel down the street. The drive was rocky and I could smell the rubber burning as the air from the tires oozed out of them.

But out of nowhere, I heard shots coming from behind us. *Pop! Pop! Pop!* The driver's-side window glass shattered. "I'm hit," I heard Monty say as shards of glass rained down on me. And before I knew it, I heard another shot, and that's when the truck started swerving. And when I looked up and saw Monty's lifeless body slumped over on the steering wheel, I knew that it was going to be a matter of seconds before this truck slammed into something. So I got up and grabbed the wheel and tried to steer it as best as I could. Meanwhile, Rich barked orders at me from the back seat.

"Move him out of the way and drive this motherfucker before we crash!" he shouted. We had gotten at least a half of a mile down the road, giving us at least a three-minute head start to escape from their grasp, but the timing of preventing the truck from hitting the telephone pole had run out. The collision rattled me a little, but I shook it off. I knew I had to think quick; in a matter of seconds, I was going to be staring down the barrel of a gun. I needed to get out of here. But before I ran off, I wanted to get my hands on that ten thousand dollars. And

I knew it would be in my best interest to get it from Monty. If I didn't, Ahmad would take it back.

While I was taking the money out of Monty's jacket pocket, Rich climbed over the girls and exited the truck on the side where I was. I thought he was going to close the door behind himself, but he didn't. He took the little girls with him and ran as fast as he could. Before I exited the truck, I took Monty's gun too. I knew I was gonna need it more than anything else. The money portion was good, but it wasn't going to save my life. So I held the gun as careful as I could and then I exited the truck, making sure that Ahmad and the other guys didn't see me.

I thought that I was going to run into Rich the farther I ran from the crash, but he disappeared into thin air. I didn't even hear the little girls crying while I made my way out of the neighborhood. I saw two police cars and a paramedic vehicle coming my way, so I ducked down behind a massive tree alongside the road. I knew that they were going to that house we just left, so I made sure they didn't see me.

After they drove by, I put some pep in my step and got the hell out of that neighborhood. I came here with plans to get my mother back, but it didn't work. So now I had to come up with a plan B. It was now or never.

28
RUNNING OUT OF TIME

People will only do things that you allow them to do. In this case, I allowed Rich and Monty to treat me terribly within hours of meeting them. I swear, I can't keep dealing with guys like this. Rich didn't like me. Monty didn't like me. Terrell didn't like me, and Ahmad didn't like me. *What is it about me and this weird dynamic that I have with men? Am I allergic to them?* Whatever it was, it hadn't been conducive to me, because I'd been having some bad reactions because of it. Hopefully, I would get it right one day. But until then, I was gonna take the bitter with the sweet.

I was afraid to take this taxi ride back to Rich's spot, but I didn't have anywhere else to go, so that was where I headed. I got in a taxicab with an older Hispanic gentleman, who, I believed, wouldn't put me in any danger by being around him. For one, I knew that he wouldn't recognize me, and two, if he did, I was sure that he wouldn't rat me out. People from other countries tend to stay out of other people's business, especially since there was a language barrier. All and all, I knew that I wasn't in any risk of this guy contacting the cops, but to be sure, I paid him in advance and added a nice tip to it, and then we headed into that direction.

I had no idea if I was going to see Rich when I got there. At this point, it didn't matter. All I wanted to do was get into that neighborhood so I could hide amongst the street hustlers and blend in with the girls that hung around in that area.

I couldn't give the cabdriver the exact address to Rich's trap house, but when we arrived within a mile of it, I pointed him to the exact location. It only took us a minute or so to get me to drive up to the building. After I got out of the car, I walked up to the door and knocked on it. Surprisingly, Rich opened the door. When he saw me, he acted like he saw a ghost.

"I thought they got you," he commented as he stood in the doorway of the front door.

"I thought they got you too," I replied in a nonchalant manner.

"Hell nah! I wasn't going to let them get me. I got that money and got out of there."

"Can I come in?" I asked him.

"Yeah," he replied, and then he stepped to the side so I could walk by him. "How did you get here?" he asked after I got out of the way so he could close the front door.

"I caught a cab," I told him immediately after I sat down on the sofa.

"I caught a cab too," he stated as he stood in the middle of the floor.

"Where are the little girls?"

"Oh, they're gone. I left them on somebody's front porch."

"What do you mean you 'left them' on someone's porch? Are they dead or alive? What?"

"They're alive."

"You're pulling my leg, right?"

"Nah, I'm serious." He tried to assure me, and I pretty much believed him. He wasn't the type of guy that would lie about something like that. He was a heartless asshole, but when it was time to lay the truth out there, he'd do it. And he wouldn't care if you liked it or not.

"I see you hurried up and changed clothes," I pointed out.

"Why not? Who wants to walk around with bloody clothes?"

"Interesting" was the only response I could come up with. This guy was insane. But I'd seen men who were crazier than he was, so I gave him a pass.

Before Rich and I could engage further, there was another knock on the front door. He walked over and said, "Who is it?"

"Choppa!" I heard the guy say.

I watched Rich as he opened the front door. Choppa was a very short young guy with a headful of dreadlocks. The locks were unkempt and so was he, from where I was sitting. His body reeked of marijuana and his actions demonstrated exactly how high he was. "Yo, dawg, I got two hos out here trying to spend a hundred dollars. So show a nigga some love so I can make a few dollars off the sell."

"Here, take these five twenties and do what you want

with 'em," Rich told him, and dropped the packaged drugs into Choppa's hand.

"Come on, Rich man, these joints are small as hell. Give me one more," Choppa begged.

"Take it or leave it." Rich stood firm.

Choppa stood there for a minute as he looked closely at the drugs. After looking down at them for a moment or two, he said, "A'ight, fuck it!" And he handed Rich a one-hundred-dollar bill. Afterward, he stood there, opened every plastic wrapped Baggie of the drug, poured them in his hand, and then he took two away from that pile and stuffed them down into his pocket.

"You're only giving 'em three of those joints?" Rich laughed.

"Yep, that's it," Choppa said, and then he walked away.

Rich laughed at Choppa once again after he closed the front door and locked it. When he sat back down on the couch, his cell phone started ringing. He answered it. "Hello."

I could hear the caller just a tad bit to know that it was a woman. But when she started talking at full speed, I couldn't keep up with what she was saying, until Rich said, "I'm glad he's doing good. But did the police come up there and talk to him yet?" Right then and there, I knew he was talking to a woman that had information on Mike's situation.

"Well, if they come up there, just tell Mike to tell them that the guy wearing a dark-colored hoodie tried to rob him. And when they found out that Mike didn't have any money on him, they got mad, shot him, and ran off."

The woman Rich was talking to said a few more words, and right before Rich ended the call, he told her to keep him posted, and if Mike needed anything, she should call him back.

Right after he disconnected the call, I acted like I was watching television, but that was far from the truth. I was watching him from my peripheral vision. Judging from his mannerisms, I could tell he couldn't care less about how Mike was doing. All he cared about was if the cops visited Mike or not. And if they had, what was their conversation about? Rich was a heartless piece of shit. So the quicker someone put him out of his misery, the better things would be for all parties involved.

"It's good to know that my boy Mike is okay," he blurted out.

"That's good to hear. I was really worried about him."

"Well, worry no more," Rich said cheerfully, and then he started chuckling loudly.

"I see you're in good spirits. What are you so happy for?"

"Because I'm thirty thousand dollars richer than I was about two hours ago."

"Oh yeah, I heard about that."

"What did you hear?"

"I heard you and Monty going back and forth about the forty thousand y'all got from that house, and how you weren't giving up more than the ten thousand that you gave him. And that he had to share that same ten grand with the other two guys he brought along with y'all."

"Yep, I said every word, and I meant it too. Because him and his homeboys came in on the tail end of that job. That job was supposed to be for me, Mike, and one other person. I didn't ask for Monty to bring that dude Paul and Jason back to the spot. But since it happened that way, then it's his job to hit 'em off with his share."

"Where's my part?" I asked sarcastically. "Remember, I set the whole thing up."

"The deal was for you to help me and I would help you get your mama back."

"Yeah, it was. But did I get my mother back?"

"Was it my fault that she wasn't there?"

"Come on, Rich, let's keep it funky. Your intentions were never to help me get my mother back. All you wanted was the stash, that's it. Not to mention, every guy that went into that house with us didn't make it out."

"That's on them. I did my part."

"Are you really gonna share that money with Mike?"

"Yeah, I'm gonna look out for him."

"How much?"

"None of your fucking business!"

"Sorry! My bad!"

"Yeah, it is," he commented while gritting his teeth at me. And then he changed the subject. "So you say that you didn't murder that nigga Terrell, huh?"

"No, I didn't."

"Well, I don't believe you. I think you did. And I think you did it because he cheated on you and you couldn't handle it."

"Sorry to disappoint you. But that did not happen. I don't know who killed Terrell, and I don't care. He was a fucking asshole, so in my book, he got what he deserved."

"You're sticking to the script, huh?"

"It's the truth."

"Yeah, tell me anything," he said, and then he stood up from the couch and started walking slowly toward me. I was getting a little nervous, because I had no idea what he was about to do to me.

"Look, I don't want no more beef with you," I told him, and I held up both of my hands. "If you want me to leave right now, I will do it."

"Don't worry, I'm not bringing no beef to you. And you ain't gotta leave either," he assured me as he continued to walk toward me.

Even though Rich just said that he had no beef with me, my intuition told me something totally different. So I braced myself for the inevitable. "I hit you pretty hard earlier, huh?" he asked me as he laid his hand against the side of my face. The bruises around my right eye and the cheek area were still purple and blue, so he could see them very well.

"Yes, you did," I replied, and pulled my face away from his hand.

"I wanna make it up to you," he insisted.

"No, I'm good," I assured him.

"Come on now, don't act like that," he said, and tried to lean toward me so he could give me a kiss on the lips. I yanked my head back.

"I told you that I'm good," I reminded him.

"Stop playing hard to get." He grabbed the bottom of my chin and tried to pull my face toward him.

I yanked my head back again. "I told you I was good. So, can you please stop? I don't look at you like that." I was becoming aggravated.

He stood straight up and gritted at me. "Bitch! Don't be acting like you're better than me. Do you know how many hos be throwing themselves at me? I can have the whole damn city of Norfolk, if I wanted," he boasted.

"Good. I'm glad," I said, and slid a couple of inches away from where he was standing. Having him standing before me gave me an uneasy feeling. I hoped my actions indicated it.

"Ho, you ain't all that!" he snapped, and took two steps toward me.

"I didn't say I was," I corrected him. In no way was I trying to cause another disturbance between him and me. I needed somewhere to stay for the night so I wouldn't be in the street. But he was really making it hard for me to be here.

"You ain't gotta say it. You're showing me right now."

"Look, Rich, I'm really not trying to fuss with you. I'm tired and I'm frustrated that I couldn't get my mother tonight. So, will you just cut me some slack so I can re-group?" I asked.

"If you ain't trying to give me some pussy, then you might as well get out."

"Are you serious right now?"

"Fucking right I am. No pussy, no overnight stay. So, what is it going to be?" From the looks of things, he wasn't going to move until he had gotten an answer.

"Rich, please tell me that you're joking." I searched his face for a twinkle in his eye.

"Fuck nah! I ain't joking. Now I'm gonna say this one more time, if you ain't trying to give me some pussy, then you gotta go. And I'm talking about leaving *right now.*"

"Damn, Rich, that's fucked up, especially since I'm the reason why you got that thirty grand," I pointed out.

"Come on, let's go," he said, grabbing me by my arm and pulling me up from the sofa. Immediately after he helped me up on my feet, he looked down at the breast area of the jacket and wondered what was bulging out. But before I could answer him, he reached over and patted my left breast. "Wait a minute, is that the dough I gave to Monty?"

I pushed his hands away from my jacket. "It's my diary," I lied.

"Yo, you can't even lie right. I can see that dough sticking out of your jacket clear as day. Now hand it over to me," he demanded. But I wasn't going for it. I wasn't about to allow this guy to take away this money that I helped him get. And besides, he gave the money to Monty, and now that Monty was gone, it now belonged to me.

"If you don't give me that money right now, I'm gonna put a slug in your head," he threatened me.

"Look, I don't have time for this," I said to him, and then I reached down into my inside jacket pocket and slowly pulled out the ten grand I took from Monty after he got shot. Before I could get it out of my jacket pocket free and clear, Rich snatched it from my hands.

"You thought you was going to keep this dough for yourself, huh?" He cracked another smile.

"Yeah, I did," I told him, and watched him as he shoved the money down into his front pocket; then he turned his back toward me and started walking toward the kitchen. Before he took one step, I took the gun from my other pants pocket and aimed it at him. "I'm gonna ask you really nicely to give me that money back," I warned him.

He turned around slowly, and when he noticed that I had a gun in my hand, he chuckled. "I see you took Monty's pistol too," he said.

"Yes, I did. Now I am gonna only tell you one more time to give me that money back."

"What's gonna happen if I don't?" He tested me.

"I'm gonna lay you out on the fucking floor and then

I'm gonna make you clean up your own blood." I needed to let this bastard know that I wasn't playing any games with him.

"I don't believe you got the heart to pull the trigger," he challenged me.

"Act like you aren't gonna give me that ten grand back and see what happens." I made it very clear.

"Do you even know how to use that gun?" he asked me, and took a tiny step toward me.

"Rich, I told you that if you move, I'm gonna lay your ass out. Now call my bluff," I threatened him.

Refusing to believe what I said, Rich took a bold step toward me and smiled. "See, I knew you didn't have the guts to pull that trigger. So hand me the gun and I'll forget about all of this," he said.

Without saying a word, I pulled the trigger of Monty's .38 handgun. *Pop!* After the bullet went through his left leg, he fell down on the floor. "*Awoooo,* you stupid bitch! You shot me in my fucking leg," he growled in a fetal-like position. He began to rock his body back and forth.

"I told you not to move. Now if you don't give me that money, I'm gonna shoot you again," I warned him once more.

"Here, take it!" he yelled, and snatched the money from his pants pocket. After he threw the stack of one-hundred-dollar bills at me, he continued to rock his body back and forth. "You need to take me to the emergency room before I lose a lot of blood." He was still in the fetal position.

"I'm not taking your grimy ass anywhere. You're gonna stay right here and take that pain like a real man."

While Rich whined like a fucking toddler, I got on Mike's cell phone and called Ahmad. He answered after the first ring. "I'm gonna kill you very slow when I get my hands on you," he hissed through the phone. I could hear the hate riding the wave signals as they vibrated through the phone.

"I'm not the one that killed your father. Three of the men responsible for killing your family were already killed by you and your men. But I have the ringleader here with me. So I am willing to trade him for my mother right now," I told him.

"No deal. I want you too," he replied.

"Where is my mother now?" I wanted to know. It had been a while since I heard her voice over the phone. I needed to know that she was still alive, or there was going to be no way I was going to make the trade.

"Don't worry, she's still alive."

"How long will it take for you to get her and meet me in downtown Norfolk?"

"I can meet you within the hour."

"Do that. And call me when you get close by. Don't try no funny shit!"

Instead of responding to my comment, he disconnected our call. I shoved Mike's cell phone back down in my pocket after our call ended. And when I turned around and looked at Rich, he gave me this weird facial expression. "When did you get a phone?" he wondered aloud.

"I picked it up from the floor after you and Monty's dumb ass picked Mike up from the floor and carried him outta the house."

"So you had that phone all this time?"

"I sure did." I smirked at him.

"Wait a minute, so you know that Arab dude's phone number?" Rich seemed confused.

"Yep, I sure do. And I set you and those dumb-ass niggas up too. Ahmad knew how many of you were in that house. He knew exactly where everyone was at too. The only bad thing was that he didn't keep up his end of the bargain. He didn't bring my mama with him, like he promised. So I'm giving him another chance to make it right. And as a bonus, I'm offering you up, since it was all your idea to rob and have his family killed."

"You sneaky bitch! Do you know that he's going to kill you too?" Rich snapped. He punched the side of the couch and hurt his fist.

"I know he is. But at this point in my life, my life is meaningless to me. See, unlike you, I love my mother. So, if I have to exchange my life for hers, then so be it." I tried to explain this to him, but it went right over his head.

"You got to be the stupidest bitch I know! None of that shit you just said made any sense to me," Rich continued, still applying pressure to his bloody leg.

He and I kept going back and forth about how ignorant I was for selling him and myself out to the guys that were coming our way. From the position I was sitting in, our argument wasn't going anywhere. So I ended the conversation by telling him to just let things fall where they might, because our lives would be put in someone else's hands. And there was nothing he could do about it.

29

MAKING THE TRADE

It took Ahmad approximately forty-five minutes to call me back. My heart started beating rapidly after I answered the call and he told me that he was ten minutes away. I gave him the address to the house and warned him about the guys that were posted on the corner of the block. "If any of them ask you where you're going, just tell 'em that Rich knows that you're coming and they'll let you pass," I told him.

"Is there anything else I need to know?"

"Let me speak to my mother, because you didn't keep your end of the bargain back at your family's house," I insisted.

He paused for a second and then I heard a woman's voice in the background. "Is that my daughter on the phone?" I heard her say. It was faint, but I knew it was her.

I heard some crackling sounds and then I heard, "Misty baby, is this you?" I could hear the fear and pain in my mother's voice. I swear, I wanted to lose it and flood our talk with cries and tears. But I held it together. She was already upset from what she had endured while she was with those bastards, so I felt it was best to stay calm. Still, I wanted to make sure she knew that I was doing everything within my power to get her back safe.

"Yes, Mama, it's me. Are you okay?" I asked her.

"They cut off some of my fingers." She started sobbing.

"I know, Mama, I know. Don't worry. I'm gonna get you to the nearest hospital as soon as I get you back," I lied to her. She had no idea that I was trading my life for hers.

"Baby, I can't wait to see you."

"And I can't wait to see you too. But for right now, I'm gonna need you to do what they tell you, until we see each other, okay?"

"Okay," she replied.

"Give that guy the phone," I instructed her.

When Ahmad got the phone back in his hand, he said, "I will see you in a few minutes, so don't fuck me over. It's you and that guy for your mama. Got it?"

"Got it," I assured him. Once again, he ended the phone call.

Anxiety stricken, I tried to collect my thoughts. How was I going to proceed with my plan of getting my mother safely out of harm's way? While I was going over my plans in my head, Rich said, "You think my boys outside are going to let that cat walk out of here with me?"

"We shall see," I commented, and then I started stuffing the money I took from Rich into my pocketbook.

When I finally saw my mother, I was going to hand her my bag with the money inside. She didn't know this, but she would find out later that she was gonna need this money to live on after I was gone. I mean, this was the least I could do for her, knowing that none of her family was going to be around to help her go on with her life. I just hoped that she did the right thing and went into hiding. She could be a stubborn lady at times and she didn't like change. Hopefully, after realizing that I was gone, she would move on with her life.

"So you just gon' drag me into your shit?" Rich asked.

"I didn't drag you into anything. You volunteered for this job. And now you don't wanna get caught in the middle of it? I mean, you was talking all that tough-guy shit since yesterday. And now today, you wanna sing a different tune. You're a weak-ass, wannabe gangsta!"

"Oh, so you think you're tough shit because you shot me in the leg? Bitch, I'd murder your ass right now if I could get my hands on a gun."

"You had a gun on you when I walked into the house, but you didn't know how to hold on to it," I replied sarcastically.

"Give it back to me and I'll show you how I'll use it," he insisted, giving me the look of death.

"Nah, I'll pass. You look better on the floor with a bullet wound in your leg. I figured it would be better to injure you enough so that you wouldn't resist what was about to come," I warned him.

"You fucking ho! I knew I should've let Monty rape your ass! But nah, I caught myself looking out for your stinky ass! If I hadn't stopped Monty, he would've made you his bitch! And he would've beat the hell out of you!" Rich roared. He tried to get up from the floor, but the pain from his leg wouldn't let him. He even looked around to see if he could find something to throw at me, but nothing was in reach. He was becoming more and more angry by the minute.

I don't know why, but I started laughing at him. I was chuckling like I was looking at a comedy on TV. I swear, I don't know where it came from, but everything he was doing had cracked me up. "Oh, so you think this shit is funny, huh?" He gritted his teeth.

"Yeah, it is," I replied nonchalantly.

"How the fuck can you laugh when you got a mother-fucker coming over here to kill us?"

"Because I've already accepted the fact that I'm going to die. And where I'm going, I'm gonna be very happy," I replied, and smiled while I was doing it.

"You're sick, bitch! And—" he tried to say.

"Hold that thought," I said, cutting him off in midsentence. I pulled Mike's cell phone back out of my pocket and made another call. "Agent Sims, this is Misty," I said, and then I put the call on speakerphone. I wanted Rich to hear my entire conversation.

"Misty, where are you?"

"I'm in Norfolk, on Bland Street. Not sure if you know a drug dealer named Rich. But he's the son of my mother's deceased boyfriend, Carl. Well, I'm hiding inside of his trap house. He and his street soldiers killed family members of Sanjay and Amir tonight inside their Indian restaurant."

"She's fucking lying!" Rich yelled, hoping Agent Sims would hear him.

"And then they took a woman named Sania hostage and made her take them back to her house. When we got there, he and the rest of his boys killed the grandmother and Sania. He didn't kill the little girls. They're running somewhere around her neighborhood, crying and afraid. So please send someone out there to find them."

"Is there someone else there with you guys?" Agent Sims wanted to know.

"No, it's just Rich and me."

"She shot me in my fucking leg and I'm losing a lot of blood!" Rich yelled out.

"He's shot?" Sims continued with the questions.

"Yeah, but he's okay. Enough about him. I hope you're on your way here, because I just got off the phone with Ahmad and he's bringing my mother here to this house. So I'm gonna need you and your agents to make sure everything goes off without any hiccups. Getting my mother back is my main priority. And if that doesn't happen, then there will be hell to pay."

"Do you know what kind of car Ahmad is driving?"

"No, he didn't say. But whatever it is, he will have a gang of guys with him, because he knows that Rich had something to do with killing his family and he knows that Rich is here."

"Are there any guns in the house where you are?"

"Yes, but I have them both. So, are you on your way?"

"Yes, Misty, but I'm gonna need you to do me a favor," he pointed out.

"What is it?" I wanted to know.

"I'm gonna need you to call me as soon as you talk to Ahmad again. I need to know what kind of car he's driving and how many people he's bringing with him. But more important, I'm gonna need to know how you two plan to make the switch."

"I can do that. But where will you guys be?" I asked him.

"Don't worry about that. Just know that we'll be watching. And when all of this is over, I'm gonna have to bring you in for Terrell's murder," he mentioned.

I let out a long sigh and then I said, "I know." And then I ended the call.

The second after I ended my phone call with Agent Sims, Rich said, "Oh, so you did kill that nigga, huh?"

"I gave him everything he had coming to him," I replied, and then I walked over to the window and peeped through the mini blinds. I didn't see anyone but the cats that hustled on the block. I saw a handful of crackheads and dope fiends running around like their heads had been dismembered from their bodies. I couldn't believe where I was, speaking about this house and in this neighborhood. My mother and grandmother made it their missions to keep me and my cousin Jillian away from places like this. But look at me, caught up in a mess of organized crime that killed all my family except for my mother, which was why I got to make this thing right.

"You think because you called the feds that they're gonna help you? They couldn't care less about your ass! All they care about is locking our asses up!" Rich shouted at me.

"I wish you would just shut the fuck up! You lost your privilege to talk when I took the gun from your dumb ass!"

Rich punched the couch again, this time bringing a greater pain to his hand. "Fuck! Fuck! Fuck!" He was yelling like a little bitch.

I chuckled. "Go ahead and bruise your hand up."

"What? Like your face? You smart-ass bitch!" he yelled at me.

"Exactly." I smiled at him.

Before he could say another word, Mike's cell phone started ringing again. I knew this time it had to be Ahmad calling me back. I took a deep breath, exhaled, and then I answered the call. "Hello," I said.

"I'm outside in the dark blue Cadillac SUV," he said.

I rushed over to the window and instantly saw the truck. I couldn't see inside the truck because all the windows were tinted. From where I was standing, the windshield even looked tinted. "Where is my mother?" I asked him.

"She's here in the back seat," he replied.

"I need to see her. Show me something. Like maybe let her stick her head out of the window?" I suggested.

"Roll down the back window and let her poke her head outside of it," I heard Ahmad instruct someone who was in the SUV with him.

A few seconds later, my mother stuck her head out of the window. I swear, it felt really good to see her face again. It also felt good to see that she was still alive. "Tell her to wave at me."

"Wave your hand," I heard Ahmad say.

Once again, Ahmad had my mother show me proof that she was, in fact, where he said she was. This brought joy to my heart, even though I knew my joy would be short-lived after I turned myself over to Ahmad. I just hoped my mother would find a way to live with my decision to do this.

"Now let's make this exchange," Ahmad instructed me.

"Okay, I'm gonna send Rich out first," I told him.

"I'm not going anywhere. You're gonna have to drag me!" Rich roared, and then he started scooting himself away from me, in the direction of the kitchen.

"No, fuck that! You ain't going nowhere." I gritted my teeth and threw the phone down on the couch next to me. I ran over to where Rich was and tried pulling him back in the direction of the front door. I grabbed his shirt, but he was strong and ended up coming out of the shirt he was wearing. Because of this, I lost my balance and fell backward on the floor. I hit the back of my head against the edge of the TV stand. *"Owww!"* I screamed, and immediately grabbed the back of my head. It felt like a sharp pain shot through the back of my head and exploded. I got up from the floor and walked around in a circle while I grabbed both sides of my head. *Boy, is my head throbbing!* "Fuck! Fuck! Fuck!" I yelled, trying to get my pain under control.

When I looked around to see where Rich was, he had made it to the back door of the house. This negro had managed that quickly to get the back door open. I raced to the couch and grabbed the cell phone. "He's trying to get away. Send one of your guys to the back of the house!" I shouted through the phone.

"Go around back," I heard Ahmad say.

I ran back to the window and peeped through the blinds again. In a flash, one of Ahmad's men hopped out of the front seat of the SUV and fled on foot, going in the direction of the back of the trap house. He had his gun already drawn. I knew that in a matter of minutes, Rich was going to be staring down the barrel of a gun and would wish that he hadn't fucked with me. It felt like a weight was about to be lifted from my shoulders, and that was the relief and satisfaction that I needed.

"Ahmad, you can go ahead and send my mother out of the truck. I'm gonna open the front door so you can see me," I told him.

Feeling a knot in the pit of my stomach, I hesitated for a second or two, and then I walked over to the front door. And when I grabbed the doorknob, I heard three gunshots. *Pop! Pop! Pop!* It startled the hell out of me. My heart did a somersault underneath my rib cage, because I knew that Rich was dead.

"Come on, Misty, I know you're scared, but the hard part is almost over," I mumbled underneath my breath. I needed this pep talk.

The back door opened, but then nothing else happened. The anticipation of my mother walking out of the truck was taking too long. "What are you doing? Send her out!" I was getting nervous.

"She's coming now," he said calmly over the cell phone, and then I saw a foot appear from the back door. I swear, it felt like everything was going in slow motion. I'm talking about some *Matrix*-type shit.

"Tell her to step down onto the ground," I instructed him.

Without saying a word to my mother, he stepped completely out of the back of the SUV. Then a second later, she appeared from behind the back seat's door. I was finally able to see her face and, I swear, it was a relief. But then I had to realize that we were not out of the woods as of yet. "Now, why don't you open the front door and come outside, because she's not moving another inch until you do," Ahmad stated. I knew he wasn't bluffing because I heard the finality in his voice.

I dreaded this moment, but I knew that it was either now or never, so I grabbed my purse that contained the money Rich and Monty had taken from Ahmad's family's house; then I slowly opened the door. "I'm gonna hang up with you now, since you can see me fully," I told him.

He didn't know it, but immediately after I disconnected our call, I called Agent Sims back without looking at the key panel or saying hello after I heard the phone ringing. What Ahmad didn't know was that I had just gotten off the phone with Agent Sims, so all I had to do was press the Send button because he was the last person I had called. That's what I did. I held the phone down by my waist area of my pants; this would give Sims a clear and detailed account of the movements that Ahmad and I were having.

What Ahmad also didn't know was that I had Rich's gun underneath the front waist area of my pants. I had to do this because he wasn't a trustworthy guy. He lied to me the first time about bringing my mother to his family's house, but that bogus-ass ploy of his went south. I couldn't let that happen this time.

"Come from behind the door, Mama," I yelled from where I was standing.

"Okay, I'm coming," she yelled in a whining tone, and then she took two steps around the back door.

When I saw her entire body, a calm wind brushed over my face. My plans to get my mother away from Ahmad were finally becoming a reality. "I see you, Mama!" I yelled back at her, but she wouldn't move.

"She's not going anywhere until I see you walk away from that door!" Ahmad yelled.

With a ton of apprehension consuming me, I tried to move a few steps away from the front door, but my legs wouldn't move. I felt paralyzed. "What is taking you so long?" I heard Ahmad yell from the truck.

"I'm coming," I managed to yell back. And right when I took that first step, I felt a strong force pulling me backward. I stumbled a bit. "Move, you dumb bitch!" I heard a male's voice say. And when it hit me that that voice was coming from Rich, I froze. I tried to turn around toward him, but he fought that from happening by pushing a pistol into my back really hard. I was able to turn my head to the side, and that was when I realized that he was using his one good leg to position himself to stand up to me from the waist down.

"Move now or I'm going to shoot you in your fucking back," Rich hissed. I knew he was livid. I couldn't see his face, but I knew he wanted nothing else but to see this guy Ahmad finish me off, once and for all. "Now give me that fucking money back," he instructed me.

"You want me to give it to you now?"

"Fucking right! Slide your purse strap from over your head and give it to me."

"What are you doing? I said to walk away from the front door!" Ahmad yelled from the truck. He was losing patience with me.

"I am going to do this," I said underneath my breath, trying to come up with a foolproof way to escape the clutch of Rich's hands.

Without giving it much thought, I shook Rich off me and made a dash for the truck. "Mom, run the other way!" I yelled while stooping down.

I raced toward the front grille of the truck and ducked down low the entire run. And from there, everything went in slow motion. I heard gunshots fire from both directions, all while taking the purse strap away from my neck.

"Here, Mom, take this!" I managed to yell at her despite all the firepower coming from Rich's and Ahmad's guns.

My mother turned around and looked at me, but when I threw the purse at her so she could catch it, it missed her by one inch. "Get it, Mama! Get it!" I yelled at her.

Thankfully, after failing to catch the purse the first time, she was able to get the purse off the ground and continue to run away from the war I had created between Rich and Ahmad.

Instead of moving from the front right tire of the truck, I hunched down behind until I felt like the coast was clear. I didn't care if I died, but I didn't want my mother to see me die. I'm sure Ahmad had her boyfriend killed in front of her, so having another tragedy happen in her face, I knew that it wouldn't have been a good idea. Planning this whole thing out this way took the proper calculations and, magically, I made it happen.

The gunfire stopped completely. But I hadn't known that it was over until I saw a set of shoes coming from the driver's side of the truck. I pulled Rich's gun from my front pants pocket and aimed it right at the feet. But I was shaking so badly that all my shots missed. Before I could decide what to do next, he was right in front of me, and I knew my life was over.

My heart was beating uncontrollably. My hands even started sweating profusely. I tried to slow my breathing down, but it just wouldn't happen. Resigned to my fate, I felt my gaze roll up from the feet, to the pants, and to the shirt. When I looked up to the neck, my heart took a nose-dive into the pit of my stomach. I couldn't believe that by looking at this guy, my life had come around in a circle. I wasn't about to meet the end I'd thought was near.

With his gun aimed directly at me, he said, "Misty Heiress, you have the right to be silent. Anything you say can and will be used against you in a court of law. You have the right to an attorney. If you cannot afford an attorney, one will be provided for you. Now, do you understand the rights I have just provided for you?"

Hearing Agent Sims's voice reading me my rights gave me a relieved feeling that I just could not describe. I'd never been so happy to know that I was on my way to jail. The whole time, I had been waiting to be killed by Ahmad, but instead of a murderer standing before me, I was now being recaptured by the law.

After Sims helped me up from the ground, I looked at him and said, "How were you able to get in this truck? I was talking to Ahmad the entire time. And where is he anyway?"

Agent Sims moved out of the way and pointed to Ahmad, who was sitting in the back seat of the truck.

"Remember when you walked away from the window so you could get Rich to come out the front door?" he asked me while he was putting me in handcuffs.

"Yeah."

"Well, that's when it all happened. My men and I were able to sneak up on them without them even noticing. And thanks to you, we came at the right time. So I wanna thank you," Sims said. "This was more work than I expected, but we'll finally be able to wrap up this case."

30
WHAT NOW?

Icouldn't believe that I was sitting in the back seat of a fucking unmarked FBI agent's vehicle. To add insult to injury, I was handcuffed and heading down to the county jail.

Two minutes into the drive, Agent Sims tried to spark up a conversation. "You have gotten yourself into a whole lot of trouble since I last saw you."

"Is that a question? Or a statement?" I asked.

"It's a little bit of both. I mean, you did manage to kill your ex-boyfriend, get in the middle of a shoot-out, and become a suspect in the murder of your next-door neighbor . . . ," he said, letting those statements hang in the air for me to either confess or debate. Instead, I gave him a bland comeback: "Trouble always seems to find me."

"You know we're gonna have to turn you over to the local homicide detectives, once we are done with you?"

"Is there a way that you could work out a deal with them, considering that I'm gonna help you guys with the federal case?"

"They're gonna charge you with murder, so there's no way that they will cut a deal with us. That's not our jurisdiction."

"Come on now, Sims. I know you can do something," I pressed him. I needed some help, and he was the only person I had access to who had any leverage.

"Do you realize that you killed a guy?" he asked again, trying to get me on the charge.

I was tired of pretending, so I finally responded, "Do you realize that I was only trying to defend myself? Terrell was abusive to me. I had a restraining order against him and he violated it on numerous occasions. It was either kill him or be killed."

"I'm sure that if you tell the detectives what you just told me, they'll probably be lenient with you."

"'*Lenient,*' *my ass!* Those crackers downtown are gonna try to put me behind bars for the rest of my life. That's why I'm gonna need you to put in a good word for me. If you don't, then I'm gonna be up shit's creek."

"I can't make you any promises, but I will see what I can do."

For the rest of the drive, silence filled the air. Agent Sims saved the rest of his lip service until after we entered the holding tank of the jail.

"I've got a female that needs to be processed," Agent Sims told the female officer sitting behind a counter.

"Put her in cell three," the officer instructed him.

"Will do. Thank you," he replied, and escorted me to the nearby cell.

While we were walking toward the cell, he said, "See, if you would've done what I told you to do, you wouldn't be in this situation. All you needed to do was testify in the drug case and you would've been scot-free."

"Look, I know all of that. Can we move past that and help me make my current situation better?"

"I told you, I can't make any promises."

"Well, would you at least try?"

"I'll see," he assured me.

He and I stood in front of the cell he'd been directed to take me to. I didn't want to go in, so I kept giving him an expectant stare, like I was waiting for a better answer. Instead, he insisted, "Here we are," and tried to wave me into the cell.

"So I guess this is it, huh?"

"Another agent and I will be picking you up in the morning, so try to get a good night's rest."

"Tell me, who gets rest while they're behind bars?"

"I wish I had the answer to that question," he replied as he took the handcuffs off me.

Immediately after he put the cuffs in the leather pouch next to his gun, he instructed me to step back so that he could close the door of the cell. "See you in the morning," he said.

I sucked my teeth and said, "Yeah, whatever!" Then I took a seat on the metal bench.

There was one other person in the cell with me, a woman who looked like she was around my age. But she looked like she'd had a hard life. And she looked like she hadn't had a decent amount of sleep in a long time. It was plain to see that she was a drug addict.

"What they got you in here for?" she asked.

"Murder."

"Damn, girl, you're hard-core. You don't look like you could harm a fly."

"It was done in self-defense."

The woman chuckled. "That's what we all say."

"Who did you kill?"

"My ex-boyfriend."

How was she in here for the same thing as me? This was crazy. "Well, you ain't gotta worry about him cheating on you while you're in here," I joked.

"You got family in the streets that gonna help you while you're in here?"

"My mother. I'm hoping that I get bond so she can bail me out." I didn't think it was possible with my extra charges, but she didn't need to know that.

"Oh naw, sweetheart, there's no magistrate in this place that's gonna give you bond."

"If I tell 'em that I did what I did in self-defense, then I'm sure they'll give me one."

"Good luck wit that! Because the people in here are racist as fuck! After they process you, you belong to them. They ain't gonna do shit for you. If you're sick, then you might as well deal with it on your own. Their food is nasty. The CO's got a bad attitude. The women in here love fighting. They will steal from you and the whole bit. So keep your eyes open at all times," she warned me.

The whole idea of possibly looking over my shoulders the entire time I was locked up alarmed me. I didn't want to live like that. I couldn't believe that I recently was about to start a new job in another pharmacy, but ended up dragged into this. *Damn! I just can't catch a break.*

After finally getting processed, I had to change into an orange jumpsuit and shower shoes. I was led up to the area in the jail where I was going to remain until all of my court cases were resolved. I felt defeated. This wasn't where I was supposed to be.

EPILOGUE

While I was in federal custody, I had to testify against Sanjay's brother and a couple of others I had witnessed coming into the pharmacy when I worked there. In exchange for my cooperation, Agent Sims offered my mother witness protection, but she refused to go. I ended up with nothing.

When the trial ended, everyone connected to the drug ring received sentences from forty years to life in federal prison. The two little girls that got caught up in the mix were returned to family members that weren't a part of the ring. And even though they were in the custody of family, I knew they'd always remember what happened to their mother and grandmother that terrifying night.

And as soon as the government used me up, they turned me over to the local homicide cops and I was transferred to a local county jail. My mother hired a lawyer to help with my defense, but that didn't help any. I was sentenced to twenty years in prison for the murder of my ex-boyfriend, Terrell Mason.

I had a few choice words for the judge after she threw the book at me. "How the hell can you sentence me to twenty years when I was defending myself? He was abusive to me and he violated all of my protective orders."

And she responded, "I'm not giving you twenty years for murder. I'm giving you twenty years for having his body chopped up and his remains discarded like he was an animal."

"No disrespect, Your Honor, but he was an animal. And he got what he deserved." When I uttered those words, all his family and friends screamed and shouted obscenities at me, so the court deputies hurried up and ushered me out of the courtroom.

I was transferred to a state prison and I came to the realization that it wasn't all that bad. I figured that if I survived all of what I'd gone through prior to this, then doing a twenty-year bid should be a cakewalk. Thankfully, I was taken to a state prison that was only two hours from where my mother now resided. She ended up selling her house and moving. I was happy about that because I was concerned about her safety. Now she was able to see me every other month. Our relationship had gotten so much better. And I was finally in a place where I didn't have to look over my shoulders. I could concentrate on serving my time in peace. Who knows? I might get out of prison sooner than everyone thinks.

STAY TUNED FOR THE NEXT INSTALLMENT IN
THE BLACK MARKET SERIES

Property of the State

Keep reading for a sneak preview of
PLAYING WITH FIRE
The latest novel from Kiki Swinson
The origin story of Yoshi Lomax
Available now
From
Dafina Books
Wherever books are sold

THE BEGINNING

I knew at first glance that my roommate Gia Santos had snorted a couple of lines of coke right before I'd opened the door to our dorm room and walked in. Luckily for her, I didn't show up with one of the other girls who lived in the building. Occasionally, one or two of my dorm neighbors would follow me back to my room to borrow a textbook, and today would not have been a good day. She looked out of it. Dazed. She blinked a few times to readjust her eyes.

"What's eating you?" she asked me as she opened her eyes wide.

I slammed the door of our room and took a seat on the edge of my bed. "I swear, Professor Reynolds is going to make me put a hit out on him if he keeps fucking with me," I spat.

"What happened?" She asked the question, but judging from her facial expression, she could not have cared less about my problem with our professor. She tilted her head back and closed her eyes.

"Come on now, Gia, really?!" I whined.

She lifted her head and looked at me. "What?" she said.

"You're not even listening to me."

"Yes, I am," she added as she focused her eyes on me. She tried her best to pretend that she was being attentive.

"What grade did he give you for your exam?"

"He gave me a 92," she replied, stretching her neck to the side.

"Wait, how did you get a better grade than me? We studied together."

"I let him eat me out right before class this morning."

"Oh, so you're back at that again, huh?" I commented. I was repulsed by the idea that she would even let him come near her in that way.

"You better get with the program, or you're gonna get left behind," she warned me. And within seconds she closed her eyes again and lay back on her bed. This time she was out like a light.

I couldn't sit there and watch her go off into a zone while I wallowed in my state of depression. My mother was going to kill me if she found out that I was failing my classes miserably. She may even be a bitch and pull me out of school altogether. Teach me a lesson, and God knows that I don't want her to do that. My dad passed away a few years ago in a bad car accident, so the only parent breathing down my throat is my mother. What will

I do? Go back home and sit around and watch her berate my stepfather? Boss our housekeeper around unnecessarily?

I swear, my mom could be the meanest person alive sometimes. It's like she prides herself on being a bitch. No one likes her. Even I don't like her. I deal with her crazy ass only because she's my mom and it's written somewhere in the Bible that you're supposed to honor your mother and father.

College spring break would be here in two days, and I wasn't looking forward to flying back to New York to see her. My dad's side of the family lives here in Norfolk, Virginia, but I'm not close to them, so what other choices did I have?

Instead of moping around in my dorm room, I grabbed my purse and left. I figured I needed to get something to take my mind off all the bad shit I had going on in my life.

On my way out of my building, I walked into Rita Reznik. She wasn't alone. Three frat boys wearing their fraternity jackets were walking by as well. It was Conner, Eric, and Tyler. They were the popular white boys from ODU's Division I football team, so they were the cream of the crop. The most admired by other guys and desired by most girls. Each one was cute. But they were dogs, and yet girls always threw themselves at them.

"What's up, Yoshi? When are you gonna let me spend some time with you?" Conner flirted.

"Yeah, you should come and hang out with us," Tyler said.

"Wait, Conner, aren't you screwing the brains out of her roommate Gia?" Rita teased them.

"Who is that?" he said jokingly. "And besides, what's

wrong with the two-for-one special?" He continued to clown around.

"She'll be interested in me once I show her what I'm working with," Tyler added as he grabbed and tugged on his genitals.

Eric chuckled in the background and started blowing kisses at me.

"Sorry, but I don't fuck little boys with little dicks!" I shot back at them.

"I'm sorry but you got me mixed up with somebody else. I've got the biggest dick you'll ever find on a white boy," he boasted.

"I find that hard to believe," Rita joked as they continued walking by.

"Hey guys, sounds like Rita is trying to keep Yoshi to herself, huh?" Conner called out.

"It seems that way to me too," Eric chimed in.

"Rita, *cock blocker* would look really nice on your resume,'" Conner commented.

"Right under 'the campus Percocet and Ecstasy dealer who makes the bulk of her money from a group of dumbass frat boys.'"

"Piss off!" Rita replied, and stuck up her middle finger.

"Yeah, yeah, yeah . . ." Tyler added as they moved on in the other direction.

"They're such jerk-offs," Rita commented as she approached me. She's hot shit on campus. She was pretty too. If you stood her next to Janet Jackson, you couldn't tell them apart. Word around campus is that her brother was a prescription drug dealer and her father was a coke dealer. I wouldn't be shocked about it. I mean, where else would she get the drugs she sells around campus? There's no prescription drug that she doesn't have. Gia is one of her customers. I cop from her too. But not as much as Gia and a couple of other girls in my dorm. I mentioned to Gia a time or two that she needed to be careful around campus. We had a lot of haters roaming around who would love to see her arrested and put out of school.

"What's up with you? Why the long face?" she asked me.

"Professor Reynolds gave me a shitty grade on my exam, and my mom is going to shit in her pants when she finds out."

"What did you get?"

"A freaking 72."

"Don't sweat it. I'm gonna take care of that for you," she said confidently.

"And how are you going to do that?"

"I told you not to worry. I got it."

I let out a long sigh. "You sure?"

"Yes, now let me get out of here. I've gotta get to my next class."

"Thank you so much! I owe you."

"I'm gonna hold you to that." She chuckled and walked away.

Hearing Rita say that she would take care of my situation took a load off my back. All I could do was wait.

It wouldn't shock me if I found out that my mother had someone watching me, because as soon as I walked away from Rita and stepped foot back in my dorm room, our room phone rang. When I answered it I found out it it was my mother.

"Hi, Mom."

"Hi," she replied quickly, and then she went into question mode. "What time does your flight arrive? I don't want your stepfather to waste time waiting on you when he could be doing something else." My mom never minced her words. She was a straight shooter and didn't care who liked it.

"The time on my ticket says that I'll get there at five thirty-five p.m.," I replied.

"Are you staying here for your entire spring break?"

"That's the plan." It took everything within me to answer that question. She has this way of talking to me like she doesn't want to be bothered.

"Do you have any special requests or things I could get for you before you get here?"

"No, you know I'm a simple person. The regular fried chicken and eggs and turkey bacon is all I need."

"You know I don't eat greasy food. It's bad for you," she pointed out.

"Has Sydney stop eating chicken?"

"No, he hasn't. But I have gotten him to eat baked chicken. There's a couple of soul food places around here that sells it."

"Where is he now?" I asked her. I'd learned over the years that if you continue to harp on a subject too long with my mother, she will dominate the conversation.

"Visiting his parents down in Florida."

"How are they doing?"

"You're gonna have to ask him. I don't meddle in the affairs dealing with his parents. They have a weird dynamic. All I ever hear them say to each other is how much they love each other. His mother calls at least ten times a day. She carries on like he's a teenager. It's annoying."

I chuckled.

"What's so funny?" She said it in a way like, how dare I laugh. What she said had no humor in it.

"Oh, it's nothing really." I downplayed it. "So when is he coming home?"

"He'll be back tomorrow."

"Wow! So you've got to make two trips to the airport?"

"Oh no, honey. He drove himself to the airport. You know I don't do a lot of unnecessary driving."

"Your anniversary is right around the corner. "

"Yes, it is."

"Have you two decided where you're going this year?"

"Spain," she replied with no enthusiasm.

I know if someone told me that they were taking me out of the country, I would be ecstatic. "How long are you guys are going to be there?"

"Seven days and six nights."

"That sounds fun. Wish I had someone to take me to Spain." I said jokingly. I wanted my mother to be happy knowing that her husband was taking her out of the country. He was very wealthy and spared no expense in going all out for my mother. I just had to convince her that she needs to be a little more grateful.

"How's school?" She abruptly changed the subject.

"School is going great," I forced myself to say cheerfully.

But my mother was no fool. She raised me, so she knows when I am lying to her. "How did you do on your last exam?" She pressed the issue.

"Not sure. Haven't gotten my score yet."

"Think you'll get it before you leave for break?"

"I should."

"How do you think you did?" She wouldn't let up.

"I feel like I did great." I replied enthusiastically. Once again, I had to act as if everything on my end was on course even though it wasn't.

"I hope so. Sydney and I are spending a lot of money sending you to that university, so don't let us down."

I let out a long sigh. "I know, Mom."

"Don't get smart with me."

"I'm not. But you keep saying the same thing over and over," I pointed out. What I really wanted to say was that Sydney was the only one forking over the money to send me to school. But I left well enough alone. I knew she'd leave me stranded at the airport if I told her what I really wanted to say.

"And I will say it over and over again if I feel like you need to hear it," she spat. "Now let me get off this phone before I say something else."

"Okay, see you in a couple of days," I managed to say before she ended our call.

I headed to my friend Maria's dorm room so we could chat. She was a political science major like me. We had a few classes together. Her career goal was to become an FBI agent. I couldn't see it because she was so laid-back. She was a beautiful and down-to-earth twenty-year-old. Now don't get it twisted, because she was feisty and she made sure that everybody knew it.

"What's up?" she asked after I'd knocked and she'd opened her door.

"I need to blow off some steam," I replied as I walked by her and entered her room.

"What happened?" she wondered out loud and closed the door to her room.

"Professor Reynolds gave me a shitty grade on my exam today," I hissed as I sat down on a chair placed by the desk. I was livid.

"What did he give you?" Maria took a seat on the edge of her bed.

"A 72."

"He can be a fucking dickhead at times."

"Tell me about it."

"Aren't you leaving for spring break the day after tomorrow?"

"Yeah," I reluctantly said.

"You don't sound like you're up for it."

"Am I ever?"

"How is she?"

"Miserable," I began. "She just never seems happy. She wakes up every day and acts like she hates the world, and I'm over it."

"Look at it like this, at least you don't have to be there with her every morning when she wakes up."

"I can always count on you to see the good in everything," I told her, because it was true. Maria strayed away from negativity.

She smiled.

"So when do you leave for Florida?" I changed the subject. Maria's family were immigrants from the Dominican Republic. Maria was born here in America. She was the first generation from her family to go to college. Her family was proud, especially since she was given an academic scholarship.

"I'm leaving right after my last class tomorrow," she told me.

"I know they're gonna be happy to see you."

"They always are when I go to see them."

"I wished I could get that same treatment."

"How many times have I told you to get her to go to counseling?"

Before I could answer Maria's question, one of her roommates walked in the room. Her name was Abby Blum. She was a Jewish girl from a very wealthy family. She was from New York but had a few relatives here in Virginia. Her family owned a lot of real estate around town. You'd think she'd flaunt their wealth, but she didn't. Nothing about her was over the top or flashy. In fact, she walked around with what seemed like the same gray hoodie and sweatpants every day. Maria boasted all the time about how smart this girl was. I'd thought about asking Abby to help me out on term papers a few times, but I can't deal with rejection so I did them on my own.

"Hi," she greeted me as she dropped her backpack on her bed and sat down beside it. She sounded winded. "You guys going to the dining hall?"

"Not me. I've gotta finish packing my stuff," Maria answered first.

"I'm not leaving campus until the day after tomorrow, but I'm sick of eating pizza and Chinese food," I replied.

"Well, I'm not." She chuckled. "I'm gonna get me a personal pan pizza and savor every bit of it." She grabbed her wallet and then left the room.

"She's sweet," I commented.

"Yeah, and she's hardly ever in this room."

"I wish that I could say the same for my roommate. Every time I turn around, she's lying around like there's nothing to do outside our room."

"She's probably high," Maria interjected.

I didn't respond. I looked down at my right foot and started wiggling it like I got a sudden itch.

"Don't act like you didn't hear me," she pressed.

I looked up from my foot. "What are you talking about?"

Maria gave me a hard stare. "Wait, is she still popping pills?" She wouldn't let up. She disliked Gia from the day she met her. And she had good reason too.

"The last time I checked, no."

"Yoshi, don't lie to me."

"I'm not lying. She told me that after her parents found out about her addiction, they put her in outpatient substance abuse classes," I managed to say. Now I can't say how I was able to come up with that terrific story, but it worked, because it got Maria off my damn back. Not only that, Maria doesn't know that I get high with Gia sometimes. If she knew, I was sure she'd stop being my friend and probably rat us out to the dean. Things would end catastrophically if that cat was let out of the bag, and I couldn't let that happen.

Maria and I talked a little while longer, and then I left so she could get ready for her trip back home.

On my way back to my room, I saw flyers posted on every wall asking for help to find a missing girl named Kristen Chambers. According to the flyer, she was a student at the university who had been missing for a month now. I didn't know the girl, but seeing that she was missing and that there was a possibility that she could be dead was terrifying. She was a pretty biracial girl who looked like me. We were almost the same height and weight. The flyer said that she was last seen when she left campus to go to a 7-Eleven store.

Reading this melted my heart away. I knew her family

must be going through it. "That's sad, huh?" said a voice from out of nowhere.

I turned around and saw a black girl standing behind me. I swear, I had no idea where she came from. "Yes, it is," I replied. "Do you know her?" I stepped back so I could stand next to her.

"No, I didn't know her. But whoever did this to her, I hope they pay for it dearly." While she expressed her feelings about the situation, I looked at her from head to toe. She was a very petite average-looking girl who couldn't have been older than nineteen. She wore a simple ponytail, sweatshirt, and a pair of blue denim jeans. She looked just like a college kid.

"What's your name?" I asked her.

"Penny. Penny Nelson," she replied, and then she held out her hand.

"Hi, Penny, my name is Yoshi. Yoshi Lomax." I shook her hand. "Which dorm did she live in?"

"The one next to this one."

"Wow! I know her family must be going through it. I know my parents would be going insane if this was me," I said, even though that was false. It sounded good though. "Do you know who her roommates are?" I added.

"I see them around on campus, but that's about it."

"This is strange because I can't believe that I'm just now hearing about this."

"Local and FBI agents have all swarmed this campus asking students and professors if they had any information on her whereabouts."

"Damn! Where was I?" I commented.

"They talked to me," she confessed.

"What did they say?"

"They wanted to know if I knew her. And if I had seen her on the day she was reported missing."

"Did they walk around to every dorm?"

"As far as I know they did."

"Do you live in this building?" I wanted to know.

"Yes, I live on the top floor."

"How long have you been living there?"

"A year now. But I took a semester off to figure out my life, and now I'm back."

"Really?"

She nodded.

"I wonder why I've never seen you before," I questioned out loud. It was becoming clear that was clueless about everything going on around me, and that's not good.

"It might be because you're very pretty and popular and everybody is always looking at you," she responded.

Taken aback by her comment, I had to replay what she had just said. I mean, I know that I'm very attractive, but what made her think that I'm popular? I didn't hang out with a clique of girls.

"Why do you think I'm popular?" I needed some clarity, because it was clear that she knew something I didn't.

"You don't hear what the girls around campus are saying about you? Every time you enter a room, girls are always talking about how pretty you are. They even wonder what ethnicity you are."

"I'm Asian and black."

"I even hear the guys talk about how much they want you."

"No way," I said, because this girl was blowing my mind. I wasn't getting all the attention that she claimed. Okay, now I was cool with a few groups on campus but not to the extent that she was saying. And to hear her claim that she's around every time people talk about me spooked the hell out of me, so it was time to make my exit.

"Yes, way," she replied in a weird way, and then she just stood there.

I swear, I am a very outspoken girl and for the first time in my life I didn't know what to say to this person in front of me. She had this Norman Bates horror film thing going on. It was really uncomfortable. "Let me get out of here. Gotta pack my things for spring break," I managed to say, and then I grabbed the flyer of the girl off the wall so I could take it with me.

"Talk to you later," she said, still standing there.

"Talk to you later," I replied, and was off in the wind.

I was so happy and relieved that I had finally got away from that weird-ass girl. It wouldn't have surprised me if she was on meds. I mean, who walks around and watches everyone's moves? Who has time to do that? That girl was definitely a nutcase.

I was so glad that Gia was up when I got back. She was on her laptop when I entered into the room. I walked over to her bed and handed her the flyer of the missing girl. "Did you know about this?" I asked after she took the flyer and looked at it.

"Yeah, I heard about it. Why? Have they found her yet?"

"No. I don't think so."

"So why you give the flyer to me?"

"Because this was my first time seeing it."

Gia tossed the flyer next to her on the bed and then continued doing what she was doing on her laptop. "I told the cops that I saw her a couple of times but I didn't know her personally."

I sat down on the edge of my bed and let out a long sigh.

"Think she might be dead?" I wondered aloud.

"She probably is. They said that she was from Connecticut."

"Why you have to say it like that?" I questioned her.

"Say it like what?" Gia seemed puzzled.

"When I asked you if you thought she was dead, you said that she probably was," I pointed out.

"And what was wrong with that?" she replied nonchalantly.

"You said it like you didn't care."

"That's because I don't. I've got too much shit going on in my life to be worried about a girl that I don't know, Yoshi. Why do you think I get high?" She paused and then said, "Because I've got a lot of shit going on in my life that I don't want to deal with. So if you're looking for me to go with you to that girl's pity party, then count me out, because my plate is full."

"I didn't come in here to fight with you. And I didn't ask you to go to a pity party either. I just wanted you to be a little bit more sympathetic about that girl's disappearance. That's all. I know you mean well, so I'm sorry."

"I'm sorry too," she admitted.

After Gia and I closed the chapter about the missing girl, I took off my sneakers and lay back on my bed. I tried to think about the good times that I used to have with my mother back when I was a child, but I couldn't come up with any. I even tried to rehearse in my mind how I was going to take the high road when she started talking out the side of her neck about something I did wrong or how I should live my life. But I came up empty. Listening to Gia tap the keys on her laptop was kind of distracting too. "Hey, Gia, do you know a girl named Penny?" I sparked up a conversation.

"Penny who?" she asked and halted her typing.

"Penny Nelson. She said that she lived on the top floor. Black girl. Skinny. She wears her hair in a ponytail. She said she's been in the building for two years," I said, hoping to jog Gia's memory.

"I think I know who you're talking about. What about her?"

"I was looking at the flyer about the missing girl and she comes up behind me and gives me the whole run-down. She tells me that the cops and the FBI spoke to her about the girl and then somehow she starts telling me how popular I am and that all the girls on campus want to be me—"

"What?" Gia interjected. She seemed confused.

"That's what I said, and then she said how the guys wanted me. I mean, she kept going on and on. I had to get away from her because she was freaking me out."

"She sounds weird."

"I thought the same thing."

"Who are you guys talking about?" a voice blurted out.

It was my other roommate, Jessica Vonn. Jessica was a black girl from Richmond, Virginia. This was her last year in college, so she had her finger on the pulse of everything going on and around this campus. She came from a middle-class family. Her dad inherited a funeral home and cremation center after her grandfather died five years ago, according to Jessica. She said she hated it in the beginning when she had to go clean up there after work hours. The stories she told me were quite funny. She didn't think so at first. Luckily for her, she's gotten used to it, so it doesn't bother her that much now.

"A weird girl that lives on the top floor named Penny."

"What about her?" Jessica went into question mode while she took off her shoes and jacket.

"I was just telling Gia how bizarre she was acting when she walked up on me while I was looking at the flyer about the missing girl," I began to explain.

"What did she say?" Jessica wanted to know.

Gia chuckled. "She was being a little stalkerish and creeped her out."

"She told me that every time I enter a room, she hears when girls talk about how pretty and popular I am. And the guys gawk at me and talk about how much they wanted to be with me. So, in my mind, I'm trying to figure out, how is she hearing all of this? She said more stuff, but I'll be here all night rehashing it."

"Don't pay her any mind. Everybody knows how crazy she is," Jessica insisted.

Agreeing with Jessica, I left that matter alone and changed the subject. "So you heard about the missing girl too?" I asked her.

"Everybody's heard about it," Jessica said.

"Not me. I just found out about her an hour ago."

"Where have you been?" Jessica tossed a question back.

"On campus like everyone else."

"Doesn't seem like it to me," she added, then grabbed a towel, bath cloth, and her robe from her locker. "I'll be back." She smiled and left the room.

"You two are the most cynical chicks I know," I said, nodding.

"But I thought your bestie Maria was?" Gia said sarcastically, and then she smiled.

I threw my pillow at her, and then I looked up at the ceiling and shook my head. "God please help me with these girls."